A Good Excuse To Be Bad

MIRANDA PARKER

Dafina Books

KENSINGTON BOOKS
http://www.kensingtonbooks.com

DAFINA BOOKS are published by

Kensington Publishing Corp.
119 West 40th Stret
New York, NY 10018

ISBN-13: 978-0-7582-5950-9
ISBN-10: 0-7582-5950-6

First printing: July 2011
10 9 8 7 6 5 4 3 2 1

Printed in the United States of America

A Good Excuse
To Be Bad

To D, D, D, S, M, and D with unfailing, fiery love

Acknowledgments

Writing about a woman like Evangeline Crawford is a serious, sleep-deprived endeavor. She rarely lets me rest until I've chronicled her last escapade, her last confession, her last word, and in the exact order she told me. So if you catch me slumped in a corner, with shoulders drooping and my head bobbing and sliding across my laptop keyboard, you now know why.

Therefore, if it weren't for the village that is Miranda Parker, I wouldn't be sharing her story right now. I would like to thank my village here.

To my editor, Selena James, thank you for not just appreciating my cornball humor, but extending me more creative license than I thought I could get away with and accepting my blind manuscript despite it being fifty pages short. I suspect Angel has haunted you, too.

To Mercedes Fernandez, although you are not my editor, thank you so much for welcoming me to Dafina last summer at the Faith & Fiction Retreat in Atlanta. It gave me great solace to know that I would be writing for a publisher that has a human face . . . and a sense of humor.

To my cover designer, Kristine Mills-Noble, I'm a big fan of your work, so I'm humbled, honored, and a little giddy. The jewel green tone, Angel's smirk, and the handcuffs brought the perfect balance of pop, fun, and sexy intrigue I wanted readers to note.

To my book cover photographer, George Kerrigan, when I received the mechanical for *A Good Excuse to Be Bad*, I was reviewing Ted Dekker's *The Bride Collector* for a book award that I judge. I trembled. Thank you for giving me some sleep back. I can tell that Angel found you, because now she's on the book!

The Kensington/Dafina sales and marketing team, thank you for getting behind Angel's story at the sellers' level. I may have written the book, but you help put it in reader's hands, where it belongs.

To Rhonda McKnight, for holding my hand and holding it tighter during moments I wanted to fall off a cliff. To finding pieces of this manuscript when my computers had eaten it up, and for getting the story to Deatri at Romance Slam Jam, where it found Selena. I owe you big.

To the late, great Katherine D. Jones and family. I would not be here if it weren't for her.

To FBCWA, ACFW, WORD, ACW Atlanta Chapter, RWA Kiss of Death Chapter, and PENWrites, thank you for making me write stories readers would love to read.

To my Book Buds, Tee C. Royal, Martin L. Pratt Johnson, Ron Kavanaugh, Ella Curry, Jacqui McGunis, Tarsha Burton, Chip MacGregor, Marina Woods, Curtis Bunn, Pam Perry, Rebecca Seitz, Troy Johnson, Tasha Martin, Carol Mackey, Ty Moody, Wayne Jordan, Rhonda Bogan, Jazz Vincent, Kevin Smokler, Angela Reid, Tanisha Webb, and Makeda Peterson, thank you for making this wide world of book publishing feel like family.

To my writer's enclave, Dwan Abrams, Stacy Adams, L. A. Banks, Kendra Norman Bellamy, J. Mark Bertrand, ReShonda Tate Billingsley, Carleen Brice, Claudia Mair Burney, Shana Burton, Bonnie Calhoun, Maggie Dana, Mary DeMuth, Virginia DeBerry, Sharon E. Foster, Ashea Goldson, Donna Grant, Linda Hargrove, Trice Hickman, Stephanie Jones, Deatri King-Bey, Sherri L. Lewis, Glenville Lovell, Creston Mapes, Shawneda Marks, JD Mason, Tia McCollors, Ane Mulligan, Victoria Christopher Murray,

Kathleen Popa, Cydney Rax, Francis Ray, Chet Robinson, Gil Robertson, Hank Stewart, Michelle Sutton, Amy Wallace, Pat G'Orge-Walker, Tiffany Warren, Eric Wilson, and Cindy Woodsmall, thank you for befriending me before I became published, for being transparent and teaching me this industry.

To Drs. David Song and Steven Patten, I write because you saved and continue to save my life.

To Tom Gregory, you changed my life forever.

To Rev. Dr. Moore and St. Philip AME Church, thank you for not being too important to hold my hand those nights when I was in the ICU.

To my godmother Earlie for making sure I had my college books, a car to drive, and for hosting my Birmingham, Alabama soiree.

To my Agnes Scott College sisters, can you believe this? Go Scottie!

To God and his angels: Patricia Woodside (the best proofreader on the planet), Veronica (who's like a fairy godsister), Vanessa, Trina, LaMonica, Pam, Sharon, Chip MacGregor, and David Long.

Chuck Palahniuk, thank you for teaching me how to be a storyteller, your advice, the purple beanie baby, the hand-beaded necklace with our names liked together, and the forget-me-knot seeds. I still keep them near when I write. And thank you for *Fight Club*.

To all the men I've had crushes on and the ones I heart now. Justus is a montage of you.

To my family, Mom, MeLana, David (my real twin), Daddy, and Aunt Doe, thank you for protecting Selah's spirit for me, for watching her when I needed to attend a book event, for helping her with her homework when I had to turn in those extra fifty "cough" pages, and for buying *Sweet Valley High* novels every week to help me through my fifteen blahs, reading my bad first poetry, enduring saxophone lessons, and being my booster club.

To my ace, Dr. Natasha B., for talking me out of bad decisions, encouraging me when I thought my life was over, being the best godmom for Selah, and being the best Best Friend Ever.

And for Selah. I love, love, love, love you. Like Bella, you are the reason the world smells sweet, the sky twinkles, and my heart sings. You are the absolutely best daughter in my world. Thank you for showing me true unconditional love.

Thank you all!

P.S. If I missed someone, I apologize. I nodded off about halfway through. Blame Angel.

1

Wednesday, 11:00 PM
Club Night Candy, Underground Atlanta, Georgia

If I weren't so screwed up, I would've sold my soul a long time ago for a handsome man who made me feel pretty or who could at least treat me to a millionaire's martini. Instead, I lingered over a watered-down sparkling apple and felt sorry about what I was about to do to the blue-eyed bartender standing in front of me. Although I shouldn't; after all, I am a bail recovery agent. It's my job to get my skip, no matter the cost. Yet, I had been wondering lately, what was this job costing me?

For the past six weeks, Dustin, the owner of Night Candy and my Judas for this case, had tended the main bar on Wednesday nights. His usual bartender was out on maternity leave. According to Big Tiger, she would return tomorrow, so I had to make my move tonight.

Yet, I wished Big Tiger would have told me how cute and how nice Dustin was. I might have changed my tactic or worn a disguise, so that I could flirt with him again for a different, more pleasant outcome. See, good guys don't like to be strong-armed. It's not sexy, even if it is for a good reason. Such is life . . .

Dustin poured me another mocktail. Although I detested the drink's bittersweet taste and smell, I smiled and thanked him anyway. It was time to spark a different, darker conversation. The fact that his eyes twinkled brighter than the fake lights dangling above his station made it a little hard for me to end the good time I was having with him.

"If you need anything, let me know." He stared at me for a while, then left to assist another person sitting at the far end of the bar.

I blushed before he walked away.

Get it together. I shook it off and reminded myself that I was on a deadline. I wanted his help, not his hotness and definitely not another free, fizzled, sugar water. It was time to do what I was paid to do.

When he returned to my station to wipe my area again, I caught his hand.

He looked down at my hand on his, glanced at my full glass, and grinned. "Obviously you don't need another refill."

I giggled. "No, I don't, but I do need something from you."

"I was hoping you would say that." He smiled and took my hand, then held it closer to his chest. "Because I've wanted to know more about you ever since you walked into my club."

"Great." I couldn't help but giggle back. "Does that mean I can ask you a personal question?"

He nodded. "Ask me anything, sweetie."

I leaned forward and whispered in his ear. "Do you have a problem with me taking someone out of here?"

"Of course not. You can take me out. My patrons don't mind, long as the tap stays open." He chuckled.

"No, Blue Eyes. I'm not talking about you. I'm talking

about dragging someone out of your club. Very ladylike, of course, but I wanted to get your approval before I did it."

He stepped back, looked around, then returned to me. "I don't think I understood you, sweetie. You want to do what in my club?"

"Take someone out."

He contorted his grin into a weird jacked-up W. "And what does that mean?"

"It means that you have someone in the club that I want, and I'll shut this club down if I don't get whom I came for. I don't want to cause a scene, so I'm asking for your cooperation."

He scoffed. "Is this some kind of joke?"

"No, it's a shakedown, Dustin Gregory Taylor, and surprisingly, you're the one who sent me. So I need you to play along with me right now. Okay? Sorry for the inconvenience."

"Sorry?" He stumbled back and let go of my hand. "Who are you? How do you know my name?"

"You're causing a scene, Dustin, and that's not good for business. Why don't you come back over here and I'll tell you . . . quietly."

He looked around the bar. The club was jumping so hard only a few people around us noticed his confused facial expression and his almost backstroke into the glass beer mug tower that stood behind him. He ran his hand through his hair, then walked back to me.

He murmured. "Who told you about me?"

"We have a mutual friend." I pulled out my cell phone, scrolled to a saved picture, and showed it to him. "I'm sure you know the man in this mug shot. It's your cousin Cade. Correct?"

His brow wrinkled; then he sighed. "What has he done now?"

"What he always does, Dusty, robs banks and skips bail. But do you want to know the worst thing he's done?"

Dustin just looked at me. He didn't respond.

"Well, I'll tell you anyway. He convinced your mom to put a second mortgage on the family house, in order to pay his bail the last time he got caught. Guess what? He got caught three months ago and then he missed his court date, which means—"

Dustin yanked the towel off this shoulder. "Say what?"

"Your mom's home is in jeopardy if I don't find him tonight. My boss Big Tiger Jones of BT Trusted Bail Bonds is ready to turn your childhood home into his Smyrna office, if you know what I mean."

"Son of a . . ." He turned around in a full 360. His towel twirled with him. "This isn't fair."

I nodded. "Life can be that way sometimes."

"I had no clue he had gotten back into trouble. He didn't say anything to me, and my mom . . . No wonder she hasn't been sleeping well lately." He rung the towel in his hands, then snapped it against the bar. "I don't believe this."

"Believe me, I understand how frustrating it is to watch your family make horrible mistakes and you or someone you love pay the price for their burden." I thought about my sister Ava. "Dustin, I have to take Cade downtown tonight. We both know that he's here in Night Candy right now and has been sleeping in your back office since his ex-girlfriend Lola kicked him out of her house. So tell me how you want this to go down, nice or easy?"

"Neither." He folded his arms over his chest. "You can't do this, not here. It'll ruin me."

I sighed. "I know, ergo this conversation."

Last year after a stream of violence and crime, the Atlanta Mayor's Office and the Atlanta Police Department issued a new ordinance against crime. Any businesses that appeared to facilitate criminal activity would be shut down. Night Candy already had two strikes against it: for a burglary gone bad that ended in the brutal murder of Atlanta socialite and real-estate heiress Selena Turner, and then there was that cat brawl between two NFL ballers' wives that was televised on a nationally syndicated reality TV show. The club definitely didn't need a showdown between a habitual bank robber and me. I'd tear this place up and anyone who stood between me and Big Tiger's money. I'm that bad, if I need to be.

"Maybe it won't." I touched his hand with hopes that I could calm him down. The last thing I needed was Cade to notice Dusty's agitation. "But you must do as I say."

Dustin leaned toward me. His starry eyes now looked like the eye of a hurricane. I shuddered. Man, he was hot.

"Listen to me," he said. "It's not you I'm concerned about. Cade has made it clear to everyone that he'll never go back to jail. He will fight. Lady, he'll burn my club down with all of us inside before he goes back in."

I patted his shoulders. "I believe you, and that's why Big Tiger sent me. See? Look at me."

"I've been looking at you all night."

"Exactly. This froufrou that I have on is a disguise."

"Didn't look like a disguise to me."

"That's my point, Dustin. I can sweet talk Cade out the back where Big Tiger's waiting for him in the alley. No one will suspect a thing, not even the plainclothes APD dudes hanging around near the champagne fountain."

He looked past me toward the fountain, then lowered his head. "I didn't see them there."

"That's because your attention was on me, just like Cade's will be once he sees me." I grinned. "All I need you to do is to introduce me to him. I'll take it from there."

"Makes sense, but there's a problem." He ruffled his hair

again. "Cade's in the cabanas upstairs, but I can't leave the bar. I'll let Ed, the VIP security guard, know you're coming. He'll parade you around for me. What's your name?"

"Angel."

"Angel, that name fits you." He looked at me and then over me. His eyes danced a little; then he frowned. "You're very pretty and too sweet looking to be so hard. Are you really a bounty hunter?"

I slid off the stool, smoothed down my hair and the coral silk chiffon mini cocktail dress my little sister Whitney picked out for me, then turned in the direction of the upstairs cabanas. "Watch and find out."

Night Candy sat in the heart of downtown Atlanta—underneath it, to be more exact—on Kenny's Alley, the nightclub district inside Underground Atlanta. Real-estate moguls, music executives, and Atlanta local celebrities frequented the club whenever they were in town. They also hosted popular mainstay events there. The upscale spot had become so über trendy that unless you were on the VIP list, getting inside was harder than finding a deadbeat dad owing child support. But getting admitted was worth the effort.

On the inside, Night Candy was its name: dark, indulgent, and smooth. Chocolate and plum colors dripped all over the lounge. Velvet and leather wrapped around the bar like cordial cherries. It even smelled like a fresh-opened Russell Stover's box. Dustin looked and smelled even better. I wished we'd met under different circumstances.

The club had three levels with VIP at the top and the best live music I'd heard in a long time: vintage soul, reminiscent of Motown girl groups with a dose of hip-hop and go-go sprinkled on top. My hips sashayed up the stairs to the music until I stopped.

I checked my watch and huffed. In three hours the judge could revoke Cade's bail. There was no time for errors. Cade had to go down now.

I texted Big Tiger. He had assured me he would be outside waiting for us. Trouble was, Big Tiger's promises had 50/50 odds. I promised myself to hire a male tagalong next time, preferably one as big as this Ed guy standing in front of me.

Whoa. I reached the stairs he guarded. Ed was a massive, bronzed bald-headed giant. He had brawn and swagger. My little sister Whitney would eat him up. Dustin must have given him the green light, because by the time I reached the top of the staircase, he was smiling and holding out his hand to help me inside the VIP lounge.

As he gave me a personal tour of what I called a Godiva version of a party room, I spotted Cade and exhaled. The Taylor men definitely had great genes. I didn't have to take a second look at his Fulton County Corrections Office booking photo to know it was him. He was drop-dead handsome—bald and dark, a bad combination for me. I'm a recovering bad-boy-holic. I hoped he wouldn't give me too much trouble, but the thought of a good crawl with this guy was enough to send me to church first thing Sunday morning.

I melted into a milk chocolate lounge chair across from his cabana and waited for his jaw to drop at the sight of me. And boy, did it. He was talking to a barely clad and quite lanky teenybopper when he saw me through the sheer curtain covering the cabana. I grinned and slid my dress up too high for a woman my age to ever do without feeling like some dumb tramp. I wished I could say I was embarrassed acting that way, but I couldn't. I liked having a good excuse to be bad sometimes.

The sad thing about all of this was that the young

woman holding on to Cade didn't notice him licking his lips at me. After five minutes of his gross act, she stood up and walked toward me. My chest froze. Maybe she had seen him and was now coming over to warn me to back off or to claw my eyes out.

Yeah, right, like I would let that happen. Homegirl better think twice about dealing with me. But I didn't want to hurt her. I didn't get all shiny and done up to scrap with some girl over a fugitive. Besides, I promised Dustin I wouldn't show out up in here. So I gripped the chair as she approached and relaxed when she breezed past. I watched her enter the ladies' room, then patted my cheeks with my palms. I was getting too old for this crap.

As soon as the child left his side, Cade slinked his way over to where I sat. I looked below at the bar where Dustin watched me. I waved my fingers at him until he dropped the martini he was making. *Man, he was cute.*

While I daydreamed of a date with Dustin, Cade stood over me. "So you know my cousin?"

I turned toward him. "Is that your way of introducing yourself to me, or are you jealous?"

He smiled and reached for my hand. "My apologies." He kissed my hand. "I'm Cadence Taylor, but everyone calls me Cade. Don't tell my cousin, but I think you're stunning."

"No, I'm not." I giggled. "I'm Angel."

"I can see that." He sat beside me. "Like a guardian angel . . . no, a cherub."

"More like an archangel."

He clapped and laughed. "Not you. You don't look like the fighting type. You have sweetness written all over you. You're definitely Dusty's type."

Oh, great. Now you tell me. I moved closer toward him. "And you have 'Bad Boy' written all over you."

He grinned. "You don't have to be afraid of me. I'm a good guy when I need to be."

I smiled back. "Can you promise to be good, if I ask you for a favor?"

He nodded. "Anything for you, Angel."

"I'm tired. I'm ready to go home. Can you escort me to my car? I was supposed to wait for Dustin, but I don't have the stamina for this club life."

"Of course, you don't, because you're a good girl." He stood up and reached for my hand. "Surprisingly, I'm not a clubber either. How about you leave your car and I take you for a quiet night drive through the city, then over to the Cupcakery for some dessert. By the time we get back, Dusty will be closing up this place."

"I don't know. I don't think Dustin would like that so much. Sounds too much like a date."

"Yeah, I guess so." He scratched his head like his cousin, another Taylor trait.

"Besides, your girlfriend would be upset if you left her here."

"What girlfriend?"

I pointed toward the ladies' room. "Her."

"Oh, her. We're not together."

I came closer and whispered in his ear. "Neither are Dustin and me."

He smiled and his eyes outshined the VIP lounge.

"Why don't you escort me to my car and follow me home instead, just to make sure I get there safe?"

He placed his hand at the small of my back. "I can do that."

Because Cade almost carried me out of Night Candy, I couldn't text Big Tiger to let him know that I was coming outside. All I could do was hope he was where he said he would be.

We stepped outside. No Big Tiger. I hit the hands-free Talk button on my phone earpiece and voice-activated Big Tiger's phone number to dial. I got nothing. My heart began to race. Where was he?

"Is something wrong?" Cade asked. His hands were all over me.

I removed his hands, but said nothing. I had no words.

Sometimes bail bondsmen needed women locators to lure a defendant out of their hiding spot. I didn't mind doing it. Honestly, I needed the money, but we had a deal. I brought them out; he rode them in. So why was I out here alone? Well, not entirely alone . . . with Octopus Cade.

Cade watched me. "Are you having second thoughts?"

"I have a confession to make." I scrambled for something to say while fiddling for my handcuffs. They were trapped somewhere under the chiffon.

"So do I." He pulled me toward him. "I can't keep my hands off you."

I wanted to cuff him, but I couldn't, because he had wrapped his hands around my waist.

"Not here, not like this." I removed his hold on me again, but held on to one of his hands.

He smiled until he felt—I assumed—my cold handcuffs clank against his wrists. "What the—"

"You've violated your bail agreement, Mr. Taylor," I said. Still no Big Tiger in sight. "So you'll have to come with me."

He chuckled as he dangled my handcuffs—the ones I thought had locked him to me—over his head for me to see. A piece of my dress had wedged between the clamp. They were broken. My heart hit the floor.

"Unless these handcuffs are chaining me to your bed, I'm not going anywhere with you, sweetie."

Then, quicker than I anticipated, he head-butted me. I saw stars and fell to the ground. A pain so bad crossed my forehead, it reminded me of labor pains. I couldn't scream. I had to breathe through it to ease the pain.

The head-butting must have stung Cade, too, because he stumbled before he could get his footing. I caught one of his legs and clutched it. I closed my eyes and groaned as he dragged me down the alley. Through the excruciating bumps and scrapes I received holding on to Cade, past the onlookers who didn't care to help this poor damsel in distress, I asked myself, "Why wouldn't I let go?"

My forehead and my skinned knees throbbed now. I'm pretty sure Whitney's dress looked like wet trash. To make matters worse, I was angry with myself for putting myself in this position. I couldn't afford to be so cavalier anymore. I knew that before I took this stupid assignment. I knew it while I sat at the bar. I knew it the day I became a mother, but I did it anyway. What's wrong with me? I couldn't leave my daughter alone without a parent. Now I had to hurt this fool to get back to my baby in one piece.

Cade stopped and cursed. My heart beat so fast and loud, I prayed it would calm down so I could prepare for his next move.

"Angel, sweetie, I think we need to have a little talk."

He pulled me up by my hair, my store-bought hair. I wore a combed-in hairpiece because I didn't have time to go to a hair salon and I didn't want to damage my hair. However, Cade's tugging made the plastic teeth dig deeper into my scalp. I screamed to keep from fainting.

"Shut up!" He slapped me. "You stupid—"

Before he could say another word, I grounded my feet then threw a round kick so high and hard with my left leg that I heard his jaw crack against my stilettos. He hit the ground, unconscious. While he was knocked out, I turned him over and handcuffed him again, but from the back this time and with the chiffon visibly gone.

I dialed Big Tiger. "Where are you?"

"Where did I tell you I was gon' be?" Big Tiger's voice seemed crystal clear. "Right here."

Someone tapped my shoulder. I jumped.

"It's a good thing I showed up when I did. You could have killed the man. I'da lost my money and then I would have had to take care of your raggedy bond." Big Tiger laughed, then helped me hoist Cade up. "Why didn't you wait instead of messing up your sister's dress? How many dresses have you slaughtered now?"

I looked at him and growled. "Say that again. I dare you."

"And your face, Angel Soft." He squinted. "I think we'd better call 911 after we put homeboy in my truck."

I walked toward Big Tiger with the intent to give him a right hook across his jaw. When I lunged, I think I fainted. I don't know what happened next and I almost didn't care until the EMS worker asked me whom I should call to let them know I was being taken to the emergency room.

"Call my sisters. Tell them where I am and make sure Ava comes to get me."

Then I faded back to black and it felt good. In my dreams, Dustin was on his knees proposing to me with some chocolates and a pink diamond.

His voice was so clear. "Angel, will you . . . be healed in the name of God."

God?

2

Thursday, Midnight maybe
Grady Memorial Hospital

I awoke in an ER examination room to find a familiar stranger praying at my bedside. I sat up, squinted, and blinked until his face came into full view. It was my pastor, Justus Morgan, not Night Candy's Dustin, as I had dreamed. Tonight had been crazy enough, but what in the world was he doing here?

I wanted to ask him, but he was at the tail end of praying for me.

"God, show your providence. Show her that she doesn't have to do it all. Amen," he whispered.

I touched my throbbing head and groaned. "I'd like to see Him try."

"As soon as you let Him, He will." He looked up and grinned.

I smiled back. Suddenly losing dreamy Dustin didn't feel so bad.

"How are you?"

I said nothing because I was fixated on his smile. Whitney and I likened Justus to a frosted glass of lemonade iced tea: tall, golden brown, and refreshing. He had cinnamon-

and-russet-colored twists that fell past his shoulders. His eyes were the color of cane syrup drizzled over golden flapjacks, and he had a dimple in his right cheek deeper than the slits in Aunt Frankie's hot apple pies. A bronzed angel was what the other ladies in the Women's Ministry called him. To me, he was perfect, and looking at that man now kneeling before me, I wished to God I were perfect, too.

Justus touched my leg, which wakened me out of my crush haze. "Are you okay, Angel?"

"I will be, but I'm curious." I sat up straighter. "Why are you here? Where's my sister?"

"Your sister Ava was tied up with an emergency of her own, so I'm here to bring you home." He stood up. "I know you weren't expecting me, but I assured Whitney that I would take good care of you. She sent these for you."

He handed me my favorite pink Hello Kitty duffel bag. "She assumed your clothes would be confiscated for evidence."

My little sister Whitney was pre-law at Emory University, which translated in real speak as her mind was set on thinking way too much. In lieu of paying for room and board, she was also my on-call au pair, but if she asked me to spot her any more cash for her sorority activities, she would involuntarily become my law records researcher, too. Nonetheless, I was glad she gave Justus some clothes for me. I didn't want him to see me in that ripped cocktail dress.

I don't know what impression he had of me, but I would die if he thought I was the woman I was paid to pretend to be.

"Actually, Justus, they took photographs. Besides, it was a simple AB charge stacked on top of Cade's failure to appear, bank robbery, and God-knows-what-else charges. I think the DA's office has their hands full with enough stuff to put him away without needing my dress."

"I'm sorry that happened to you," Justus said; then he patted my leg again.

I looked down at his hand on my leg. I hadn't realized how touchy-feely he was. But I noticed that every touch from him excited me more. That realization troubled me very much. Was I becoming just as perverted as the criminals I seized? Justus was my pastor, not some dude I met at a bar. This crush with my pastor was stupid. I had to stop it now.

I shifted in the bed.

I assumed he noticed my discomfort, but instead of removing his hand from my leg, he held me tighter and leaned closer to me.

"I know because we're here in a hospital that you're not physically okay, but how are you feeling?" he asked.

"Sore and embarrassed."

"I'm sorry." Finally, he removed his hand. "Don't be embarrassed. What that man did to you was wrong. Perhaps you need a pick-me-up." He reached down beside the bed and pulled up a glass vase filled with white roses. "I was told these were your favorite."

"Thanks, Rev." Smiling hurt, but I couldn't help it. He had a way with me. I shook my head. "You're such a nice guy."

Justus pointed upward. "He's nice, not me."

I rolled my eyes. "Please tell me that you're going to be human today."

He chuckled. "What does that mean?"

"No offense, Rev, but I can't deal with the preacher talk tonight. I've already had my Jesus moment. Okay?"

"Gotcha. But in the future, call me Justus. That way we won't start the conversation so preachy." He winked.

"Okay." I placed the flowers on the bed stand, then unzipped the bag and looked inside. Whitney had packed a white tee and a pair of jeans. I smiled. Dull, just like I liked it. "How's Bella?"

"Bella's fine. According to Whitney, she's asleep. She doesn't know that you're not home, but you'll have to explain the shiner on your forehead."

I reached for my purse, which was also on the nightstand, and pulled out my compact. I looked at myself and gasped. My face was swollen, and my forehead looked like someone had sketched a tic-tac-toe game on it.

"I look hideous. I can't be seen in public like this."

He shook his head and chuckled.

I frowned. "What's funny? My face?"

"No, your face is gorgeous. Your reaction to what I said about the shiner on your forehead was funny, but that's beside the point."

A normal woman would have found a compliment in what he just said about me being gorgeous, but I'm not normal. I had to say something smart. "And your point is?"

"When your sister called me and told me what happened, I . . ." He blushed, then looked away. "I shouldn't have said anything. Bella will be fine. I'm sure you will come up with a reason that won't cause her to worry about you."

"No . . . that's not what you meant. Go ahead and spit it out. I'm a big girl."

"It is what I meant." He paused and rubbed his head; then he looked at me, opened his mouth, closed it, then exhaled. "I didn't think you would flip out about the scars on your face when I mentioned them to you. I was just preparing you for when Bella noticed. After all, she is a child and they notice everything. She will be as worried as I was."

I looked up. "You're worried?"

He nodded. "More than you know."

"Don't worry." I pulled my legs in closer. "Scars can heal or be hidden."

"You don't have to hide from me, Angel. I see you."

"What if I don't want you to?"

"It's too late." He paused, then stood up. "Now, stop being so extra. I gotta get you home before Whitney rings my neck."

I lowered my head. "Now on top of feeling ugly, I feel foolish."

"Just feel better." He bent toward where I sat, then rested his hand on my left shoulder. Touchy-feely. "I'm going to step outside so you can change into something—"

"Less revealing. I wondered when you would get around to that."

"Calm down," he scoffed. "I was about to say change into something more comfortable."

How embarrassing. I covered my head with my hands. "I'm sorry, Justus. For whatever reason, I can't seem to keep my foot out of my mouth. That's no excuse for being so abrasive with you. It's not right."

"In my experience, we act out because we're hurt. What's really hurting you?"

"My head hurts."

He sat down beside me again. "No, I mean, what's hurting your heart?"

"I can't tell you that." I pursed my lips. "No offense, but you wouldn't understand if I told you."

He touched my hands. I jumped. "Oh."

He removed my hands from my eyes with his hands; then he touched my forehead with one palm. I peeked and held my breath. His eyes were so close to mine I saw the twinkles from the hospital light shimmer in his eyes. Did all the men in Atlanta have such nice eyes?

He lowered his hand and sat back. "Feeling better?"

I nodded.

"Then try me. I may understand more than you know."

The sour bleached scent of the hospital room no longer destroyed my sense of smell. Justus's heady cologne warmed up the room and stirred something inside me that I hadn't felt before—an urgent need to spill my guts.

"To be honest, I'm self-conscious about you being here. It's quite the surprise, but more than that I'm really bummed that Ava isn't here. She's only ten minutes away, but she didn't come. She didn't want to come. I don't understand her anymore."

"From what Whitney told me, Ava had a good reason for not being here. But if it's any consolation to you, I'm glad I was the second choice. Actually, I was shocked."

So was I. I would thank Whitney later. "Well, I'm full of surprises tonight."

"I have a feeling you're full of surprises any night."

"Why do you say that?"

He blushed again. "Get dressed and I'll tell you on the drive home. By the way, Bob Buisson, one of our church members, has towed your car home for you. No charge. And I have your gun and all the tiny weapons you had on you when you arrived at the hospital. They're in a plastic bag. I've already put them in my car."

"Got to be more careful." I covered my face with the hospital sheets.

"It's fine." He walked toward the door, then turned around. "Did you hear my prayer for you earlier?"

I nodded. "Some of it."

He shrugged. "I don't want to sound preachy, just want to remind you that what we think we see isn't always the truth. Give Ava the benefit of the doubt. Truth reveals itself in due time."

I bobbed my head, but didn't buy it. The benefit of the doubt never applied to Ava, and as for time, she hadn't come clean with me yet about what happened at the *Sentinel*.

As soon as Justus left, I reached for the hospital phone and dialed my home.

Whitney answered on the first ring. "How is she?"

"I'm fine, Whitney. It's me."

"Oh, I thought it was Justus. Cool. Cool." She paused. "Were you as surprised as me that he came?"

Her velvety voice held a hint of mischief. Good thing she was on the right side of the law.

I shook my head. "I'll deal with you later about that. Where is Ava?"

"She couldn't come. Don't get upset, but I think she and Devon are having some problems."

"Not the Adam and Eve of Holy-wood. Can't be."

Ava was the wife of Bishop Devon McArthur. He ministered to the largest church in Atlanta, Greater Atlanta Faith. The church had 30,000 members and had made my sister and brother-in-law Christian household names. They became famous with their couple's ministry program and Wedding Guild. There was no way they could be having marital problems. Ava was just being Ava, too goody-goody to come down to grimy Grady Hospital to see her unlady-like twin. That's the problem.

"Angel, not for nothing, I believe her," Whitney said. "When I called and told her what happened to you and where you were, Ava was so hurt and scared for you, but she couldn't come. She was crying. In fact, she offered to send a driver to bring you home, but then I thought of Justus."

"Yeah, you sure did."

"You can thank me later, but anyway . . . Angel, something is going on at Ava's. She said she would tell us when you're feeling better. So you get your butt home, so we can find out."

"Okay. Did you call Mom?"

Our Mom lived in Marietta but was spending the week in Myrtle Beach with her new hubby. I couldn't remember his name. Saturday they would travel to Italy for their honeymoon. I was happy for her and a little jealous, too. If we didn't tell her about my beat down before one of our nosy aunts did, I would be in more trouble than Cade Taylor.

"Yes, ma'am. She said she would deal with you when she returned."

"Whatever," I huffed. Honestly, I was a bit scared. "Justus is waiting outside and I haven't gotten dressed, so I need to go. Thanks for the clothes."

"You're welcome, but one more thing."

"One more, Whitney."

"Ask him to drive you home slow." Whitney giggled, then hung up.

It was such a nice ride back to Sugar Hill, I didn't want it to end. The sky was a deep, but clear, romantic midnight blue. The Atlanta smog had taken a nap, because I could see the big, full moon guiding us home. The stars sparkled so bright they reminded me of Dustin; then I realized I was heavily medicated and seriously craving male companionship. As I watched Justus run around the front of his truck to open my door, I reminded myself again that he was my pastor and nothing more.

He opened the door. "Did I get you home safe and sound?"

I nodded. "Yes, sir, you did."

He smiled and leaned down toward me. "Good."

My heart raced as his arms moved around me. Wow, the

cologne he wore made me swoon in a good way until I noticed his eyes weren't on me, but my seat belt buckle.

"May I?" he asked.

"Sure." I sucked in my tummy and chided myself for thinking the man was about to kiss me while he removed the safety belt from around me.

When he was done, he helped me out of the car and up my steps. He even unlocked the door for me. I shook my head and chuckled. I had had the pleasure of two gentlemen's company tonight. Maybe this was God's way of telling me that my prince may come after all.

I turned toward him. "Justus, I don't know how to thank you."

"Stop sitting on the back pew in church."

I shuffled my feet. "That might be hard."

"Why?"

"Because most of the time I don't feel like I belong there."

"Angel, if you're so self-conscious about your job, then why do you do what you do?"

"Justus, I do what I do to take care of my family. Let me throw you a lifeline . . . I made five thousand dollars tonight. That's my mortgage for three months, and it took me all of one week to track that guy down and bring him in. What other work outside of degrading myself would allow me to do that?"

"Dressing up like a go-go dancer to lurk in nightclubs for bail jumpers doesn't seem to shine a spotlight on what's so incredible about you either. Explain to me how such a dangerous and dirty profession empowers you?"

"You think I'm incredible?"

"Don't avoid my question, Angel."

I wasn't avoiding the question. I was wondering—hoping—he crushed on me, too. Then I wouldn't feel so foolish. But the look in his eyes didn't suggest longing for me, just for an answer.

I huffed. "Every time I bring a lowlife who can't respect women to justice, I feel like the world is becoming right again."

"Vengeance will not bring Bella's father back."

"What did you say?" I stepped back. I felt dizzy and swooned for real that time. Just before I stumbled off the porch, he caught me. "Let go." I scrambled out of his arms. "Did Whitney tell you my business? Because that's not cool."

"I apologize. This is not how I meant for this conversation to go. I just want to understand you better. I didn't mean to offend."

I walked across my threshold, but didn't turn around. "Let's just call it a night. I'll see you at Thursday Communion, Justus."

"You will be there?"

"Yes, good night." I nodded, then closed the door behind me.

Whitney had fallen asleep on the living room couch while waiting on us to arrive. Before I awakened her, I stood by the foyer window and watched Justus return to his truck and back out the driveway. I didn't want to be so cold to him, but that's exactly how I felt, cold and distant after he said what he did. His words and the tone of judgment in them was why I sat on the back pew in the first place. I wanted to wrestle my own demons in my own time, especially what happened to Bella's father. I had no intention of dealing with that demon anytime soon. It was too much. It still stung.

I waited for Justus to turn out of my yard, but he didn't. He stopped short of the curb, got out the truck, and marched back to my front door.

I opened the door before he could ring the doorbell and wake up the house. I stepped onto the porch and closed the door. "What in the world are you doing?"

"Do you like to read?"

I frowned. "What?"

"Pearl Cleage is reading at the Margaret Mitchell House tomorrow night. Would you like to go with me to hear her?"

My heart skipped three beats. I loved her writing. Yet, I was confused by the question and where it came from. "What's this all about?"

"I'm changing the subject like you asked of me," he said.

"I don't understand."

"Angel, did the doctors check your head? Give you an MRI? Because you may have a concussion."

"Of course I have a concussion, but still . . ." I paused. "I don't understand where all of this attention from you is coming from."

He walked up one step toward me. "I admit that I'm intrigued by you. I want to know more about you than what I've learned in the little bit of time I spend watching you from afar at church. And since I don't know when I will have the opportunity to see you like this again, I thought I'd ask. Will you allow me the chance to know you?"

My mouth dropped. I felt it go numb.

Before I could answer him, my cell phone rang, flattening the sizzle out of the past two minutes. Ava's name appeared on the caller ID. I grumbled, rolled my eyes, and took the call. "Ava, you have some nerve."

"Can we crash at your place tonight?"

"We? Who?"

"The kids and I. Only the kids and I. Don't ask why."
She sighed. "Please."

At that moment, I felt time pause, like my answer to her
held the weight of the world. I shook my head in angst and
looked back at Justus. "Sure, just get here."

After Ava hung up, I shrugged. "Do you take rain checks?"

3

Sugar Hill was an old church, a beautiful church in a quaint little town north of Atlanta. I had prayed to find a church like Sugar Hill. A church that from the moment I walked inside the sanctuary, I couldn't help but lift my eyes toward the steeple mosaic and fall to my knees in awe. A place that made me forget the world outside wasn't created to trouble single mothers, but to support them; a place that reminded me why I moved way out in the boondocks in the first place. Solace.

My soul needed sanctuary. Bank robbers hanging in nightclubs weren't our typical miscreants. They were mostly mothers strung out on meth and fathers too broke to be a joke, regular people who made one bad turn too many and had no one to catch them when they hit the wall.

Thankfully, I had family, a certain skill set, and I had this place, not to mention First Thursday Ladies' Communion and Brunch, which was convenient for mothers who worked near the church. The brunch was designed to relieve young mothers who were swamped with Sunday-school duties, diaper changes in the nursery during regular service, or sleeping in because they were out all night haul-ing bail jumpers to jail. At the First Thursday Ladies' Communion and Brunch, we could commune with each other, share survival tips, and eat lunch like grownups for a change while our children were either in school or the church nursery. And I didn't have to dress up and dip out before all the Holy Rollers informed me that I was #1 on their prayer lists. Perfect.

But today, much like my life, I had lost my focus. I should have been seeking advice on preparing for Bella's upcoming first day of kindergarten or how we would sur-vive if I stopped taking contracts from Big Tiger. Instead, I marveled over the new shepherd of our little flock, Rev-erend Justus Too-Hot-to-Be-Holy Morgan, and wondered did he really ask me out on a date last night?

The tip of his hand touched mine. I shivered and shut my eyes tighter.

"This is my Body. Take it," he said.

My chest stiffened. *Lord* . . . I tried to expel every un-compromising thought about Justus's body out of my head. Yet, my heart and my longing . . . *have mercy* . . . I had much work to do.

I felt a nudge on my right side. I didn't have to peek to know it was Mrs. Toliver, my wannabe-surrogate mother. She was one of the few African American mothers of this church and one of the few other women here who had taken it upon themselves to meddle in my life, whether I wanted her to or not.

I opened my eyes. Justus held a loaf of bread out to me. I squinted. I hadn't become comfortable taking Communion that way.

I grew up in a small, agricultural town four hours south of Atlanta. We—like most of the state of Georgia—lived differently than the people in Atlanta. In my home church, we didn't eat off a bread loaf during Communion. No, we ate stale, white crackers until a few years back when we switched to white, tasteless discs.

Come to think of it . . . those discs and crackers in an uncanny kind of way reminded me of Ava. Tasteless. She had called me twice this morning, although she was supposed to come to my house last night with the kids. I was curious about what changed her mind. I was pissed off that I postponed my sort of date with Justus for nothing. She had some nerve. When it came to me, she had little taste.

I thought about calling in my rain check with Justus. Yet, despite the fact that today was Thursday, it didn't feel right to spring my new availability on him here.

Justus continued to hold the bread toward me. The bread looked warm and yummy. Justus looked warm and yummy. I blushed and lowered my head. Did the man know what he was doing to me? *This has got to stop.*

He continued our monthly ritual. His eyes shimmered through me. "Eat this in remembrance of me."

I nodded faster than a bobblehead and ate. The sooner I got out of here, the better.

He leaned toward me and touched my head again. "Be encouraged, young mother."

Something about the way he looked at me and the way he said those words told me that he meant it. I remembered his concern for me the other night and his question about my profession. I could see in his eyes that he was reminding me that he was praying for a better way for me. It was the nicest, purest thing I'd ever heard from a man in my life. I lowered my head and cried. *Was Justus right? Was I being too risky? Was I really doing the best I could for Bella?*

I knew that I couldn't be a father to her, no matter how hard I tried, no matter my black belt or my ballistics training. I couldn't be him and was beginning to wonder if Bella needed a dad. The thought of Bella's disappointed face when I attended a Father's Day, Father/Daughter dance, or Donuts for Dads event made me feel worse, not blessed. I wanted to be more for her because Bella was so many things to me. She was everything. Being her mother had taught me a truth that I wished to God I had learned eons ago: Second chances are hard to come by. When you get one, take it, then change to honor the chance.

Immediately, I thought of Ava. After all, I did owe her and she owed me a chance to make things right between us. I got off my knees and ran toward my purse, but couldn't find my phone. I had left it in the car, so I raced out the sanctuary to find another one.

There was an old beige rotary phone that sat at the welcome desk in the narthex. I found it behind the desk, picked it up, and dialed.

But as soon as her voice purred through the phone, something weird happened. Someone behind me called my name. I held the phone to my head and searched the room. Had the Communion juice made me crazy?

Someone tapped my shoulder. I spun around. I jumped. Justus.

"Hello," he said.

"Hello?" Ava asked through the phone.

"Yes," I said to them both.

"Angel, I'm sorry. I didn't realize you were on the phone."

"I'm not, really." I removed the phone from my ear, but could hear Ava screaming my name. I put the phone receiver over my heart to muffle her voice. "What do you need, Justus?"

"When you're done with your conversation, can I speak with you in my office?" His deep voice held a quiet power over me like the last, low thunder after a storm. "I need to discuss a private matter."

I nodded and lifted the receiver to my mouth. "Ava, I'll call you back."

I heard her shouting something about tonight and needing my help as I hung up the phone. I'd call her back. I promised myself I would, after I met with Justus.

Justus's pastoral study smelled of lavender, magnolia blossoms, firewood, and holiness—at least my version of it. Once we entered the room, he turned around and smiled. His face lit up as I smiled back. I shouldn't get too excited. He looked like that at every church member. Yet, I hoped he was sweet on me and that his invitation to see Pearl Cleage was still on the table.

He walked me toward his lounge area. "Have a seat."

He motioned a greeting with his hand, which also reminded me of my granny. She always talked with her hands, as if we couldn't get the gist of her stories without the grand gesturing. I sat down on the love seat in front of the table, feeling all warm and fuzzy over her memory.

Justus sat in a stiff-backed mahogany chair to my right; then his phone rang.

"Excuse me, Angel. I need to answer this. It'll just take a second. Make yourself comfortable." He stood and walked toward the door.

"What? Wait a minute." I hopped up.

He spun around. "Excuse me?"

"No, excuse me, Justus, but I just hung up on my sister to have a chat with you at your request. Come on now. You're leaving me for a phone call?"

His eyes shined brighter. I could see fire behind his cheeks. He lowered the phone from his ear. My heart fluttered. I hoped I didn't just piss off my pastor.

"I didn't tell you to hang up on Whitney."

"Ava," I corrected. "Hang up on Ava. She didn't show up last night, so . . ."

"Wow. Really?"

I nodded and threw my hands on my hips.

He watched me, then glanced at his phone. "Angel, I'm sorry, but I have to take this call. I will make this up to you and Ava. I promise. Just don't leave, okay?"

"Did I say I was leaving?"

"Thank you." He walked toward the door, put his hand on the doorknob, then stopped. "Again, make yourself comfortable."

Of course I would. I grinned back, then snapped a frown when he left the room. Who was he talking to that made him drop everything in an instant? I turned around and searched the room for answers.

At first glance, I couldn't tell that he had moved in. Brother Allen's old mahogany desk, the swivel chair, his wife Anne's floral settee, and the matching bookcases were stationed in the same places they were before our old pastor left this church to plant churches in France. The only items that appeared to belong to Justus were the books on black theology, civil rights, and the history of rap music on the coffee table, and of course, the black Jesus bobblehead that sat on his desk. I chuckled at that.

Justus returned. He walked in, closed the door, and met my eyes. I was locked in to him again. He sat down, looked up at me, and said nothing. Although he wasn't smiling anymore, his face glowed. I felt warmer than August in Miami.

"Have you thought about what we talked about last night?"

Of course, I had thought about Pearl Cleage all night, but I didn't want to embarrass myself. I had a bad habit of reading more into things than there really was.

I shrugged. "We talked about so many things."

"We did." He grinned.

God blessed Justus with intoxicating eyes. They charmed you and didn't release you until he was done with you. He'd been here at Sugar Hill for a few months, but I had picked up his mannerisms early on. For instance, he usually reserved this Jedi eye charming thing for gut-check sermon lines right before the Invitation. I watched his handiwork from the back pew most Sundays, but today as he leaned toward me, I knew he finally had me where he wanted me and it was working. I wondered what he wanted.

"However, right now I want to talk about what happened to you last night at the club. I think I have a less dangerous assignment for you."

I sat back very disappointed that what he wanted to discuss had nothing to do with wanting me as a girlfriend. Yet, I was curious. "What are you talking about?"

"I want to hire you."

I chuckled. "For what? Someone's been taking loose change out the collection basket again?"

"No, nothing like that. What I need from you isn't even church related. It's personal." He paused. "I need that special service only you provide."

I could feel my eyes roll to the back of my head. I smirked to hide my disappointment. "After last night, I thought that you wanted me to stop."

"Perhaps I was being premature. Maybe your talents can best be served for a different purpose. A good one. And what I was thinking of definitely fits the bill."

I thought about my daughter's dead father and my complicity in him being six feet under. "Believe me. I need to stop. What happened last night was a definite indicator that I have been walking down the wrong trail." I shook my head. "I could be a white-collar private investigator for small businesses or one of those lady detectives who decoy themselves to catch cheating husbands. You know? I don't have to do this to make money, just like you said."

"I take back what I said."

I looked up. "What?"

"Angel . . ." he paused. "Is there any way I can persuade you to take on one more case?"

I wanted to refuse him, but his eyes were tugging on my heart big time. I sighed as I watched him. He didn't have a clue what he was getting himself into.

"What is it?"

"I need you to tell me anything you can about my niece's new boyfriend."

I laughed hard. "Are you serious?"

"Very, and I have good reason to be concerned."

"Would you mind elaborating?"

He reached for a book on the table and opened it. There was a letter inside. He handed it to me.

I glanced at it. It was a love letter between his niece, Kelly, and some boy. "It looks like your niece is in love." I handed it back to him.

"I found this love letter in Kelly's jeans pocket two days ago while folding laundry."

I cackled.

"Don't ask . . ." He paused. "I know I shouldn't have been prying, but there have been events lately that warranted the action."

"I'm sorry." I chuckled. "The sight of you folding clothes tickles me. Do you have kids . . . um, of your own?" I asked.

"No, I'm not married."

"Neither am I, but I have a child."

"Oh, right. . . ." His eyes widened; then he lowered his

face. "What I meant was, I have kids in my house for now, but I don't have kids. I've never been married, so, of course, I don't have kids."

My neck snapped at his last statement. Did he just judge me?

"I heard you the first time, but maybe you didn't hear me. So let me repeat myself. I've never been married and I have a child." I reached for my purse and stood up. "I don't know if this is your way of ministering to me, but I draw the line at being judged."

He caught my arm. I looked down at him. His gaze had changed. It was warmer, more endearing.

"I'm sorry. I didn't mean to offend you. I was telling you something about the kind of man I am. I wouldn't have a child and leave her mother to take care of her on her own, not if I could help it. I wasn't putting you down. I wouldn't do that to you. Understand?" His eyes stole the last bit of good sense I had left. "Please stay. I need you."

He looked so pitiful, while his hand fit strong and snug around my arm.

I huffed. "No need to apologize. I am what I am."

"You shouldn't feel ashamed of being a single mother."

"No, I'm ashamed of my pride. It clouds my judgment sometimes."

"Well, I have a habit of sticking my nose in places it doesn't belong." He raised his niece's letter. "So now you've discovered my vice."

"It's fine, as long as you know my rates aren't cheap."

"Even for your pastor?"

"No, but for Justus, yes."

I sat back down. I reached for my bag and pulled out a composition book small enough to fit in my hand and my favorite wacky pen of the moment. Last month, I found a sweetie-pie fat pen designed with a wild-haired, green-eyed, tongue-wagging man's face on the front. It made Bella laugh.

I clicked on it and opened my book. "Tell me about Kelly."

Justus wrinkled his brows and stared at something on me.

I tried to see what it was until I clicked my funky pen again.

He raised his eyebrow, chuckled, and sat back. "She's sneaking out of the house at late hours to meet a guy."

"She lives with you?"

"Yes." He nodded. "Trish, my younger sister, Kelly, my niece, and the twins . . . boys."

"Wow." I muttered, "I'm a twin, too," under my breath. Wasn't sure if I should reveal that.

"Right." He looked away. "My brother-in-law is in Iraq. My sister just opened a bakery in Edgewood. She's overwhelmed, so I thought I would help her out until Mike returns. Mike's her husband."

"How honorable, but I'm sensing that you're not too enthusiastic about your family arrangements."

"I can't complain. It is what it is. I'm just grateful I can help her."

At this point, I felt like a big doofus jerk. No one at church had spoken about his sister or his full house. I couldn't live with myself if I made him pay me full price. If I weren't so broke, I wouldn't charge him at all.

I smiled. "I guess I'll give you a discount, since I didn't see that one coming."

"You're an angel, literally." He leaned toward me as if he were going to hug me again, but he stopped and laid his hands over mine. His hand hug felt just as good.

I slid my hands from his hold. "You're very touchy-feely."

"Usually I'm not, but with you . . ." He chuckled and scratched his head. "Not like this. Maybe I'm relieved that someone of your caliber is willing to help me with this delicate situation."

"You might not think so after what I have to say."

"What do you mean?"

"Your niece. She's at that age. You know? First love. She's missing her dad, probably angry that her mom moved in with you. Different school, right? She's probably milking you and your sister for sympathy points. If I were in her shoes, I would, too."

"She is, but I'm more concerned about this boy. She's had boyfriends before, but the sneaking out, the intensity in this letter . . ."

"I know, but you need to consider that these boys are a smoke screen. Meaning you can follow every boy that runs behind her skirt tail, but the problem isn't just the boy. Kelly can't be sneaking out the house. Period."

He nodded. "I know, but I don't know what to do, and Trish is tired. I told her I would handle it, so that's why I called you in here. I need to do something productive."

"Then you need to let Kelly know that the life her parents designed for her hasn't changed."

"And how do I do that?"

"You don't need me to find this boy. You need to scare the bejesus out of him the next time he calls. If you haven't already, take Kelly's cell phone from her. If she broke curfew, she shouldn't have the phone. When he calls, you intercept."

He chuckled. "That's all good if we're talking about a teenager, but he doesn't sound like a boy."

"So you've talked to him before?"

"Yes, Kelly has lost her cell phone privilege, all phone privileges, but the boy called the house phone."

"Ooh, now it's getting interesting." I laughed. "Boys these days are older than you and I. They know more and have done more, so, of course, they sound like they know more, but they don't."

"I get that, but this guy doesn't sound like a boy to me."

"What do you know about him?" I asked.

Justus placed his arm over the seat. The tip of his hand was a touch away from my shoulder. The energy in the room pulled me toward him. I stopped myself and scooted back. I needed to concentrate on his words.

"Like I mentioned before, Kelly's phone had been taken away from her as a form of punishment. So he called on the house phone two nights ago. Late. I picked it up and overheard a man—not a boy—talking to my niece about meeting him tonight. It wasn't just the deepness in his tone, but the way he talked. It's how I would talk to . . . a woman."

"So what did you do?" I asked.

"I told Trish. We grounded Kelly, but then I found the note. He asked her to come to his place." He paused. "A fifteen-year-old move in with a what-year-old? He has to be too old for her if he has a place of his own. I wanted to hurt him, Angel. I want to hurt this man/boy/whatever. All I know is when a man wants something, he wants it. He becomes consumed with the wanting. You know what I mean?"

I nodded. My stomach churned. "Exactly."

"I need you to find this guy for me tonight. I need to be sure he's not a pedophile. I need to quell this anger." The glare in his eyes told me that he was serious.

I scratched my head. "Tonight?"

"Yes, is that a problem?"

"Not if you call the police. Do that. Save your money. They'll help you."

"Why, because they're often here at the church?"

"Well, yeah. This place has more security than the Tyler Perry estate."

Then he looked at me with a connection that ran through my veins. "What would you do if someone took Bella's innocence?"

"Vengeance is the Lord's, Rev," I said, knowing full well I would throw a pot of piping-hot grits on anyone who hurt my baby.

"I'm not going to hurt the guy." He took my hand. "I just want to find him. You can locate him faster than the police. Everyone knows that."

"Everyone like whom?"

"Your sister Ava, for one. When I talked to her last night when you were hurt, she said that. She even said that she wished she had talked to you sooner about something you had warned her about."

Ava. I stood up again.

He jumped up. "Did I say something wrong again?"

"No," I lied. "I promised Bella I would eat lunch with her today after VBS. Her lunch starts in a few minutes, so how about I call you?"

"Can you help me tonight?"

"I'm a single mom. I can't do tonight. Too short notice. Understand me?"

"Yes, very . . ." His voice hinted desperation and longing. "Well, can you at least tell me what I need to do for now?"

"Keep doing what you're doing. Take turns keeping watch over your niece. That's all I can say off the top of my head. Check with my assistant, Cathy, for an appointment. She knows my schedule better than I do."

"I can do that. Okay. I can do that, but I do want to talk with you. What about this evening? Trish is off tonight. Plus, she and Kelly have some mother/daughter cotillion meeting at the church. The boys attend vacation bible school at night, so I'm free."

"Why aren't you taking no for tonight as my final answer? I don't want to work tonight. Shoot. I don't even want to cook or leave my home to eat."

"Good, then I'll cook dinner for you, Bella, and Whitney."

"Why would you want to do a fool thing like that?"

He smiled. "Isn't it obvious?"

I giggled and scratched the back of my neck. I did that when my mother's wit told me I was about to make a life-changing decision. "Sure. What time?"

4

I hadn't forgotten to call Ava back. I just didn't have the time. But I had some questions of my own, and if she was as desperate as she sounded on the phone earlier, she would find me. At six o'clock, she did.

She stood in my foyer with shades on and wrinkled her nose when I asked her to have a seat in the living room.

"No, thank you, sweetie. I don't have much time. I have a First Wives' Prayer Meeting at the governor's mansion within the hour." She turned to my hanging mirror in the walkway and checked herself out.

I shook my head. Only she could pull that look off.

Ava wore a red hat and a matching red pencil skirt suit that looked too tight for kneeling down to pray. I checked my watch. The governor's mansion was more than an hour's drive from my home. Either she was lying about trying to get to the meeting on time or she was in some serious trouble she was too shame-faced to tell me. At any case, she had me waiting with bated breath.

"If that's the true, then why are you here? As a matter of fact, what happened to you last night?"

Her mouth dropped. "Aren't you glad to see me now?"

"Seeing you briefly between more important matters in your life? No, I'm so over that. Can't you tell?"

"Fabulous. I knew I shouldn't have come here." She turned toward the door and sniffled. "I knew you hadn't changed." She sauntered toward the foyer.

My sister missed her calling. She should've been an actress. I sighed and walked toward her. "Don't leave."

She stopped. "Are you sure?"

"Yes, I'm sure." I rubbed her back. "I missed you and I wanted to ask you something."

She turned around and took off her shades. "Ask me what?"

I gasped. Her left eye was swollen and bluish. "What happened to your face?"

She cowered. "It was an accident."

I lifted her chin so I could get a better look. "Doesn't look like an accident."

She brushed my hand away. "Is this what you wanted to ask?"

"No, I wanted to know whether you wanted your husband's body found tied to a tree stump or at the bottom of Lake Lanier."

"Stop it. It's not what you think." She pushed me aside and kept walking toward my family room. "Where are Whitney and the baby anyway?"

"Whitney's either on campus or in the streets. You know her, but the baby's . . ." I followed her through my house. "She's napping. Today was the last day of vacation bible school. She's pooped and I don't feel like waking her."

"Good. Mom always says young ladies need beauty rest and good bible study, but that little sister of ours, now, she needs Jesus."

"She needs you to come around more, too," I whispered. "She needs better guidance."

"Maybe . . ."

Ava strutted her pump-wearing, Bible-toting self toward my kitchen. The walk changed into a stagger; then she laid her head on my countertop and cried.

I stood there watching my sister—and former soft place to fall—bawl all over my marble countertop and did absolutely nothing to comfort her. I didn't know how. Ava never cried like this in front of anyone, let alone me. A huge knot squeezed my chest. I couldn't breathe. I couldn't speak. I wanted to scream.

"I'm going to kill Devon," I growled.

"No." She grabbed my hand. "Will you listen to me for a change? My husband didn't hurt me. I was in a car accident."

"Uh-huh. Then why are you slobbering all over my countertop?"

"Why do you always believe the worst of him?"

"Because the only time I hear from you is when he does something wrong." I reached inside my kitchen towel drawer next to the refrigerator and began to pat the countertop dry. "And you hadn't told me what happened to you last night."

She whimpered nonsense. My brain wasn't ready for all this foolishness.

"It's not Devon's fault, so stop bashing him, please. He's going through enough."

I stopped patting and put down the rag. "Okay, Ava. If you say so."

She lifted her head. "Good."

I stood behind her and stroked her hair, which was in better condition and smelled better than mine. Strawberries. She sniffed some more and said nothing. I waited for her to come to me like she did before things had changed between us, before getting on her nerves didn't turn into a fistfight.

She finally picked her head up, turned to me, and whined. "Stay out of my head. These extensions are Indian and cost more than your mortgage."

"How illuminating." I patted her head. "I was expecting to hear a humble appeal come through those pearly white teeth, but what was I thinking?"

I wouldn't give her the satisfaction of knowing that I wanted that hair whether it was salon bought or not. To be honest, despite that horrible Jessica Rabbit outfit she wore and the eyeliner now raccooning her face, Ava looked pretty good. Avalyn Marie Crawford McArthur, my slim, but shapely, bronze twin held the grace of a Southern belle and the class of a bourgeois countess. All unlike me. I still had a fondness for mayonnaise sandwiches, shoebox doll-houses, and bad boys with big dragon tattoos stretched across their backs.

She looked at me. "I need your help."

Even when her lips quivered and tears streamed down her face, she cried "like a lady," to use Mom speak. By the way her shoulders shook, I could tell she had been crying long before she reached my house.

I kept a basket of lace handkerchiefs in a curio near the half bath. Handkerchief collecting was my new passion. I found them at different estate sales and antique shops all over the state. Mostly up here in North Atlanta. That's how Bella and I stumbled upon our little hitching post of a home.

I grabbed my most recent conquest, an Irish cotton shamrock corner, off the pile. Mom would get a kick out of it since she prided herself on the fact that our great-great-grandfather escaped his Scotch Irish plantation owner father and married a Seminole Geechee-swearing swamp princess. On a side note, I was surprised that she hadn't called to chew me out for disturbing her honeymoon. This was her third with her fourth husband.

She read in some magazine that the secret to marriage longevity was taking honeymoons instead of celebrating anniversaries. However, she skipped the anniversary idea and decided that taking honeymoons on a whim would be more fun.

Ava had stopped crying by the time I came back into the kitchen.

I sat on the stool next to her and placed my hands in hers. "Seriously, did you and Devon get into a fight? Is he cheating on you? I promise I won't kill him. I just need to know."

"Of course we didn't, Angel. Let me remind you, he is a man of God."

"Let me remind you that we all are children of God, and if he had hit you, then I'd hit him, too."

She huffed. "Your constant dance with violence. What has it gotten you?"

"A broken heart." I slid my hand away. "I don't need to remember what I feel every day."

The doorbell rang. I stood.

She touched my hand. "Angel, please forgive me. I wasn't talking about Bella's father."

"Whatever . . ." I stepped back. "Did your man hit you or not?"

"The bishop would never hit me." She snatched the hankie back and wiped her eyes.

"The bishop . . ." I took a deep breath and cleared my mind of that last remark. Any woman who referred to her husband as a job title had issues. I handed her another hankie and walked toward the door. "I'll be right back."

I walked back down the foyer, then looked through the peephole. Justus stood on the other side. My stomach flip-flopped. He carried a casserole dish in his potholder-covered hand. Did the man know how handsome he looked?

I opened my door. "Hi, Justus."

He smiled, then extended the dish toward me. "Mac and cheese, as promised."

From where I stood, I could smell the cheese and butter bubbling over crusted parmesan.

I shook my head. "Ava's here. Come inside. I'll introduce you, since you two haven't met in person yet."

He nodded. When he walked beside me, I inhaled magnolias and cozy fires. Wow. If his cooking tasted as good as he smelled, I didn't know what I'd do with myself. I ushered him toward the kitchen, but Ava was not there.

Like a thief in the night, she had snuck out the back kitchen door. I looked out my opened door and stepped onto the patio. The hot muggy air held onto Ava's soft peach perfume and tickled my nose. Where had she run off to, and why the disappearing act?

Justus patted my shoulder.

"She ran out the back door, Justus." I turned to him. "Is that not the craziest thing you've ever seen?"

"I'm sure she had good reason to leave like she did. Maybe she felt uncomfortable when she heard my voice."

"No way. Ava's never uncomfortable around handsome men. Something's definitely up."

"Handsome? You think I'm handsome?" He laughed softly.

I waved him off. "You know what I mean. She's a natural flirt, gravitates to men like a moth to a flame. Normally, she would have sniffed you at my door before you rang the bell. But she's off her axis, apparently."

"She'll find her way back to you."

"I just hope it's not too late." I shuddered.

It wasn't cold outside nor was a cool breeze stirring. Yet, I had a chill I couldn't shake. Ava was hiding something important.

"Maybe I should go after her."

"For her to leave the way she did, I don't think she wants to be found right now."

"But her behavior isn't like her. I'm really worried now." I leaned over my patio railing. I couldn't believe she ran out like that.

I turned my attention back to Justus. "Something's wrong. I feel it."

"Come here." He pulled me into his arms. "If you need me, I'm here for you. Remember that."

The way he held me felt just right. Not in a kinky way, but a safe way, like I didn't have to worry about taking care of every little thing when he was around.

"If you don't want to have dinner now, I understand," Justus said.

"Are you kidding me? I haven't had someone else cook for me in a long time. Just give me a minute to collect my thoughts."

"Okay." He walked back inside.

I kept a pair of binoculars in a hanging flower basket on the patio. I swept my patio and backyard with them. They gave me no insight as to how Ava managed to wiggle that pencil skirt of hers down my steps, snake through my child safety-protected backyard, open the locked fence, and back out of my driveway in the itty-bitty time it took to walk Justus through my backdoor. I bit down on my thumb. Did she get a personal trainer or something?

"Macaroni!" Bella's sweet voice caught me off guard.

When I walked back inside, I found her seated at the dinner table. She had snuck downstairs after her nap or I hadn't noticed her come downstairs, because I was too preoccupied with how great Justus looked. She licked her lips while Justus spooned macaroni and cheese in her special plastic dinner bowl. I cannot lie. The sight of them melted me.

I had decided to stop cutting Bella's thick curly brown hair last year. Now it fell well past her shoulders. Thank goodness Whitney had brushed her hair back and parted it into two cascading ponytails before she left, else she wouldn't be able to see the food in front of her. I wouldn't be able to marvel with pride over her baby doll brown eyes, deep dimples, and button nose. She was a cutie. I was honored to be her mom.

After Justus placed some strawberries and peaches in another plate for Bella, he walked over to me. My heart skipped a few beats as I watched his swagger. When he wasn't in his church garb or preachy frame of mind, he had great promise.

"Since Bella's here, I assume that we will talk about my niece at a later time," he said.

"You don't mind?" I asked.

"Actually, I was hoping for another chance to cook for you."

"I better taste your cooking first before I ask for second helpings."

He laughed hard.

"Mommy, food's getting cold."

"Honey, I think it might be too hot for me."

Justus beamed and I enjoyed drinking him all in.

At midnight, my questions about Ava were answered. Ava showed up on my doorstep again. This time she wore a floor-length peach silk marabou robe, my niece and nephew strapped to her hips, and the most apologetic pout a twin could make.

Once inside, Ava peeked down the foyer and looked up toward the staircase, which compelled me to check my foyer and search my staircase. *Wait a minute.* I shook myself. *You know what's in your house, girl. What's wrong with you?* My older sister—by a mere four minutes—continued to have the knack of making me second-guess myself, even when the obvious hit me smack dab in our thirty-four-year-old faces.

I turned toward her, really looked at her, and observed the situation. She came to my house unannounced, with her children, but without her husband.

I asked her the only obvious questions anyone with good sense would ask. "What are you doing here, and where is your husband?"

No reply. Not a good sign for a preacher's wife, or at least the ones I knew.

Six years ago, a local paper had botched a tax scandal investigation of Atlanta Faith Church, which I called Big Faith. Since then, anywhere Ava went or anything she said, my cronies from television and radio were sure to note and file away. I was once a reporter. I knew the game. So when this infamous, provocatively dressed preacher's wife snuck out in the middle of the night with the celebrity preacher's kids to visit a sister whom her husband promised to never speak to again, it didn't look like Big Faith was involved at all. Looked more like big trouble.

I didn't like any kind of trouble, big or teeny tiny.

I decided to ask another question. "Is something wrong?"

Ava shifted her kids on her hips and spoke so soft I had to read her lips. "I don't know."

Granted, it's not hard for me to read lips. All it took was a basic knowledge of the human face—which was fairly easy, since Ava and I shared the same face. Yet, I was confused. We were in the North Atlanta burbs. Ava was safer than an angel at dawn here. Yet, she just scoped my place like Satan was lurking behind the couch. She searched my eyes like our being twins never mattered, like I hadn't battled hell to save her or that Bible-spouting husband of hers six years ago. And the best answer she could come up with was she didn't know? Who was she fooling?

"You don't know what? Why you're here or where your husband is?"

She bit her lip. "I don't know anything anymore."

"Well, you've come to the wrong place. Honey, you know I've been fresh out of answers since Y2K."

She chuckled and shifted the kids again. "How about a fresh pot of coffee and a place to rest until I figure some things out?"

"Now, *that* I can do." I pointed toward my staircase. "Why don't you put the kids upstairs? Lil' D and Taylor can sleep in the guest room next to Bella's. You can bunk with me. Whitney's room is the pits, so don't look at that mess. I'll pull out my generic instant coffee and some stale coffeecake that's been hovering in the back of my fridge. How 'bout that?"

She hesitated before she nodded. "Sounds perfect."

As we approached the stairs, I thought of sleeping Bella. She had longed for another sister or brother since she realized all her friends had sisters and brothers. Why *we* women could not be satisfied with what we had was beyond me. Fortunately, she'd get her wish tonight.

From where I stood, all I heard was her soft snore and her vacation bible school music stampeding down the floor—this year's theme was Western Roundup. Their finale pool party was tomorrow. We had to giddyap by eight in the morning, so I needed to be asleep like now.

"Let me help you." I stretched out my arms to take one of the kids from Ava.

She turned away from me and clutched them tighter. It reminded me of the time she didn't want me to play with her porcelain dolls. It reminded me of how awkward and unworthy I often felt around her. Why did I let her in my house?

"I wouldn't hurt them. You know that," I said.

She nodded, but wouldn't release one child to me. Whatever.

I pointed toward the stairs. "After you."

Once we reached the second floor, I stopped. "I'm going to check on Bella. Okay?"

She nodded with a slight hesitation again, then continued toward the guest room.

An old statistics professor of mine once taught me that over sixty-five percent of communication was nonverbal. Fifty-five percent of what a person meant was in their facial expression. Ava hadn't looked me in the eyes since she got here, and that last bob was suspect.

"Avalyn Marie McArthur?"

She turned around and winked at me. "I'm good, Angel."

I sighed. That Betty Boop wink of hers always calmed me down. For a moment, we were little girls again, sneaking off at dawn to fish in our granny's creek. No puberty, boys, or any of those things that eventually separated us. We were in sync back then. Why couldn't it be that way again?

I winked back and then went to check on my child. Maybe Ava missed me as much as I did her. Maybe that's why she was here. Or maybe I was jumping to conclusions again. I'd been doing that a lot lately.

That's the only negative about being a retired reporter. I couldn't stop questioning every doggone thing. Like lately, I could swear that Ms. Hattie Mae, my neighbor across the street, stayed up at night watching passersby out her window. Or take Darlene Eades, the mother of three under three, two doors down. I had never seen her without a well-rested smile. Creepy.

Bella slept soundly. I kissed her cheek and left for downstairs. When I got down there, Ava wasn't there. I checked my kitchen, the den, every room, including the patio. So I went back upstairs to see if she needed any help with my niece and nephew.

But when I got upstairs, I couldn't find her there either. I found three suitcases, however. I assumed she brought them in while I was upstairs.

"Ava?" I searched the guest room.

No Ava. I went back upstairs and searched my room. She wasn't there either. Then I heard a car door slam outside.

I ran to the window and looked outside. I groaned. *You gotta be kidding me.* Sure enough, my perfect sister politely was backing of my driveway without a word. Gone again, but this time she left her kids behind.

My heart pounded. What in the world was going on?

I raced out the room, down the hall, and slid down the banister. It wasn't pretty and it chafed. Despite the discomfort, I yanked the front door open and stumbled onto the porch. But I was too late. She peeled off into the night just as I hopped off the last step.

"Avalyn!" I screamed at her taillights speeding down my normally quiet street. "I can't take care of three kids and Whitney."

5

I stood on my porch for thirty minutes, waiting and praying for Ava to come back. My hands shook. My head swam. My mind raced. My sister had me bent with few options.

I called her cell phone; she didn't answer. I wanted to call her house, but there was no way she was there so soon, and I wasn't sure if my calling would cause trouble. I wanted to call Mom, but then I remembered that if I did that, then I should also prepare for her to kill me, or worse, tell me how I continue to fail her as a daughter. Or, I could travel to Ava's place in Decatur to find out what was going on and, if need be, kick D's butt. Sounded good to me, except I had to tell Whitney what just happened.

I took a slow walk to her room. Our little sister was no joke. Unlike Ava and me, she grew up in Atlanta instead of the country. Because she had always lived in the city, she had very little patience, except when it came to Bella. Her whole logic about life was different than Ava's and mine, too. Although I learned to develop a thick skin, I believe Whitney was born to fight. At least that's what Mom said when she made her come live with me.

I knocked on her door.

She flung it open. "What?"

"You're awake." I hopped back.

Whitney didn't look like Ava and me, not because of the obvious. We had different dads. She was longer, leaner, darker, and oozed sexiness. Even with her hair in a ponytail and wrapped in a bandana. She looked like Atlanta.

"I couldn't help but be after all that jumping and running Bella was doing in the house. Do you know when I went to her room, she was sound asleep? How does a kid make all that noise, then look so innocent and quiet in the next minute?" She shook her head, then tilted her head at me. "How much do you know about her daddy?"

"Whitney, it wasn't Bella making that racket, it was me, Ava, and her kids."

Her eyes widened. "Ava's here?"

"Nope, not anymore. She left about a half hour ago."

"Why was she stopping through this late? Did she and Devon just come back from a road trip or something?"

"Ava came here with the kids without Devon. She was dressed in a froufrou nightgown looking sad, real sad. I went to check on Bella, and before I knew what was happening, she left us with the kids and disappeared."

She grabbed me and pulled me inside. "What in the world? What's up with her? Let me call her." She reached for her cell phone.

"Wait." I caught her hand. "Ava has a bruise on her face. She says it was an accident, but it looked like a handprint to me."

Whitney reached for her shoes under her nightstand. "Let's go."

"Hold on!" I snatched the shoes from her. "If it is what we think it is, we have to be careful. I think we need to call the Dekalb County Police first."

"Bump the police. Pack the up kids. Let's go. I got some

hurt for him." She ran out the door and down the hall. "Meet you in the garage. I need to get some tools."

"Wait . . ." Maybe I should have asked her to be my heavy last night when I needed it. "Don't you wake up those kids."

The phone rang. I looked at it. It was Justus. I smiled.

Whitney returned to the room with the other cordless phone on her right ear and a grin on her face. "Hold on, Justus. She's right here . . ."

She stood beside me, muted the phone, then elbowed me without dropping any of the tools in her arms. "Why didn't you tell me Justus was here today?"

"Because I didn't have time to. Plus, Ava's disappearing acts almost blew my night with Justus.

"Your night?" She grabbed me by my pajama top. "Did y'all go on a date? And you didn't tell me?"

"No, technically no. He brought dinner here."

"Shut the front door," Whitney squealed. "And now he's making a booty call."

I snatched the phone from her. "He's a minister. You can't say stuff like that."

"Hmm . . ." She pursed her lips. "He's a man, ain't he?"

"Girl, get a grip. He is a man, not one of your wangster boy toys."

"Whatever." She looked at the phone. "I bet you five dollars he's waiting on the phone."

I frowned. "And what would be the point of this bet?"

"As long as we've been talking . . . if he's still holding on, he wants more than just to talk with you." She giggled. "Ooh. Why would he want you at one in the morning? You know what that means? He wants you for life, wifey." She laughed louder.

"Stop it. Please get that thought out of your head." I checked the phone to see if he was holding. "It probably has something to do with his niece. He came over here today to convince me to work for him. Apparently, some mysterious Romeo has her nose wide open. The child probably snuck out the house tonight."

"Ttttt." Whitney shook her head as she dumped a steel chain and two hammers in a duffle bag. "Been there, done that."

I plopped myself back on her bed. "I can't help him right now."

"So what are you going to do?

"Tell him the truth." I lifted the receiver and unmuted the call. "Hello, Justus. Is something wrong?"

"Everything is fine. Actually, I'm calling to find out if you're okay. I heard you screaming."

"How did you hear me? Are you outside my house again?"

"No, not exactly. I needed to take a jog." He chuckled. "For some reason, I couldn't sleep. Why are you awake? Is it because of Ava?"

"Are you psychic, too?"

"No, but I saw someone that resembled you back out of your driveway in the same nice car I noticed parked in it when I dropped by earlier today."

"Oh, yes." I shook my head. "Yes, you did. How is Kelly, by the way?"

"She's fine. She just got home. From where, I have no clue."

"You gotta be kidding me."

"No, I wouldn't kid about the real reason I'm jogging around the neighborhood at one in the morning." He huffed. "I needed to burn off some steam before I returned home."

"I'm sorry." Whitney knelt beside me and leaned her head on the other side of the receiver. I rolled my eyes at her. "I know how taxing family can be."

"I'm scared for Kelly, and that makes me feel helpless," he said.

"Again, I know exactly how you feel, but I can't talk. I have to see about Ava. Something is horribly wrong."

Whitney tapped my shoulder. "We need to get to Decatur before something else bad happens to Ava."

"You're right. I do," I said to Whitney, then stood up.

"What do you mean?" Justus asked. "Where are you going?"

I waved Whitney off again. "I'm going to Ava's home, to see if she's okay."

"No, we all are," Whitney shouted.

I turned to Whitney. "What did I tell you?"

She folded her arms and pouted. "She's my sister, too."

"I know that." I huffed. "Justus, I need a favor. Whitney has finals in the morning and she needs her sleep. Plus, if something goes down, I definitely don't want her caught in between. She's pre-law, if you know what I mean. And to be honest, I need a tagalong that won't piss Ava off."

"I see." Justus sighed. "Why don't you call the police? They're better suited for this sort of thing and they can arrive at Ava's within minutes. Realistically, you're an hour away. By the time we got there, who knows what could happen."

"We?" I sat up straighter. "As in you would be my wing man if . . . ?"

"No, you don't." Whitney shook her bag. "I'm ready to roll. He can stay here and watch the kids."

I shushed her. "You're staying here and protecting the house."

Whitney threw the bag on the bed. "Why don't you admit that you want a good excuse to be with Justus tonight?"

"Hush!" I tried to cover the phone, but it was too late. I cringed. "Justus, are you there?"

"I'm outside your house right now," he said. His voice was deep and dark like Ms. Ida's six-layer chocolate cake.

"Now?"

"Nope, now I'm at your door." He hung up.

The doorbell rang.

I held the phone in my hand. My mouth fell wide open. "He's downstairs."

"Who?" Whitney asked.

"Justus."

"Girl, stop."

"I'm not joking, so you better cool it when I let him in the house or one of those hammers in your bag will mysteriously find your backside."

I threw on a robe, bopped back downstairs, and opened the door.

"Angel . . ."

I had never met a man who could say my name and make me feel like a queen at the same time. My jaw dropped. His locks were pulled back into a ponytail. He wore a Polo track suit jacket with matching shorts. He hugged me.

I exhaled into Justus's close cuddle. I liked my new friend too much.

Justus released me. "Are you ready?"

I nodded and reached for my keys. "I'll drive."

Justus and I sped down southeast I-85 toward Dekalb County. The Atlanta skyline vanished, returned, and then faded again into the night over hills and around curves and kudzu. The drive reminded me of Ava's disappearing acts earlier. What was going on with her? I was so afraid for what it might be. In my past, I had seen things, things hidden behind the sanctity of marriage, things that would turn a single woman cold to falling in love. My arms shivered and my legs twitched as I recalled those horrible things. I had to get to my sister fast. I gripped the wheel and floored it.

Justus sat in the passenger seat. I glanced at him. His jaw was clenched. I looked down past his legs. His feet were dug into my floorboard. My speeding had unnerved him. I shook my head in chastisement, then lifted my foot off the gas and slowed down.

"Sorry," I said. "I'm anxious."

He nodded. "No apologies. I understand."

I smiled. I really liked the little bit I knew of him. I glanced at him again.

"Thank you for coming with me. I know this seems unorthodox, but I didn't have anyone else to turn to tonight." I headed eastbound on Spaghetti Junction. "Whitney needs to be home with the kids and my mom is away."

"What about the brunch ladies? Are you friends with any of them?"

"Not like I should be."

"What does that mean?"

"It's hard for people who share their secrets with you on a professional level to also want to be friends with you."

"Is everyone in the group your client?"

"No, but it's an excuse. I have many." I sighed. "I need to do better as a friend to those women. I don't know how to be vulnerable and tough at the same time."

"You will in time . . . I'm honored you thought enough of me to let me be here for you."

"Well, you're my pastor." I smirked. "If I can't come to you with this kind of mess, then what good are you?"

He laughed. "So true."

I noticed the time on the dashboard. If Ava had gone home, she would be there by now.

"Could you use my phone to call Ava's cell for me?" I asked. "I want to let her know we're on our way."

"Sure." He reached for my phone, dialed, then waited. "Your sister isn't answering the house phone or her cell. Are you sure she's home?"

I nodded. "Call it twin-tuition. She's there."

My gut, however, bubbled and screamed. *Don't go down there, girlfriend.* I sped up despite myself.

Justus gripped the seat. "Slow down, Angel. We'll get there when we're supposed to." His voice was soft, yet stern.

I eased off the gas.

He sighed. "Thank you."

"I'm sorry. Can you call my home and ask Whitney whether or not Ava has called?"

"Okay." He huffed again. "I understand your motive for rushing, but I've heard great things about Bishop McArthur. I don't think he would ever hurt your sister. Is there a history of violence between them?"

"Not with them. With me. Devon and I have a long, bad history."

"What?"

"It's a long story."

"We have about thirty minutes to go before we reach Decatur, so take your time, literally." He nestled into the passenger seat.

"Once upon a time . . ." I sighed, then told him about my life—why up until this week Ava had stopped talking to me, and the real reason I launched Angel Watch Bail Recovery Agency after taking a contract gig with Tiger.

6

Friday, 1:30 AM
The McArthur Estate, Stone Mountain, GA

I hadn't been to the McArthur Mansion in a minute, but to say that they had had an extreme makeover would be a flat-out lie. From the security gate, we saw magnolia motley lining the front façade, a marble water fountain that twinkled in the night, and a home that made my place look smaller and less approachable than Granny's old outhouse. And the gate looked like something from a *Mission Impossible* movie. I stared at the gate. When did all this happen?

"Do you know the password?" Justus pointed at the security pad at the foot of the gate.

"Nope." I pressed a few buttons until the gate opened.

Justus's left eyebrow almost lifted past his forehead. He chuckled. "Yes, you did."

"No, I guessed. You know, twin-power." I touched my forehead while the gates opened, then drove forward. "Sometimes I think Ava's in my head."

"Is that true? Can you guys read each other's minds?"

"Nope, but stranger things have happened."

"Of course. What was I thinking? My nephews . . . the things they come up with. It makes me wonder sometimes."

"Mmmm . . ." I sighed as I veered right into the curve of the front drive. "Ava and I aren't close enough anymore to feel anything but disdain for each other."

"There must be something there between you, because your guess was a good one."

"It was, wasn't it?"

I parked my car in the front drive, a bit away from the fountain. I didn't want water messing up my new wax job. Justus stepped out, walked around to my side, then opened the door. He held his hand out for me. I hesitated before I took it.

He looked at me. "Having second thoughts?"

I looked down at my hands. They trembled. The lie about the keypad entry and Ava's drop-off had my nerves bad. I shook my head. "Nope, I'm good to go."

Yep, I lied again. Call it a talent. Yet, this time Justus didn't seem to buy it. He wouldn't let my hand go. He stood in front of me and said nothing, but I could tell his eyes were searching for the truth. He had great eyes.

"Justus, let's go. It's too quiet out here. I don't like it." I searched the grounds as we walked toward the front door.

The place was lit like an elegant Christmas tree. I wondered how they slept with all these lights on in the front. We stopped short of the double entrance doors and he turned to me.

"Before we go inside, I need to tell you something that I've wanted to say long before you called me tonight," he said.

My heart skipped again. "What is it?"

He opened his mouth, then a toe-curling shriek rippled through my body. It was a woman's scream. I dropped his hands and turned toward where the sound came from.

"What was that?" Justus asked.

"Ava." I leaned on the doorbell.

I didn't have a key or a clue how to get inside, but I saw two huge planters flanking the door. I reached for one. It looked heavy, but I was capable of throwing it. Thank goodness I had carried Bella's forty-pound body all over the place. I lifted that planter off the ground so fast and without a sweat, but Justus caught my arm.

He took the planter out of my hand and placed it back down. "No sense in you going to jail for breaking and entering. Let's call 911."

"You call. I'm going in." I leaned down to grab the planter again.

"Wait . . ." He walked toward the door, jiggled the knob, and opened it. "This is how most robbers get in."

I watched him in disbelief. "I thought you didn't look like the kind of person who always walked the straight and narrow."

"I haven't always been saved." He grinned. "Another thing we have in common."

"What about 911?" I asked.

"I got it. Go."

Without hesitation, I tiptoed inside.

No alarms went off when I walked inside, which meant for me that either Devon left the alarm off with hopes that Ava would return, or that Ava had already returned but forgot to turn the alarm back on. If the latter, I wondered why she forgot, especially since she acted like a bodyguard on adrenaline in my home. I had a sinking feeling that the correct answer wasn't a good one.

As I walked through the foyer, I listened for more screaming. The only sound I heard came from upstairs. It was a moaning that gave me more shivers. I hadn't heard that sound since Granny died.

Something caught my shoulder from behind. I jumped, then panted.

"It's me," Justus whispered.

I spun around and punched his right shoulder. "Don't scare me like that."

I winced. It was solid muscle. I wrang my hands.

He took my throbbing hands in his. "Careful. You may hurt yourself."

"Whatever." I slid my hand away from his. "What did the police say? Are they on their way? And you're supposed to stay outside."

"Yes, I called the police, but I'm not letting you go up there alone. Actually, I think we both should go back outside and wait for them."

Boom. Something fell upstairs.

I looked above me, then back to Justus. "Stay. I mean it."

Then I tiptoed toward the staircase and looked around. On the inside, the McMansion was pretty and quiet like a snow day, even in the dark. A white baby grand piano sat in the grand room, which led to a white rose-covered sitting room. I wondered if Taylor and Lil' D ever played in there. Probably not. Ava was the kind of person who lived and died by rules and room restrictions. The children more than likely had their own playroom hidden in a wall around here somewhere. There wasn't even a scent of crayons and burnt cookies in the air.

I saw a picture of Bella on a table in the living room that made me feel like a horrible aunt. The noises became clearer now, and I followed it up the staircase until I reached the end of the hall. I felt for my cell phone stun gun in my back pocket. It wasn't my real phone, but a decoy Taser and flashlight. It was girly pink, too. If I only remembered one thing from my ten years in Girl Scouts, it was to always be prepared. I definitely was tonight. This baby could put out 900,000 volts.

Justus pointed toward the last door on the left.

I stopped. "What are you doing up here?" I grunted through my teeth.

"Shhh . . ." He pointed at a gold-plated nameplate on the door. It read, THE BISHOP'S STUDY. I looked at Justus. This was where the noise came from. I felt my lips tighten. I knew Devon was behind all this drama. I didn't want to go in there. I didn't want to be right for the first time in my life.

Justus looked at me and mouthed, *Ready?*

My heart raced. I could hear it pounding in my ears. I stepped back. I clutched Justus's hand. I was too scared to answer. I stood there frozen. What was wrong with me? I wasn't afraid of anything, so why was I scared now?

Justus twirled me around until I was behind him. "Stay back here. I'll knock."

I nodded, but totally forgot his request when I heard Ava scream, "Devon!"

I pushed Justus out of the way, swung the door open, and saw nothing but Devon's plaques hanging on the wall. It was dark, except for a dim light around the corner. I stepped around and peaked.

"Devon," Ava wailed some more. Her voice came from the other side of the wall. "Rachel?"

"No, Ava, it's me," I yelled.

My heart fell into my tennis shoes. It beat on my toes. I stepped forward and then back. My toes tingled now. My head throbbed so loud I could feel my heart beating now.

Justus grabbed me. "Stay behind me for real this time."

I nodded. I couldn't speak; I felt helpless. Out of all the dangerous situations I had involved myself in, I couldn't pull my wits together to do what I could usually do in my sleep. I wasn't afraid of what would happen to me. I was afraid of what I might see had happened to Ava. I was more afraid of what I could do to Devon, if it was as bad as I thought.

"Angel?" she asked between sobs. "Don't come in here."

"It's too late." I clutched Justus's shirt, then walked around the corner where she was.

I peeked, then gasped. I wasn't ready for what I saw. Devon lay on the floor in front of his desk. Ava knelt beside him, praying and crying. Dark, thick blood oozed from his side, past her hands, knees, and through the once-white carpet. It was too much blood for me. I became nauseous and light-headed. I stumbled back. Justus caught me.

"Is he dead?"

"Not sure, but it doesn't look good," Justus said.

"I'm going to have to get a closer look."

He caught my hand. "Angel, trust me. You don't need to see this."

The last time I had seen Bella's father alive flashed through my mind. I jolted and dropped Justus's hand.

"Angel, what's wrong?"

"Nothing." I stepped forward. "Justus, don't get it twisted. I've seen worse and he needs medical attention now."

"Then I'll do it."

"Why?"

"Because I'm trained to."

My brows puckered. "To do what?"

"I was a Navy Hospital Corpsman for the Marine Corps."

"Are you kidding me?"

"Nope."

"Well, then check to see if he's bleeding. If he is, then he's still alive."

"I know." Justus rolled his eyes. "Just stay back there."

He walked toward Ava.

"I'm calling 911 back. They should be here by now." Justus knelt over Devon's body. "There's a lot of blood, but *he's* not bleeding. I think he's gone."

I lowered my head. This couldn't be happening again.

Justus whispered the Twenty-third Psalm. My chest tightened more then and my throat burned. He recited that psalm during devotional service on days when I felt most broken.

Once I could control my tears, I asked, "How long has it been since you called 911?"

He checked his watch. "Maybe seven minutes."

"They should be here any minute now, then. Call them again and tell them there's a possible death at the residence."

I didn't like saying those words. I didn't like the implication for Ava once Justus made that call. I couldn't believe that she would come back here to kill Devon. Ava didn't have a mean bone in her body. Our mother's evil streak resided in me and Whitney.

I stepped closer toward Ava; then I hopped back like I just saw a big Okefenokee Swamp rat.

A knife rested near her right foot. It was an eight-inch blade Wüsthof cook's knife, to be exact. I knew the knife well, because seven years ago I found myself in the middle of a Southern Living Home Décor bidding war with my bunco buddies over that last available must-have knife. It was my wedding gift to Ava. Now I wished I hadn't shelled out $150 for the thing, and instead had bought a cheaper one that didn't cut so clean and sharp.

I took a hard look at Devon, Ava, the room, and became nauseated. "What's wrong with this picture?" I mumbled. Something in here didn't seem right.

Ava looked up at me, her eyes now smothered in black goop. "Where are my children?"

"They're fine," I said. "They're sleeping, just as you left them."

Justus added, "Whitney's caring for them."

She looked at Justus. "And who are you?"

"I'm Ava's friend, the one who picked her up from Grady Memorial the other night," he said.

"He's also my pastor."

"Friend and pastor who likes to drive you around Atlanta at all times of night?" Ava asked, although it seemed more like judgment than a question.

I sighed. "Yes, he didn't want me driving here by myself. I had to find out why you ran off from my house like you did."

"How thoughtful . . ." She sniffled. Her eyes looked more troubled than before. She kissed Devon's head, then caressed it. "Now, could you please leave us? I need to say good-bye to my husband."

"Honey, I'm not going to leave you. I'm not. Not like this. EMS and DeKalb County Police should be here any moment now. You don't need to be here in this position when they arrive. You need to move."

"I'm not going anywhere. This is my position . . ." She sobbed and rocked back and forth again. "Get out!"

I shuddered from her shout. "No, we need to see if Devon's okay. We want to help him."

Ava shook her head. Her eyes were closed now. She clutched Devon's white bishop's collar and cried. "It's too late. He's dead. He's dead, Angel. You can't help him now. Leave."

Her words ran cold through my body, but my mind was on fire. Questions filled it. The curious cat in me couldn't contain myself, but I had enough common sense to ask those questions later. I had to help my sister right now.

"Then let me help you."

We heard something out in the hallway.

She looked at me, then at the door. "You're too late for that, too."

Justus turned around and gasped. From the heavy shadow cast on the wall in front of me, I could tell we were not alone anymore. It had to be EMS.

"We're in here. Please hurry. My brother-in-law is seriously wounded." I straightened my clothes and walked closer to Ava. "Honey, you need to let him go so EMS can help."

"Don't move," a man said from behind me.

His voice was heavier than the lead in my feet. I heard the familiar metal click of a Glock backing up his demand for us to stay still. His high-pitched squeak and nervous short breaths took me off guard. He didn't sound like emergency services or the DeKalb County Police responding officers for that matter, though I could be wrong. So I studied a framed photo of Devon on the wall in front of us until I could get a better view of our trigger-happy friend. He was a large, familiar dark blob with eyes, who definitely was not DeKalb County PD. I tsked. He was one of Devon's bodyguards, Terry Mapp, as a matter of fact. I sighed once the full realization of him came into view. If he could shoot a gun, he'd shoot himself by accident. I'd met this guy before. I had hauled his sister Betty to jail for bail jumping a shoplifting charge.

I threw my hands on my hips. "Terry, put the gun down."

"Angel, how did you get in here?" His eyes widened; he noticed Justus, then returned to me. "I should've known. And who do you have with you, one of Big Tiger's thugs?"

"No, he's my pas—"

"Sir, calm down," Justus cut in.

I shushed Justus. "Hush. This fool'll kill us and not know how he did it."

"We need your help. Bishop McArthur is critically wounded," he continued despite my warning. "Please help us before it's too late."

"It's already too late, Terry. The bishop's dead . . ." Ava said. Her voice had become heavy, stone. "So put the gun down or come over here and shoot me."

Terry hurried past me and Justus.

"No!" He dropped the pistol.

The gun bounced on the floor and went off.

Before I could duck, Justus threw me to the ground. I gasped, but found it hard to breathe. Justus was literally on top of me. His locks smelled of hibiscus and sandalwood. I could feel the definition of his six-pack and the indention of his ginormous cross pendant both hidden under his shirt. My arms were splayed out across the floor. I lifted my left hand to see if it had landed on top of any bloodstains; then my eyes found its way to Devon. His eyes were closed. A blood trickle from the corner of his mouth had dried.

I turned away and patted Justus's back.

"I can't breathe."

Justus didn't reply or move.

"Justus, are you okay?"

The doorbell rang.

"Oh no." I wheezed and then heard footsteps and walkie-talkie sputter from the window. I stroked his hair. "Please, don't be dead, too."

He mumbled, "I'm not. Are you hurt?"

"Kind of . . . your body has me pinned to the ground and my legs are going numb."

He lifted up slowly. His face was a kiss away from me. My lips tingled.

"Was that the doorbell?" He frowned.

I nodded, while chiding myself for even thinking of stealing a smooch at a time like this. *Bad girl.* I glanced at Ava. My heart tugged again. *Very bad, horrible, insensitive girl.*

"I think it's the EMTs," Terry said.

"More than likely it's the police, you idiot. I can't believe you have a permit for that gun."

"I'm sorry about that." Terry picked the gun up, checked the safety, and put it back in his holster.

"I'm sorry my brother-in-law believed you could protect them."

"Are you blaming this on me?" Terry shouted.

"Hello, is anyone up there?" a man asked from somewhere downstairs. "This is the Dekalb County Police."

"Oh God," I whispered. "The door was unlocked."

Justus hopped up and swooped me up so fast my unbrushed ponytail bounced. "See to Ava."

I nodded.

"We're upstairs at the end of the hall. We need emergency services. Are they with you, too?" Justus asked.

"I can't hear you," the officer shouted.

"In the bishop's study," I spoke louder, but not too loud.

"Where?" he asked.

I shook my head. This place was so big two people couldn't hold a conversation unless they were near each other.

I tried to get Ava's attention, but she rocked Devon in her arms, and from what I heard, she seemed to be praying or slowly losing her mind. At that point I couldn't decipher between the two.

"I'm going downstairs to bring them back up."

Justus caught my hand before I walked out. "Wait."

I gasped. "What?"

"It'll be better if I go with you," he said.

"Justus, no . . . stay with them," I whispered.

"Angel, yes. I called them. Remember?"

"But you don't—"

Terry ran out. "Help!"

Justus and I both looked at each other. His jaw had dropped. I didn't have to look down to his knees to know they were buckling.

I should have shot that fool when I had the chance, I said to myself as I watched Justus, Ava, and Devon's dying or dead body next to her.

"Everything will be fine. I promise." I pasted the same smile on my face that I gave all the girls before I hauled them back to jail.

"Everyone, show me your hands now," a commanding voice shouted from behind me.

I raised my hands in the air. This time I knew our situation just turned difficult.

7

Although Devon's study was large enough to be a master bedroom and two guest rooms, the droves of armed Dekalb County policemen filling up the hallway could not join us inside. The responding officer walked slowly toward us, while his partner stood underneath the threshold. No EMTs were in sight. However, I heard someone talking medical jargon to someone else in the hallway, so I assumed they were here. I hoped they were here. Yet, I couldn't be sure because I was preoccupied with staring down the rather large S&W barrel moving closer and closer toward my nose. Justus stood to my left, whispering a prayer of deliverance, I'm sure. On the other hand, Ava continued mumbling and praying as if we weren't there, as if these cops wouldn't shoot her if she wasn't still. But then again maybe she wanted to be shot. . . . And Terry Mapp . . . he had better hope I didn't see him anytime soon.

However, the gun-wielding uniform standing in front of me was a sight to behold. He was a strawberry-blond, hazel-eyed gentleman about my age, who took great care of his skin and body, despite the black poly-blend uniform pants he wore. He also had a dangerous twinkle in his eye that reminded me too much of myself. Under normal circumstances, I would have sweet talked him into moonlighting with me. But then again, he had a .40 caliber Smith & Wesson pointed at my face. I didn't think he was in the mood to hear my career move proposition, and the gun's position had begun to piss me off.

"Put your hands back up, ma'am," he said.

I looked down. I hadn't realized that I had folded my arms over my chest. I unfurled them slow and steady for him to see.

He smirked. "Thank you. Now . . . what's your name?"

"Angel Crawford. I'm Mrs. McArthur's sister. She's the owner of this estate, and she and her husband, my brother-in-law, are on the floor behind me. They need immediate medical attention."

"Again, thank you for bringing that to my intention. Before I can help them, I need to know, are you armed?" the officer asked.

"Yes. . . ." I bit my lip. "I have a Taser and maybe some tear gas, um . . . some woodchucks, a pocketknife. I'm not sure which knife, actually. Maybe my gun. I haven't checked my purse in a couple of days. They all should be in my purse on my shoulder, though. Do you want to check?"

He looked back at the other officer standing behind him. The other officer shrugged.

"Angel, carefully hand me your purse so that I can give it to Officer Todd."

"Angel, out of curiosity, why do you have so many weapons in your purse?"

"I'm a bail recovery agent in this county, sir." I shifted my legs. "I work every now and then for Trusted Bail Bonds.

"Tiger's girl, hmm . . ." He harrumphed, then called for more backup. "Did you fire your gun before we arrived?"

"No, Devon's bodyguard, the man you met running down the hall, did that. I hope you didn't let him get away."

He wrote down something in his note pad. "And you?" The officer referred to Justus. "Who are you?"

"Reverend Dr. Prince Justus Morgan. I'm the one who called."

"Prince?" both the police officer and I asked simultaneously.

"Don't ask."

"I'm Officer Brady and that's Officer Todd behind me." He lowered his gun, put it back in his holster, and whispered, "Is that Mrs. McArthur inside with the knife?"

I shut my eyes. I forgot about the knife.

"I'm afraid so." I heard myself whimper. I threw my hands over my mouth. I began to cry again.

"Angel, it's okay," Justus said. "It's okay."

"No, it isn't." I shook my head. *We might be going to jail.*

"Unfortunately, guys. You'll have to stop talking to each other for now," Officer Brady said.

"No problem. It won't happen again." I cleared my throat.

Brady turned his attention to Justus. "You're the one who called, right?"

"Yes, we did," he said. "I don't mean to be rude, but the bishop and his wife need medical attention, officers."

"That's why we're talking to you two. We need to make sure this place is safe for EMS, which brings me to the matter of the gun shot we heard from outside. Is there anyone else inside who could be armed?" Brady asked.

I looked past his service revolver in his holster and his very quiet partner who stood in the middle of the hallway. He had his gun in his hand, but not pointed at me or Justus, ready for both of us, I assumed. Past him there were two emergency service technicians standing at the end of the hall and a few more cops at the top of the staircase. My heart bounced around pretty fast, so fast I had to inhale and exhale slowly until my hands stopped shaking.

"Angel?" he hissed.

I jumped. "Yes! It's safe."

"What happened in there, Angel?" Brady's partner, Officer Todd, asked me, but I was too focused on watching Justus walk farther down the hall with another uniform.

I knew that responding officers often separated scene witnesses and could-be suspects from each other, so that one's account did not influence another. I wondered what Terry told them about me. I wondered if I should have told Officer Brady that Terry almost shot me?

I shook my head. "I'm sorry. I wasn't paying attention. What did you say?"

He continued to empty the contents of my purse in a series of quiet plops and splats on Ava's nice table. There wasn't as much in there as I had thought: my wallet, keys, a can of mace, duct tape, mini binoculars, pack of gum, lip gloss, waterproof sunscreen, my cell phone, the usual . . .

"Todd, come here!" Officer Brady shouted from inside the room. "We have a problem. The bishop's dead. Call in the Dicks."

I cringed.

Officer Todd now stood in front of the door, so I couldn't see anything. I tsked.

"Angel, I just need you to answer some questions to help us give the best account of what happened to your brother-in-law before we wrap up things here. And since it appears that I don't have to explain everything to you, like I'm sure we would with your two male friends down the hall—"

"You don't have to explain what to me?" I interrupted.

"You're a bounty hunter. You see things that the bodyguard and your pastor boyfriend don't have a clue to look for. I'm hoping you can help us out, so I can get my job done and all of us can get out of here before it gets too crazy." Just then, the M.E. walked past us and into the study.

"It's already too crazy, and Justus isn't my boyfriend." I paused and then tried to peer over his shoulder, but even on my tiptoes I couldn't see Ava. I sighed. "How bad does this look for my sister?"

"You knew that answer before we arrived, Angel."

"But I was . . . I was wrong . . ." I sniffed, then kicked the wall floorboard too hard. "Shoot." I winced and grabbed my foot.

Officer Todd touched my shoulders. "Actually, Angel, after a little thought, I think we have all we need from you, so come on," he said. "Let me take you downstairs."

"But wait . . ." I looked around. Few police officers were on the floor now. I peeked over his shoulder and observed Devon's study. Ava was now seated in a chair. Her hands rested in her laps, handcuffed. I gasped and turned toward him. "Are you arresting her?"

Instead of answering, Officer Todd led me away from the study.

8

Friday, 3:00 AM

Not so fast. We hadn't moved two feet before I spotted a dark fedora on an overdressed man standing in front of Terry.

When Terry pointed at me, I lowered my head. I knew I needed to stay upstairs and in the loop on the investigation. But how . . . ?

Feigning a case of vapors, Officer Todd allowed me to recover in a chair down the hall. From my position, I could see only the back of the detective. He left Terry and walked over to a woman dressed in fitted blue jeans and a white M.E.'s jacket. She carried a silver briefcase and had a high-pitched, crystalline, yet peachy, southern kind of voice.

The detective nodded his head toward the body. "How bad is it? What's your best guess as to the time of death?"

"I won't know that until I do an autopsy. My best guess is a few hours ago."

"Can you give me something more concrete? The victim wasn't run of the mill, if you know what I mean."

"I wish it were that simple. But who knows, Sal?" She motioned for the other members of her team to enter the room. "For all I know, this man could have caught the Holy Ghost and had a stroke before he was stabbed. He could be on blood thinners or blood pressure pills, which would make him bleed out faster than normal. There are too many variables for me just to take his temp and tell you when he died. All we know for sure is that he died today, not too long ago. Tell the church his spirit lives. Will that work for you?"

I looked at Justus, who'd just knelt beside me. His attention was definitely on her, too, more like a grimace.

"Can we suffice it to say that what we have here is a homicide?" the detective asked.

She nodded, "Pretty much."

"Cause of death?"

"It appears that he was stabbed to death and he was killed where y'all found him. I counted ten stab wounds, including three deep, penetrating abdominal knife wounds to his right side. But I won't know for sure until I complete the autopsy."

My own side ached after hearing that horrible detail. I gulped. Could Ava do something like that?

"So how do you know he was killed here?" he asked.

"That nice white carpet and his First Lady's snazzy shoes carry a good estimate of the amount of blood a man his size could lose before dying. Is that good enough for ya?"

"Your attitude never is," he scoffed. "But I'll take the rest. Have a good night, Browner."

She waved at him and breezed past us. I took a mental note of her name tag. Browner. Dr. Natasha Browner. She nodded at two men who were also wearing gray coroner's golf shirts. They wheeled a white body bag out of the door on a squeaky movable cot.

"Devon," Ava cried.

I shivered. Tough as I tried to appear, girlfriend wanted to cry really badly.

The overdressed detective completed his conversation with Terry and then walked toward me. I stopped breathing. Not because I was scared, but because once again I had lost my focus. The man reminded me of my father.

The detective strutted prettier than a pinstriped peacock. He wore the midnight blue pinstriped suit well. His hat hung low at the brim like Colombo, like my dad's did. Only in Atlanta could I see detectives wearing hats. Southerners sure loved tradition.

The brim covered most of the detective's face. I wanted to see his eyes, learn his age, anything I could use to prepare myself for his questions. I prayed that my stomach wouldn't erupt on the detective's nice silk shirt. The man must have his own money, because Dekalb Police didn't pay enough for silk anything.

He stopped short of stepping on my toes. I flinched.

He look at me and smiled. "No need to ask you how you know the victim."

He had a slight Peruvian accent, which dripped a familiar touch of disdain for me. It didn't matter. My brother-in-law had just been killed and my sister sat in the Crown Victoria shaking like a tail feather. I needed answers, so he could take his sarcasm and shove it up his lollipop.

"Good. So we can lose the small talk and you can ask me the big questions."

He stepped back and grinned. "You don't know who I am?"

"You're the man arresting my sister for a crime she didn't commit. Detective . . . ?"

He took off his hat. I exhaled. His dark brown eyes housed small flames. I'd met him before. He was a well-dressed man with a sexy swagger, sizzling voice, and sleepy eyes. If I didn't already know him, I would have mistaken him for the devil.

"You can call me Salvador, like you used to call me back when you worked at the *Sentinel,* but I'll take Detective Tinsley, too, from the new and improved Angel Crawford."

I wanted to crawl in the back of a cruiser and call it a night. I had to change the game somehow, regain some of my power. I straightened my shoulders. My chest and my confidence had no choice but to lift.

"Are any of those squad cars over there for my friend and myself, Salvador?" I asked.

He turned around, faced the gray sedans taking up most of the front drive, then swiveled back and raised his brow. "No, matter of fact, you aren't a suspect. Your friend isn't either, but I sure would appreciate it if you would let me ask the questions."

I nodded. "Sorry."

"Don't be." Detective Tinsley signaled the officers standing near us to help out somewhere else on the property. "I wouldn't expect less from you."

"Expect what? You know I won't incriminate my sister." I retorted.

"No, Angel, because I know who you are and what you're capable of."

"What am I capable of?" I tried to look dumbfounded, but I could tell by the expression on his face that he wasn't buying it.

He looked at Justus, who was with me again, then back at me. "Getting your sister convicted."

My chest burned. He was righter than right on that one. I suspected even Ava knew it. That's why she cautioned me to stay out of it.

"That won't be a problem, Detective. I learned my lesson six years ago."

I watched Justus. He smiled peace into me.

It didn't help.

"The best I can do for my sister is watch her kids like she asked me."

Salvador took out his PDA and asked, "When was the last time you saw your sister, excluding here?"

"A few hours ago."

He typed my response. "Where were you?"

"At my home."

"Where is that?"

"In Sugar Hill."

"Wow, that's far. Do you see each other often?"

I wanted to lie but had already told Justus the truth.

"No," I said, and prayed that Tinsley would not ask me what I would ask next myself.

Detective Tinsley stopped typing and looked up. "So the rumor is true?"

"What rumor?"

"That you've grown a conscience."

Justus stepped forward. "Officer, excuse me. My name is Reverend Justus Morgan, and to me, your remark is a bit out of line. Ms. Crawford's brother-in-law has been murdered. This is a very charged situation as is. Those comments don't help either of us."

"My apologies, Reverend." Tinsley looked at me.

I didn't move.

"So your sister, whom you're not close with, was at your home tonight because she wanted you to watch her kids? Why?"

"She didn't say and I didn't ask. Is there anything else?"

"Yes." He closed his PDA and looked at me. "If you're watching the kids, then why are you here?"

9

Friday, 3:30 AM

Justus came closer to me and placed his hand in the small of my back. He made me steady again. If the circumstances weren't so bad, tonight would have been one of the most romantic nights of my life, which is sad. I chuckled to keep from crying.

"Maybe I can give you a little information to help jog your memory," Salvador said. "Will that help?"

I wanted to go home and crawl under the covers. That would help. I nodded instead.

"According to Terry, Bishop McArthur called him tonight and told him that your sister had taken the kids and run off." He paused. "She was leaving him."

He stared at me; I gulped. "News to me."

"Terry said that he had advised the bishop to call Mrs. McArthur's cell and threaten to order an Amber Alert on the kids if she didn't return."

"Come on. Everyone knows that's not how it works. Ava wouldn't fall for such a stupid ploy." I sighed. "An Amber Alert . . . please."

"Maybe or maybe she did, but what he said makes good sense."

"Please tell me that your deduction skills hadn't fallen off since the last time we met."

"Not at all, and I guess it's safe to say that you're still as sharp as a razor blade."

"Touché. Therefore, you know that I think Terry is dumber than hot rocks and I find him suspect. Did he tell you about his gun, the one he dropped when your guys showed up?"

He smiled; Justus frowned. I had forgotten he was standing between me and Salvador. I turned away from both of them. I couldn't let Justus's disapproving scowl throw me off, and I definitely couldn't allow Salvador to realize that I had a soft spot where Justus stood, else he would use it against me later.

"He didn't have to, thanks to you. However, what he did tell me about you was interesting, and he's not as dumb as he looks."

"Yeah, right." I folded my arms over my chest again and then dropped them once I realized what I was doing. The arm fold was a classic defense move, so I rubbed my pants legs instead, which looked even guiltier than the arm fold. *Great.*

Salvador didn't open his mouth while I fidgeted. He rubbed his chin. I knew I was giving him an eyeful.

I sighed. "Well, are you going to tell me what he said or not?"

"By the way you act, I don't know if I should or recommend you for a psych evaluation before I question you."

I bit my lip. "Stop playing. I'm a little shaken up. That's normal for these circumstances. Tell me what that fool said."

Justus grunted.

"I'm sorry," I whispered to him.

Salvador looked at Justus, then me and grinned. I lifted my chin. "I was talking to you."

"Of course you were." He stepped closer to Justus, coming to stand beside him.

I was facing them both. If I played chess, I'd think I had just been checkmated.

"Angel, according to what you just said, Mrs. McArthur must have been planning to hide out at your house. After the bishop's call, she left the kids with you. Most likely feeling angry and scared, she went home. They argued again. Fought. He died. Could be self-defense, a crime of passion, or she was just sick and tired of being sick and tired in that marriage. At this point, the why doesn't matter so much. What matters is that your sister had a motive and, according to you, a perfect opportunity to kill him. *Comprende?*"

I folded my arms behind my back. "How do you know that it wasn't me who killed him? Everyone knows I couldn't stand the man."

"You have a point." He put his PDA back in his pocket. "But Dr. Browner already cleared you and your friend for murder."

"There's no way she could do that so fast."

Salvador's brow wrinkled, yet he continued to grin. "The only fingerprints on the alleged murder weapon belong to your twin. I don't need a lab report to tell me that. However, I do have an accessory to murder theory that Dr. Browner could agree on. Want to hear that one?"

"That's not fair. And you know it." I turned from him.

"It's hard, but it's fair, Ms. Crawford. And I need you to answer my questions instead of questioning me. Because whether you believe it or not, I'm looking out for your best interest. Don't worry. If your sister's not guilty, then have faith that the truth will set her free."

He had just recited the last line of the last *Sentinel* article I'd written. I looked at him and became nauseous. "Truth is relative." My stomach churned.

Salvador nodded. "It can be."

He continued talking, but my nausea made me deaf. I couldn't hear a word he said. I turned to Justus.

He mouthed, "Are you okay?"

I shook my head.

"Ms. Crawford, do you need medical attention?" Salvador took off his hat and placed it in his hand.

I turned toward him, then spewed Justus's mac and cheese over the detective's silk shirt, upchucked peanuts on his pinstriped suit, and ralphed what was left of that stale coffeecake onto that cute fedora he held in his hand. It was disgusting. I truly felt bad about that.

While Salvador's team retrieved some clean clothes for him out of his car, I was allowed a brief moment to talk to Ava after an EMT checked me out and gave me a plain white T-shirt to wear to complement my pajama bottoms. It didn't matter how I looked, because I wanted to get to Ava before they took her downtown.

The police were walking her out of the house around the same time I left the EMT ambulance. Officer Todd saw me and motioned me over. I don't know where Justus was at that point.

"Detective Tinsley is allowing you five minutes with her before we take her downtown. But we want to get her to the car first; then I will take you to her."

"Thank you, Todd..." I patted his shoulder. "And again, let Salvador know that I'm sorry."

"Yes, ma'am. Follow me."

We walked down the line of squad cars that took up most of the drive. My heart quickened as I walked alongside Officer Todd. I stopped. "Are you sure I'm not being arrested?"

"Do you want to be arrested?"

"No."

"Then stop asking stupid questions."

I nodded. "Yes, sir."

It didn't take long to find Ava. She sat with her head bowed in one of the seven gray police sedans lined along the front drive. I saw her back quake and quiver. My stomach flip-flopped watching her.

This was really bad. I stopped walking and looked away. My stomach was empty, so I had to be careful not to dehydrate myself, which would land me at Dekalb Medical Center quick, flash, and in a hurry. But watching her mourn in that police car made me feel like a big fat failure. I had never failed my sister until today. And what got me was that I had failed her in the worst way, because there was no way to make this right.

There were no do-overs when it came to death. I couldn't bring Devon back from the dead; I couldn't turn back time. All I could do was stand there and watch my sister's world fall apart. My head swam, but I was willing my body to heal, because I had to come up with something. I had to find a way to fix this.

I made my way toward Ava, but despite the sun rising, I had trouble seeing. Now the police lights seemed to flash over the grounds like the disco ball at a skating rink, except Devon wasn't splitting his pants trying to impress Ava with his horrible skating skills again. No. He was dead.

I finally reached the car Ava sat in. The door was open, so I could see her cuffed hands in her lap. My stomach decided to take a roller coaster ride. I decided to ignore it.

"Get back," Officer Todd said. "You're too close, Angel."

I stepped back. I wanted to lean in and take hold of her

hands, but the officers standing beside me made me stand at a distance, close enough to look inside and fake a whisper.

"Ava?" I called for her.

She didn't look at me. Her eyes were closed. She mumbled something familiar. I leaned closer and listened until I remembered what it was. She was humming an old hymn we learned in our parents' church.

The Mother Board used to chant it when the church decided they needed prayer when we were little girls:

> *A charge to keep I have,*
> *A God to glorify,*
> *A never dying soul to save,*
> *And fit it for the sky . . .*

Watching and listening to her sing those words made me a bit nostalgic for Granddaddy's old church, for a simpler time. Back then, to be a preacher's wife in an African American church was synonymous with being the First Lady of the United States. The church was the only institution that black people could own for themselves. Back in Granny's day, we didn't need senators or lawyers or police. We needed the Black church, including a woman who represented the closest thing to purity and grace sharecroppers and wounded souls could see and touch. The preacher's wife was the face of southern black aristocracy. Seventy-five years later, my sister embodied the role until tonight.

I began to sing along with her, badly, of course, until Ava looked up and stopped. "Angel . . ."

"Ava," I exhaled.

She lifted her cuffed hands and extended them, but I couldn't touch her. The police kept me at a distance. All I could do was smile back at her. A tear fell from her face. That broke my heart.

I saw sorrow and terror in her eyes. The last time I saw her face like that was the day Daddy died.

"You'll be all right." I assured her.

Yet, she looked a good mess. Her usual perfect coif sat scatterbrained all over her head. Her so-called waterproof mascara ran down her face and onto the pink feathers on her robe. Where in the world did she get that robe from, anyway?

And then something profound hit me. Ava couldn't have killed Devon. Not tonight she couldn't. Unkempt hair, trashy pink nightgown. Unh-uh. She would never look that bad on purpose, especially if she knew the press would be pulling into the driveway, while she sat in a police sedan looking like this.

"Officer Todd, it might be good business if you shut the cruiser door, because someone has let the press in."

"Someone send the press back. I don't think Karen is here yet," he said through his phone this time. Karen was one of the police department's spokespersons. I met her once at an Atlanta Press Club meeting.

If Ava intended to do this, she would be dressed to kill, literally, if nothing else. If Devon's death was a crime of passion, she would be dressed to die for . . . for sure. Ava wasn't an unpredictable hothead like me. She planned things, thought every detail of her life through as if she were playing chess with angels. That feeling in my gut grew stronger as my mind remembered every odd thing in Devon's study and the glimpses of the mansion that were out of place. Ava didn't kill Devon, and I no longer needed twin-tuition to believe it.

Officer Todd whispered, "We're about to get her away from all this drama. Make sure you bring her a change of clothes to the jail."

"Can I go inside to retrieve some?"

"Can a dog lay eggs?" He pulled out his phone again. "Go to the store, Angel."

"I had to try."

"And I was warned."

"Can I ask one more thing?"

"We are about to shut the door and the rear windows don't go down. Jesus, Angel." He growled. "Hold on for a sec, guys . . . Jeesh! This is it, Angel."

"Thank you so much, really."

"Go." He whispered angrily.

I returned to Ava, then leaned toward her as close as I could and whispered, "Why didn't you tell me that you were leaving Devon?" I paused and frowned. "Why were you leaving him?"

She began mumbling to me, not looking at me at all.

I knelt down in front of her and tried to find her eyes. She wouldn't open them. She was stuck out on the third realm of prayer or somewhere.

I sighed. "I know you're hurting, but you have to snap yourself out of it. If Granny were here . . ."

Her eyes popped open. "She'd be in my shoes."

I stumbled back, almost tripping over Officer Todd.

"Are you okay?" he asked.

"Yes." I cocked my head to the side. "What did you say?"

"You heard me." She looked away. "You act as if you have no idea of the burden we bear."

I shook my head. "Who? Preacher's wives?"

"No, First Ladies. There is a difference," she said.

If circumstances were different, I would've yanked her out of the car and smacked her pretentious self across her forehead. I glanced at Officer Todd, then pulled myself together. He wasn't smiling at me anymore. I collected myself and blew out my frustration with my sister.

"This isn't the time for our annual debate. I want to help you. What do you need me to do? How can I help you?"

"Protect Devon's name," she said.

"Have you bumped your head?" I shouted. I didn't need to look around to know all eyes were on me. I closed my eyes and whispered, "What if I say no?"

Her mouth trembled. She mouthed. "Then I'm going to confess."

"What?" I looked at her and at Officer Todd. "Did you say you wouldn't talk until your attorney is present?"

She looked at Officer Todd and laid her head in her lap.

I hissed, "Why would you do that, Ava?"

She kept her head down, mumbling and trembling. I touched her arm. Chill bumps ran down it. Was she going into shock?

"That's it, Angel. I told you to get back."

"But something's wrong with her. I think she needs medical attention."

"It's cool out. We need to shut this door and keep her warm."

"Let me just get the instructions I need to take care of her children before you do that."

"Make it fast, Angel. It's been long enough."

I tried to recount everything that had happened this weekend: Ava coming over unexpected with the bruise on her face, Ava showing up later that night without even calling, Ava undressed and carrying her sleeping kids. I tried to rub the goose bumps away—then I realized what I'd been missing. Fear.

Fear brought Ava to my house. That was the only thing that made sense. Something scared her, scared her more than that big gash in Devon's side. But there was no way in hell I would let that fear force her to take the fall for his death.

I wanted to ask her if she killed him, but I didn't. I knew she wouldn't tell me as long as Officer Todd was nearby anyway, so instead, I asked, "Why is this more important than your freedom?"

Ava looked at me. I didn't need to read her lips to read her mind: *Because I love him.* Four words that have doomed most of the women I knew.

"Being in love doesn't amount to a hill of beans when your children's future is on the line." I shook my head.

"Saving Devon's name saves my children's future."

"But he's dead, honey."

"Look around you, Angel." Ava paused. "This place doesn't exist. It doesn't matter if his legacy and vision stops. He deserves better . . ." She sniffled, trembled, and cried again.

Officer Todd tapped my shoulder. "Don't sound like bedtime instructions to me."

"I'm getting to it," I stuttered.

Ava's arrest and Devon's murder had me so nervous. I couldn't fathom how Ava would get through this. The drive to Dekalb County jail was always a long, dark, and lonely one for the innocent. I knew that for myself.

"It's okay." I touched Ava's hand. "We'll follow you to the jail, to make sure they take good care of you. Who do I need to call at Greater Atlanta for you?"

"Call Elvis. Elvis Bloom," she said with a stronger voice than before. "He's the bishop's personal assistant. He'll know what to do, but you have to get to him before the news. You know how they do. You were one of them. Remember?"

"Yeah, I do." I grinned and nodded. "Can you give me his contact information?"

She directed me to lean closer. She whispered his number in my ear and something else I couldn't quite make out, because I heard more voices coming up the drive, then helicopters and some old familiar *voices*. I groaned. The *Atlanta Sentinel*. I should have known they would be here. I'm surprised they hadn't gotten here earlier.

"Anything else you need from me?" I asked.

She clutched my arm. I grimaced. "Take care of my babies. Don't let anyone—I mean anyone—take them from you."

I pulled her clawed grip from my arm. "Don't worry. My place is tighter than Deacon Ness's wallet. Remember?"

"Yes, I do." She smiled. "That man never wanted to pay Daddy his Sunday sermon checks on time."

"Only when Mom showed up at his door looking crazy. Now, *she* didn't care about staying in her place."

"And you're just like her," Ava said. I stopped and frowned.

She looked me in the eye. Ava had definitely come back now. She peered straight through me. "I need you to call Mom."

A large lump lodged in my throat. "I know."

Lord knew I didn't want to call that woman. Neither one of us did, and calling her during her honeymoon was a death sentence.

"And I need you to stay away from this or you'll leave me no choice," she whispered.

I gulped.

"Time's up, ladies, for the final time." Salvador dialed on his Blackberry. "It's already a madhouse waiting at the center."

I looked at Ava. She smiled slightly at me. Her eyes were redder than an Aruban sunset.

Salvador slapped the back of the cruiser and Ava's police escort disappeared out of the property.

I cowered behind Justus when the *Atlanta Sentinel* news

van pulled into the drive. My head throbbed. If they saw me here, I would have to deal with their ribbing me about my newest failure. How could I have let this happen? I needed to get out of here.

Justus tapped my shoulder. I turned toward him and threw myself in his arms. Another cry had been trying to come down since the moment I saw that body bag I assumed had Devon's dead body in it. Although Devon and I rarely got along, I'd never wanted him dead, and definitely not murdered. I didn't want Ava to live the same pain I had for the past five years. I clutched Justus tighter, let myself go, and cried a good cleansing cry this time.

Justus pulled away and looked at me. His eyes twinkled even at this hour. They gave me some comfort despite the horrible knot in my gut. He wiped my tears with his hand. "What did your sister say?"

"She doesn't want me to find Devon's murderer. She's willing to take the fall if I get involved. I don't know what to do." I covered my face with my hands and cried more.

10

"What's the matter with her?" I choked back more tears. "She's really pissing me off now."

Justus and I stood on Ava and Devon's property. We were the only things not tagged with crime scene tape or markers.

I couldn't see so well. Justus allowed me to wipe my eyes with his sleeve. I thanked him, while massaging my forehead with my fingertips. The headaches were returning and with good reason.

"Can you back up and start from where Ava wants to take the fall for a murder she didn't commit?"

"I can't. It would make my headache worse. In a nutshell, Ava doesn't want me to search for Devon's murderer, although she admitted to me that she didn't kill him. Instead, she wants me to protect his name. What does that mean?"

"I don't know. Perhaps she's in shock. Did you ask her if she saw the person who stabbed Devon?"

"No, but I should have. I got caught off guard when she asked me to protect Devon." I threw my hands up in defeat.

"What was she thinking? She wants me of all people to help him. By the way, she hadn't told me the real reason behind the bruise. I guessed I should have asked that, too. Justus, you're the minister. You know my sister's kind. What's up with her? What do you think she means?"

"First, take a breath. You can't make good decisions when your mind isn't clear."

"Justus, how can my mind be clear after what has happened?"

A helicopter roared above our heads, a little too low for my comfort.

"Okay, bad choice of words. I meant you need to find a way to calm yourself. You can't find the answer you seek when you're not thinking things through."

"Now, if that isn't a double standard." I grunted.

"What are you talking about?" he whispered, then looked around to see who was watching us.

The policemen continued their work. I saw Salvador in my periphery.

"You didn't say that when you asked me to find Kelly's phantom boyfriend yesterday? How is she, by the way?"

"She's home now. Not sure about tomorrow night, since Trish will be at the bakery."

"You haven't met the boy/man yet?"

"I haven't had time, seeing that I have been with you yesterday evening and all of tonight."

"You need to get home."

"No, I don't."

"Yes, you do. Take your own advice for a change and take care of your family. I'll figure this out."

"Stop changing the subject. I had something important to say."

I folded my arms over my chest. "Proceed, but make it quick."

"You taught me something that night. Now let me be your teacher."

I blushed. "You have to stop talking to me like that."

He shook his head. "You're incorrigible."

"Obviously, I am. Did you hear Salvador? If he could pin this thing on me, he would. I know it." I shuffled in my seat. "I think he wants to ruin me more than ruin Ava. And you know what else I think? What he said about me launching my own investigation could be right."

"What do you mean?"

"It's been so long since I've worn my reporter's cap, I've forgotten what to do."

"If it's any consolation, Sister Jenkins in the Suddenly Seniors group said you found out who was using her bank account to pay their phone bill, and I also overheard one of the ER nurses at Grady Memorial talk about how you took that bail jumper down by yourself the night I brought you home. From where I sit, you do know a little something-something."

"That's different. Trolling for teen pedophiles is a snap, but this is a murder. A capital murder of a big-time bishop. On top of that, it's my sister's husband. To make matters worse, we found her with his freshly dead body. Did you see all that blood? Looked like a crime of passion to me." I huffed. "It will take a miracle to fix this."

"Aren't angels sent to perform miracles?"

"Justus, I'm no angel."

"Your mother named you one."

"And if you ever met her, she'd tell you she wished she could take it back."

He smiled. "Not from where I'm looking." His cheeks glowed in the rising sun now.

I blushed again. "Then you need glasses."

"Look, I'm not a detective or anything of the sort, but I

have faith in you. In fact, I'll do whatever you need me to do to help you."

"Like what?" I chuckled.

"I could visit Ava at the jail, if she wanted some outside spiritual counseling. I could organize babysitting services for the children. I could contact the Young Mothers Communion Group to bring over dinners." He cleared his throat. "I could be your assistant."

"My assistant?" I giggled. "Thanks for the laugh. I needed that."

"No, it's not a joke. I'm serious."

"Oooh nooo." I shook my head. "I'm not investigating anything that requires a sidekick. Have you forgotten what Detective Tinsley just said? I'll put Ava in the doghouse if I start snooping around this thing. And just so you know, I have a secretary, Cathy Blair. She can take care of lunches."

I bit down on my thumb. It was another lie. Cathy would never lower herself to do such a thing.

"Don't get me wrong, and I'm not calling you a liar or anything, but I don't believe you."

Crap.

"About Cathy?" I asked. "You think I would lie about that?"

"Oh, I believe that. I've watched her go in and out of your home. I'm talking about your reason for not investigating this case privately having something to do with Salvador's chastising you."

"How smooth, but let's be realistic here." I pointed at all the police staff trampling over the front yard. "Those people are professionals. I troll bars in search of slimy, adulterous, deadbeat dads and ladies whose looks have run out of luck."

"You're selling yourself short. You do more than that." He stopped and patted my shoulder.

I looked back. Salvador was coming toward us.

"We need to leave," I said.

Justus placed his hand on my back and directed us toward my car. "You need to solve your brother-in-law's murder."

"So you don't think Ava did this?"

We stopped at the car. "Do you?" he asked.

"I don't know, and I don't have credible clues to prove otherwise right now." I looked down at Elvis's number scribbled on my pad and the name Rachel, something Ava said after she screamed Devon's name. It was a start, but definitely not enough. "I need more."

"Mmm . . . let me think about that." He began to rub my back with one of his hands in a circular motion, tender and soft. It felt so good, I almost dozed while standing.

"Oops." He stopped. "I'm sorry. I wasn't paying attention to what I was doing?"

"It's okay." I struggled to get my footing.

He opened my door. "I think I better drive us to jail. Is that fine with you?"

"Sure. Thanks." I slid into the passenger seat. I was torn by what had just happened, but comforted because he was here with me.

"While I drive, you can take a catnap, since I'm pretty sure you won't sleep until you get Ava's charges dropped."

"Mhmm . . ." I purred, then laid my head back against the headrest. It definitely wasn't a pillow, but it sure felt good. "You think you know me, don't you?"

"I wish I knew you more." He shut my door.

My heart fluttered. Lord knew I didn't want to go to hell for crushing on my pastor, but he continued saying things that made me wonder about the possibilities. I lifted my head enough to open his door from the inside and watched him take a seat. Everything about him, especially his lavender scent, soothed me all over again. He couldn't be my sidekick. That would be too much trouble for us both.

He shut the door and then looked at me. "Come on, let me assist."

"Justus, you're killing my snooze." I groaned and opened my eyes.

Through the windshield, I saw Salvador standing a few feet in front of my car. His arms were folded into his chest. I should have known that he wasn't going to let me off that easy.

"Then give me a chance," Justus interrupted my thoughts. "Can you find out what Detective Tinsley wants?"

"Yeah . . . be right back." He popped the door and hopped back out.

I closed my eyes and waited for the worst. Justus was too diplomatic to go head-to-head with Salvador. Any minute now he would be standing over me with his wisecracks. I exhaled and tried to relax as best as I could.

My car door opened; then I heard my ignition turn on.

I opened one eye. "Are you going to keep me in suspense or will you tell me what Salvador wanted?"

"It depends on whether or not I'm your sidekick now." He drove around the fountain.

If Salvador didn't stop us now, he would be seeing me soon, which wouldn't be a surprise.

If he chose to keep the case open, he would have to come to my house, because it was also a crime scene. I hoped he would at least let me have a few winks of sleep first and get the kids away from the house before showing up. But who was I kidding? My head ached again. I needed to call my attorney, to delay Salvador's arrival. Then I remembered he was my new stepdaddy. I groaned.

"If I decided to—you know—let you assist, what kind of

skill set do you have that I don't have that I might need to solve this case?" I tilted my head.

He continued driving toward the gates. "I have a way with the police officers."

"So do I."

He grinned. "I don't have to manipulate them to do what I want."

I pursed my lips. "Do I do that?"

He nodded. "Oh, yeah. Based on what I saw tonight, you use your feminine skill set very well."

I blushed. "Watch out now."

His eyes widened. "You don't scare me, Angel."

"Not yet."

"A man isn't afraid of a woman. He may be afraid of the way he feels about the woman, but never afraid of her unless she's carrying a weapon."

I observed him before I considered shooting another snappy comeback. It wasn't needed. His Jedi mind trick had worked the second he showed up at my doorstep last night.

"If I were to retrace Salvador's tracks and find leads of my own against my sister's will, how soon can I call in your favor to assist?"

He grinned. "Say the word and I'm your man."

"The word."

"Yes, ma'am. My first duty as your assistant is to remind you to call Whitney and your mom."

I felt nauseous again. "Pull over."

Justus pulled the car over short of the mansion's exit. I unbuckled my seat belt and stumbled out of the car.

"Are you okay?" he shouted.

I dropped to my knees. The ground was wet with morning dew. Bits of rubble from the pavement ground against my knees and palm.

I groaned. "No."

Despite the discomfort, I couldn't get up.

The car door slammed. I looked up to see Justus running toward me. I lowered my head and didn't fight him when he lifted me in his arms and carried me back to the car.

Justus lowered me onto the backseat. When I opened my eyes and saw another *Atlanta Sentinel* reporter van speed past us, my stomach turned again, but this time in anger. Those people were relentless. I wanted to get out of the car and scream. I tried to sit up instead.

"Stay." Justus touched my leg. "You're sicker than you think you are."

"No, I'm not." My head throbbed now. "I don't know. I don't know what I'm doing. The kids, the funeral, I don't know. I . . . I'm confused. I don't know how to tell them."

I was tired and in shock. I couldn't pull my head together for trying to digest everything that had just taken place and all the things I had to do. And Mom was coming. It was too much. Justus was sweet enough to help, but there was so much to do in little time. I needed to call Elvis before Tinsley, before the press, before I stroked out.

Justus turned to me. "I think you should wait until your mother comes to decide how you will tell the children. However, you have to tell Whitney now."

"No, I can't do that. She will flip out and the children will know that something's wrong."

"Can you at least text her?"

"And tell her what?"

"To get some rest. That you're on your way home soon and not to turn on the news."

"Is that what you tell Kelly? No wonder she sneaks out the house and dates bad boys." I flipped my phone out and dialed.

Whitney picked up on the first ring. "Girl, I've been calling you and Ava all night."

"I had my phone off, but I had a good reason, so don't go there."

"It better be good. What's up with Ava?"

"It's not good, but she's safe. That's the most important thing."

"Wooh . . . I'm gonna kill Devon," Whitney said.

"No, you're not, but here's what I need you to do . . ."

Actually, I did not know what to say. How could I tell her without telling her that Devon was dead? How could I not tell her and risk she find out in a few minutes from a newsfeed, blogger, or social networking service tied to her phone.

"I need you to trust me and not turn on the television, not check a text, tweet, or e-mail on your phone until I see you face-to-face."

"It's that bad?" her voice squeaked.

"It will be if you don't do as I say. And please, if the kids wake up, don't let them turn on the television."

"I'm scared, Angel."

I wanted to tell her, don't be, but I would be lying.

"Don't be scared. We're coming home soon."

I decided the lie was better than the truth for now.

11

Friday, 5:15 AM
On our way to the Dekalb County Detention Center

The roads were pleasantly quiet in Decatur, but the new day was rolling on despite my wish for it to slow down. I could be normal and go home. Who wouldn't want to go and hide under their bedcovers until the boogeyman disappeared?

Mama didn't raise me, nor Ava, that way. So I couldn't leave Ava here until I exhausted all scenarios that could release her from jail before her children missed her. Worst-case scenario, I would bail her out after she was formally charged. Trouble with that plan, however, was in my recollection, one of Salvador's tactics was to threaten to hold a person of interest for questioning long enough to disrupt their family's routine. He could legally hold her for two days before he presented charges to the DA's office. Since it's Friday, that more than likely wouldn't happen until Sunday morning. Let's be honest. The DA wasn't filing anything on Sunday, which meant he or she wouldn't get around to it until Monday at a time . . . I have no clue. Once those charges are made, then the magistrate judge's file clerk will put it on the docket calendar. And only God knew when that would happen . . .

"Justus, we're legally screwed," I groaned.

My slight concussion roared between my ears and my stomach made it clear that it didn't appreciate the incessant pain. Justus watched me carefully. He knew I wouldn't be able to hang around much longer. He held my hand as he drove, and he made sure he never bounced over any bumps in Decatur's poorly paved roads. That was sweet.

We stopped at a red light.

Justus turned to me. "Angel, I'm concerned about your health."

"You don't think I am?" I slid my hand out of his hold.

"You've only made one call since we left your sister's, and you're practically holding your head in your hands now."

"I didn't realize I was." I lowered my hands from my head.

"We've been going nonstop since midnight. There hasn't been time to take a breath. If I weren't with you experiencing this for myself, I'd swear we were morphed into an episode of *24*." He began driving. "Angel, I don't swear."

"I know exactly what you mean. My head feels like it's on a perpetual rollercoaster ride."

"Then maybe after this we go home."

"Maybe."

He sighed. "Angel."

"Justus, if you're tired, drop me off at Big Tiger's and he'll bring me home after I'm done."

"Your concussion has clearly made you loopy if you think I will agree to that."

"Then what do you want me to do, tell the kids what?" I folded my arms over my chest. My lips were so pursed my cheeks hurt.

"You should tell the kids that their mom will be away for a while longer. Who knows? With faith, Ava could be released on bail later today. Then she can speak to the children herself. But you"—he patted my hand—"see to yourself."

"With faith . . ." I scoffed. "How about some facts, Justus. Ava could be stuck in the pen for days. This is the weekend. If they detain her all day, then charge her tonight after it's too late to get on an early Saturday docket, she will be here through Monday at least. Justus, we've had clients in lockup for two weeks before a bail hearing. That's too long." I flipped my phone out. "Maybe I should call Devon's assistant to see if he can help."

"You should have called him first."

"Tttt . . . Sidekick, you could have called him while I was talking to Whitney."

"I couldn't call and drive and pay attention to you at the same time."

"Use a Bluetooth, Justus. Besides, what are you paying attention to me for?"

Justus slammed on the brakes. My car skidded slightly to the right. I could smell rubber from my tires.

"What are you doing?" I screamed.

"Pay attention, Angel. It's a red light." His voice was stern.

"Oh." I rubbed the back of my neck.

"One more thing . . . don't ever ask me again why I pay attention to you, why I care for you, or why I won't leave you."

A chill ran down both of my shoulders. I shivered. "Can I say anything?"

"No . . ." Justus checked the rearview mirror. The light was green, but we weren't moving. "Let's pray before we go a step further."

"Let's not. Okay?"

"I don't know how to respond to that request, Angel, when I know that prayer is the right thing to do."

I folded my arms over my chest. He cleared his throat. "I'll just pray in silence for a minute then."

"You do that."

Justus began to pray while my mind tried to rewind the events of last night and come up with a plan of action to clear Ava's name. I had nothing. I watched Justus and wished my problems could be solved as easily as he believed.

My heart thrummed mulling over what he said before his prayer request. Although I still didn't clearly understand what he meant.

Out of courtesy for him, though, I waited until he stopped praying before I reached for my cell phone and dialed Mom. I probably should have called Elvis first like I had planned, but since I have my guard up after nipping at Justus, I might be tough enough to make that call.

I put the phone to my ear. My knees twitched. *Oh no.* I heard the phone ring. My jaw clinched. *Not good.* Then the phone purred and clicked. I stopped breathing. My nose sweat. I was in trouble.

Before I could tell her the bad news, she said, "Evangeline Grace Crawford, you must have lost the last bit of your mind for calling me this early in the morning."

I rolled my eyes to the back of my head. Its usual position when I talk to her. "It's an emergency, Mom."

"Something wrong with my grandbaby? Whitney?" Her voice raised an octave. I heard her bed sheets ruffling through the phone. She had sat up. "Say something."

I jumped. "No, it's Ava. Devon's been murdered."

"Sweet Jesus!" Then she cursed.

Our mom Virginia had this weird habit of praising God

and cursing the world and anybody near her at the same time. The new hubby must have been in a deep sleep, because she screamed my name and the fact that her honeymoon had to be delayed until she took care of everything, like she must do, even though she has three grown daughters about five times. Yet, I hadn't heard a peep from him.

I can't remember his name to save my life.

"Well, where is my Avalyn? Put her on the phone. I tell you what." She huffed. "You girls run behind the wrong kind of love. Didn't she learn from you? What in the world happened? Who in this world would kill a pastor? Don't let the devil ride this morning." She took a breath. "What are you going to do about this, Angel? I know you're going to fix this mess. Where is Avalyn? Where's Whitney . . . ?" She was about to start it up again.

I slumped down in the passenger seat and tried to remember every question Mom asked. I didn't know when she would finish so I could answer, but I better be able to answer them all and in that order. Then she coughed.

I sat up in my seat.

"Ava's on her way to Dekalb County jail. She's been detained to be questioned about Devon's murder because she was on the scene. No, of course, she didn't kill him. Whitney is at home with all the kids."

"Holy hell, and what are you going to do about all this?"

"I'm on my way to the jail to find out what's going on."

"Let me repeat myself, dear. I don't think you heard me clearly. What are you going to do about *all* this?"

My stomach knots returned. "I'm going to fix it, Mom."

"You better, or it's me and you."

"Are you coming here? Now?"

"What other reason would I have to cancel my nine-o'clock hibiscus spa, ask my dear Carrolton to end our very short stay here in Grand Dunes, and have Dorothy, my travel agent rearrange our honeymoon to Italia."

"Italy, Mom." I huffed. "Our new dad's name is Carrolton?"

Click.

I looked at the phone and scoffed. "Unbelievable."

"Did she hang up on you?" Justus asked while he made a left turn.

My lip quivered. I pursed my lips to keep them from falling apart. "She's going to kill me if I don't take care of this mess."

I reached in my glove compartment and pulled out a fresh memo pad and pen. I kept them there because I never knew when Big Tiger would call me to pick up a client. I needed to jot down all the tasks I had to complete.

Justus glanced at me. "Explain to me why your mom would expect that?"

"It's been like that as long as I can remember."

We stopped at a light. "Wait a minute. I thought Ava was the oldest child. Wouldn't she be the one responsible for her sisters instead of you?"

"She is, by four glorious minutes, but she was sick when we born, according to Mom. I had no problems, so I went home and Granny took care of me, while Mom stayed at the hospital to take care of Ava. I don't know . . ." I looked out the window. I could see the detention center from here. "We haven't been maternally close since."

"How is she with Bella?"

"Everything I wished I had in a mother." I pointed at the jail. "We're close now."

12

Friday, 5:45 AM

One thing that I hadn't lost since my departure from the *Atlanta Sentinel* was my ability to store information in my head. Ava gave me Elvis's phone number, but I also remembered that the first three digits of that telephone number told me an approximate vicinity of where he lived. From there, I could determine that he was living somewhere between downtown Decatur and Candler Park. That area was near my alma mater and fifteen minutes from the jail, mostly traffic lights. Somehow that information put me at ease. At least I knew something about the guy. He was young, but old enough to have a decent college education; he had some money saved, but treasured the trinkets of a higher standard of living, was upwardly mobile, probably drove a hybrid, and hung out with the Atlanta Jaycees on Buckhead when he had a moment free; and if he wasn't gay or overweight, he had a bevy of ladies, single and married, at this disposal. I hoped that Ava was right, that this man could help or at least set her up with one of Big Faith's many attorneys.

Justus and I were three traffic lights from the detention center now, so I dialed.

Elvis picked up on the first ring. "Hello? This is Elvis."

His voice was groggy, but very intriguing. He had one of those British/East London accents. It was a surprised, crisp delight for me. I'd been there before on a weekend date some years ago. My heart ached in reverie.

"Sorry to disturb you, but my sister Avalyn McArthur wanted me to call you."

"I know," he said.

I pulled a face. "What do you know?"

"She's left him. Bishop told me last night that she was going to, but I can't believe she ran to you. That's so unlike her."

I paused and swallowed that slight insult down. "He told you when?"

"I'm sorry, I shouldn't have said that. I don't mean to be rude, but I was told to keep the McArthurs' private matters private, especially from you, but if the First Lady asked you to call, well, that's another matter entirely."

He just insulted me again. I held my breath.

Two small fists punched me between my eyes. My headache progressed. You know the kind. It's mixed with dizziness, nausea, and a huge rush to find somewhere to lay your head down or curse out every smart Elvis within earshot. I should have requested a pain reliever at the mansion earlier when I had the chance.

We stopped at a traffic light. I saw a billboard of Ava and Devon holding each other and smiling down blessings on me above the Red Lobster Seafood Restaurant.

"Devon's dead," I grumbled.

"What?" he asked, his voice a high-pitched bark. "Did you say . . . dead?"

"Yes."

He yelped again.

I flinched at the sound of his high-pitched bark. He

sounded like a scared puppy, not sexy at all. I began to wonder whether I had this guy pegged all wrong.

Justus began driving again.

"Elvis, no offense, but I don't have a lot of time to chop it up with you. I have to take care of my sister."

"Right." He paused. "Absolutely right. You don't care for the bishop, so . . ." He began to make those sappy dog noises again.

I rolled my eyes again. Truly, I was just as hurt about Devon's death as Elvis was. I didn't have the patience or hearing octave to listen to Elvis mourn on my phone. Justus touched my arm. His empathetic energy must have transferred a little into me, because I calmed down and gave the man some breathing room to grieve

"What happened? Is First Lady Ava and the children okay?" Elvis asked.

"The children are fine. Ava's pretty shaken up. That's why she asked me to call you. She needs your help."

"I'm so sorry for my rudeness before. I sincerely apologize. I'm on my way to the estate."

Justus came to an abrupt stop. Another traffic light.

He pointed. "Look." Another billboard.

I shook my head. "Elvis, you can't come to the mansion. It's a crime scene now."

"Of course. Where are you and she? May I speak with her?"

"See, that's another problem. Ava has been arrested for Devon's murder. She's not speaking to anyone right now, and I really would like someone to be there with her before she says the wrong thing to the police when they question her, because . . ."

I looked at Justus. His attention was on the MARTA bus that just turned in front of us. Greater Atlanta Faith's blue and gold logo with Devon's brilliant white smile underneath with a speaking bubble that said, NO GREATER LOVE IS THIS, was panted across the side. A mobile billboard.

I dropped my head. We were about to enter a media storm.

"Elvis, she's thinking about confessing to this murder."

"Bloody hell." Then silence.

My brow wrinkled. "Elvis, are you there?"

"I'm here," he mumbled.

"Good." I exhaled. I wasn't in the mood for any more intentional hang-ups. "I'm sorry to lay all this on you, but you're the only person Ava asked me to call."

"Of course." His voice shook now. "Can you meet me at my family's restaurant? It's in downtown Decatur. The Biscuit Depot. Can't miss it. It looks like a railcar. You can get me up to speed there."

"That's your place?"

I had been in there before, but never saw a guy in an apron or moving around in the back office.

"Yes, it is. You've been there?" he asked.

My stomach growled at the thought of a good old Irish breakfast: eggs, sausages, rashers, black pudding, and pan-fried potato bread. My mouth watered. Yet, I cringed. It was breakfast time in my house and I wasn't there. I had three children at home, a teenaged sister who might as well be a child, and Mom on the way. Mom . . . I felt sick again at the thought of her bursting hell wide open to get to my house. I needed to get home.

"Elvis, believe me. With all that's going on, I really need to see you, but I can't. I'm almost at the jail where Ava is being detained; then I have family obligations and I'm dead tired." I covered my hand with mouth. "Sorry. Bad choice of words."

"No apologies," Elvis said. "This whole news is bad."

Justus patted my hand. "Are you okay?"

I lowered the receiver from my face. "He wants to see me now, but I'm tired. I'm so tired, man."

"Then you're tired." He held the steering wheel with his left hand and extended his right toward me. I took his hand. Don't know why, but it felt right. I felt rejuvenated a teeny bit.

I placed the phone in my right hand and put it to my head. "Elvis, can you meet us at the jail instead?"

"Of course. I'll call the church attorney and one of the First Lady's armor bearers to meet us there. How will I find you?"

"Look for a washed-out version of my sister."

Silence. Again I felt like a heel. "Look for a red SUV, a tall, copper-colored man wearing locks and a track suit, and a woman wearing Hello Kitty pajamas, a gangsta tee, and a ponytail on the fringe of losing its tail."

Justus snickered.

"Okay, I'll meet you in the visitor parking lot in fifteen minutes."

The nausea dissipated. "Thank you."

"No problem. First Lady needs to know that we are her family and we are here for her. Where are the children?"

"They're with family," I said.

"That's what I said."

"Honey, I'm the queen of wisecracks. Don't do that. Don't play." I puffed. "Let's just start over."

"Sorry." He stopped. "Would you be offended if I had someone bring dinner from the restaurant for the family later?"

I grinned. "Thank you for asking. We'll see . . . but for right now, let's get this thing handled with Ava."

"Right. We can exchange particulars once we meet. Good day, Angel." Then he hung up.

As long as I had been talking to Elvis, we finally reached our destination.

Justus turned into the drive that led us to the massive parking garage. "You look better. What did he say?" Justus asked.

"He's going to meet us at the jail and bring one of Big Faith's lawyers with him and Ava's armor bearer. Before he gets here, can you tell me what's an armor bearer?"

"It's a new term for an assistant. Really, it's an old term. It goes back to Prince Jonathan and King David in the Bible, but you don't want to hear that preachy talk. Forgive me." He smirked. "Anyway, the name is making a comeback in contemporary nondenominational churches."

"Okay, Bible Yoda, and so how does this relate to Ava?"

"Bible Yoda, that's cute." He shook his head. "With Ava's increasing responsibilities at Greater Atlanta, she probably has one or a few devoted to help her fulfill her commitments and commissions."

"So, hypothetically, you're acting as my armor bearer right now?"

"No," he chuckled. "I'm acting as your shepherd. I'm here to guide you down the right path, nourish you, and keep you safe."

"Well, I'm definitely hungry. We can get breakfast afterward. This Elvis guy owns a restaurant not too far from the jail."

"Sounds like a plan." His focus was on driving my car through this prison maze. "I'm curious. Why do you call Greater Atlanta Church, Big Faith?"

"It's easy to remember. Why?"

He frowned. "I don't see why changing the name of a church is easy to remember."

"It's easy for *me* to remember." I turned to him. "The name has a meaning. Back in the day, I reported on many churches. To help me keep from confusing them, I gave them nicknames that I could remember, not just the name, but the thing about them I didn't get."

"And what don't you get about your sister's church?"

"It's not so much her church, but what it represents; the notion that the reason bad things happen to good people is because their faith wasn't big enough."

"And you don't agree?"

"I think it's dangerous, particularly with this economy, to say something that might possibly make desperate people question their faith. Bad things happen. I've seen it first-hand."

"I know," Justus mumbled.

I turned toward him. His attention remained on the road. I noticed he was biting his lip.

"You've read my old *Sentinel* column articles, haven't you?"

He shook his head. "Just the ones you wrote about orga-nized religion."

"You know, I wrote those articles a long time ago, and I quit the *Sentinel* soon after."

"I do, and I assume the reason why you and Ava don't get along is because of those articles."

"Partly . . . we have a lifetime of resentment between us. The articles merely buttressed one aspect of our disagree-ments and an episode in my life that I regret." I slumped back in my seat.

"Want to talk about that?"

I shook my head. "Nope, it has nothing to do with what's going on right now."

"But it does shed a light on what's going on with you. Perhaps those unresolved issues are what's clouding your judgment now or may give us a clue as to why Ava is will-ing to sacrifice her freedom rather than expose her church."

"Justus, you're reaching."

"Humor me."

I scoffed. "Okay, but I don't want to talk about this anymore or you'll be fired as my sidekick."

He chuckled. "That's not fair. From what I know about sidekicks, I'm doing a great job."

I rolled my eyes. "Someone told you wrong."

"No, come on. Think about it. Sidekicks are supposed to be your conscience."

"Justus, I'm not Perry Mason, and you are definitely not Della Street." I referred to my favorite, now-classic television detective series.

"No, not yet, anyway, but if there ever was a time to get some past troubles off your back, this is the best time. How many people do you know has their pastor chauffeuring them around?"

The man had a point.

"Here goes . . ."

I turned in my seat toward him. I knew he couldn't look at me and drive, but I wanted to read his body language. If I saw a hint of judgment, then I would end the conversation.

"When I wrote those articles I was in a bad place in my head. I wasn't objective. I wasn't doing my job, and so I quit. But it's amazing how my past continues to haunt me well after I've buried that skeleton way down in the ground. It's not right."

"I like to think that the past releases us once we understand the true meaning of grace. You can't bury what must be raised."

"See. There you go." I huffed. "I know what grace is. Now, can we move past the preachy talk?"

"Oh yes. I forgot how you can't stand the preachy talk."

He veered into the detention center parking area. "Let me complete my thought, then we can end the preachy talk. Okay?"

I nodded.

"I don't doubt that you know what grace is, but I don't think you understand what it means for you. Knowing and understanding are two different things. If they were the same, there would be need for only one."

"Uh-huh. You said the same thing this past Sunday in your sermon."

He turned off the ignition. "And yet you still haven't heard it."

"And I'm not today." I turned away from him. "We were supposed to be talking about getting Ava out of jail and here you are sneaking in a Bible lesson."

"No, I'm not."

"This is what I'm talking about when I said that you couldn't be my sidekick."

"Why can't I be your sidekick?"

"You're not thinking about what *I* need. You're trying to shove what *you* think I need down my throat."

"No, I'm not."

"You just did."

"I was trying to help you, but you don't want to be helped."

"I don't want to be judged."

"You're so pigheaded."

"And you're about to be put out of my car, Rev."

"Oh, here we go. We're back to you calling me Rev. You're . . . you're—"

"I'm what?!" I roared.

He looked over my shoulder. "You're causing a scene. Everyone on this level is watching us."

"So what? I don't care what anyone here thinks."

"That's obvious." He looked away from me and lowered his head.

"Well, at least you've finally taken me off that pedestal of yours."

"Why would I do that?"

"Aren't you angry with me?" I asked.

He shook his head. "No, I'm not angry that I can't make you soak up my sermons and learn more about our God through them. I am disappointed that you would rather be right than vulnerable with me. I know you're mourning. I get that, so . . ."

I watched him for a few seconds. "How am I supposed to return to that?"

"You're not. That's what sidekicks do."

"And what is that?"

"Feel for you."

I chuckled. "Thanks for the laugh."

He turned to me. "I didn't mean to."

"Well, it was funny and we need to go."

"Where?"

"To the right parking garage."

"This is the right parking lot."

"No, my sensitive grasshopper. It's not the one I use when I'm bringing someone in."

"Oh, sorry." He turned on the ignition. "Maybe I should have let you drive."

"No problem. I'm beginning to like the way you drive. It makes me feel all vulnerable and open to share all the short-cuts, secret entrances, and back alleys I know," I teased.

"I'm glad you find me amusing again, but I was serious about what I said earlier."

"I know you were." I checked the time again. In fact,

while we head around the corner to enter the right parking lot, let me ask you something a little more up your alley."

"All right." He began backing the car out of the parking spot.

"Do you think that someone in Devon's congregation is trying to frame Ava for his murder?"

"You think the murderer is a member of his congregation?"

"That's the only thing that could justify why Ava is willing to take the fall."

"She would sacrifice herself for a member of Greater Atlanta?" He looked at me.

I looked back. "Isn't that what shepherds do?"

13

Justus parked in the parking lot off Camp Circle behind Sheriff's Headquarters and the Dekalb County jail. Unfortunately, only parents of arrested minors could accompany detainees, so we couldn't go inside. But I wanted Ava to know that we were there. I wanted her to know that she wasn't alone, although I'm sure she was feeling the loneliest she had ever felt.

We stepped out the car in time to watch the sunrise. Somehow I wasn't in awe like usual.

"Look over there." Justus pointed at a man stepping out of a black Mercedes. He looked just as out of place as we were. "Do you think that's Elvis?"

I stepped forward, squinted, did a double take, and then leaned even farther forward.

"Oh no." I threw my hands on my hips and dropped my head. "It can't be."

"What's wrong? It's not Elvis?

"No, it's Roger Willis, Devon's attorney." I pursed my lips. "That man almost got me fired."

"For what?"

"Punching him at a press conference."

Justus looked at me.

"Don't look at me that way." I popped my trunk and reached inside. "You would have had to be there to understand."

"I bet."

I kept a small black duffel bag in there. It housed some of my bounty-hunting disguises. After talking with Justus about my challenges with the job, I didn't feel so comfortable sharing the contents of my bag with him.

I pulled out the bag and slammed the trunk. "Let's go, Justus."

Roger approached us with a huge smile; I didn't smile back. He shook hands with Justus, then extended his arms toward me.

I played nice and shook his hand back. They were as weak as I remembered.

"Never in a million years did I think we would meet again, and especially under these circumstances." He grinned.

His large eyes, chubby cheeks, and long neck made him resemble a Cheshire cat. Call me prejudiced, but in my opinion, I never trusted Roger Willis. Sure, he was one of the most successful attorneys in the Atlanta Metropolitan area, but he wasn't folk. He wasn't family.

"Well, at least this time we're on the same side." Now I sound like the cornball still smiling at me.

"After I handle things inside, I need to talk to you both about what you saw."

"Sure, we'll wait."

"That wouldn't be a wise idea. I don't know how long this will take. The best thing for you to do at this point is to go spend some time with your family."

"Willis, please."

"I'm thinking of your best interest."

"Sure you are." I handed him the duffel bag from my trunk. "Can you take these clothes in with you? I'm sure the clothes that Ava wore here will become evidence, so here's something better to wear once you've brought her out."

"Better?" Justus cleared his throat.

My face flushed. I wouldn't dare look at him. "Maybe not better, but wearable."

Willis checked his watch. "No problem, but I can't guarantee that she will be released. She may be charged and then we have to bail her out."

"I got the bail part down, but I don't think she will be charged, if you are as convincing as many think you are."

"It is highly unlikely that she will not be charged. Come on, Angel. She's covered in blood with the murder weapon at her foot."

"Who told you that?" I raised my voice.

"You're not the only one who knows people."

"And you're not the only lawyer in town."

Willis's grin now looked like a facial deformity.

"Angel," Justus whispered.

"What?" I kept my eyes on Roger while he studied Justus.

"But I'm the one she requested." He stepped forward, then hesitated. "Look, I'm sorry for what happened back then. Everyone knows it wasn't your fault. . . . I mean everyone."

"Don't go there."

"Then you stop going there. You have to take the chip off your shoulder if you want to help you sister." He grunted. "But I don't think you're selfless enough to do that."

"I want to help her; I want to get her out of here before her children wonder about their parents. Plus, if we don't get her out today, she'll be here until Monday the latest."

"Don't you concern yourself with that." He put his hand on my shoulder. "Angel, I will do everything in my power to get her released as soon as reasonably possible, while you go out there and find me anything I can use to have her out of here, if the DA decides to file a charge. Now, if you'll excuse me, I'm going inside to find her. Hopefully I can speed things along."

"Do you know how long it will be?" I asked.

"It depends, but I'll contact you as soon as I know more."

Justus handed Attorney Willis his card. "Let Mrs. McArthur know that I'm more than happy to come down here and pray with her."

I rolled my neck at Justus.

He shrugged. "What now?"

"She's not going to be in here long enough for anyone to be praying with her," I said.

"Right." Justus returned his attention back to Willis. "Stay in touch."

"Wait a minute, Willis." I looked around the parking lot. "Where's Elvis Bloom? I thought he was coming with you."

Willis's eyes wondered off toward the sky and he flicked his last limp, overgreased gray hairs on the top of his head to the left with his hands. I chuckled, but I didn't find anything funny about his gesturing. I've seen it from him too many times to count. He was withholding something important from me. He had a ball to drop.

"Greater Atlanta called an emergency meeting about my sister? Eh?"

"Nope." He reached in his pocket and pulled out a stick of gum. "The meeting was planned."

I glanced at Justus, then back at Willis. "As of late yesterday, like, I don't know, soon after my sister took the kids to my house?"

"Leave it be, Angel." Willis began to chew. "I don't want you wrecking things."

"Wrecking them how?"

Willis lifted his chin toward Justus. "It's too early in the morning to cast stones."

"Then don't and just tell me the truth. The pastor can handle it." I didn't look at Justus for confirmation. My blood was boiling, so I didn't care what he thought.

"The church is concerned that Ava's reunion with you had something to do with the tragedy that happened last night."

Justus stepped forward. "That's absurd and you can't prove it."

"Don't have to. Her past history with the McArthurs is enough to warrant the concern, and I have it on a hunch that the detective on this case hadn't entirely ruled Angel out as a person of interest."

"What gives you the right—?"

"I'm Avalyn McArthur's lawyer, which gives me the right." Willis peered at him under his glasses.

"Hold on, Willis. Does that mean the church won't help her as long as I'm around?"

He smirked. "Why do you insist on asking me questions you already know the answers to, Evangeline? I never understood that about you."

"But I'm trying to help her. I'm looking for Devon's real killer. I'm trying to get her out of jail for good.

"Angel, the only thing you can do well is take a person back to jail, not keep someone out."

"What did you just say?" Justus asked. His voice had

grown louder than before. I could see officers stopping to hear our matter.

"Calm down." I touched his arm. "It's fine . . . Justus, it's fine."

He clutched both of my arms. "No, it's not fine. This is not right."

The expression on his face made me tremble.

He paused. He took his hand off me carefully, as if I would break, and turned to Willis. "This will not stand."

"Evangeline, ask yourself this question. What's more important, Ava's emancipation or your chance at redemption?" Willis eyed me. "Let me throw you a hint. Too many people, including your sister, believe you're incorrigible."

"This isn't the first time I heard that tonight." I glanced at Justus.

Justus sighed and put his hands in his pockets.

"Willis, the kids are with me, so I can't entirely disappear from Ava's life. That would hurt the children."

"We're aware of that." He spoke to me as if I was interviewing him on the record, no personality or soul in his voice.

"Are they aware that I have changed?"

"That's still up in the air, and thus the cause for concern." Willis continued, "If you want our help and unless you plan to join her inside, play the reformed sister role perfectly. That includes you staying out of the limelight, especially at the *Sentinel*. You understand?"

My heart fell. "I understand. I'll leave Ava's innocence in your hands."

"That's a start," Willis said.

"No, Angel. Don't listen to him," Justus whispered. "You can't give up because of what he said. He doesn't speak for the entire church."

"Oh, but I do." He checked his watch. "I have to go now. Elvis has been informed to contact you once the meeting is over. He'll more than likely help your family coordinate final arrangements for Bishop McArthur."

"What about the armor bearers?"

"Who?" Willis grimaced.

"The . . . never mind."

"Very well," Willis said before walking toward the jail.

"Willis . . ." I called after him.

He stopped, turned around, and tapped his watch. "Time is billable, people."

I nodded and tried not to seem thrown by what he just said to me. There was no time to cry, mourn, sleep, or think at this point. To make matters worse, Ava and Devon's church had given me an ultimatum: Get out the way or Ava was on her own. I didn't have funds to pay for a defense lawyer as good as Willis. Besides, if Big Faith wasn't in her Amen corner at the trial—if it got down to that—a juror would equate the church's indifference as a sign of guilt. She would lose without them. But if I didn't find Devon's killer, then what? She'd take the fall to save Devon's persona?

Unh-uh. No way. I couldn't let that happen.

Where would I start? Time had slipped away too much already fooling with surly Willis. I could still snoop around without them being the wiser. How dumb did he think I was?

I wasn't sure if he was playing me for a sucker, but he seemed not to know anything about the armor bearers. I wondered if the church had spoiled my name to them already? If not, I definitely could start there. I just need to figure out how without throwing up any smoke signals. Hopefully after Willis talked with Ava he would have a change of heart about me like she had. I didn't have anyone else to talk to regarding Ava and Devon outside of Elvis. I doubt he would talk to me now, but what else did I have to work with? Definitely not stupid Terry.

"Thank you, Roger, for your advice, but Ava made it clear to me in her yard, in front of Detective Tinsley and almost the entire Dekalb County Police Department, that she wanted me as far away from the case as possible, so let the church say amen on that. They don't have to be concerned about me."

"Is that true, pastor?" Willis asked Justus.

I held my breath.

"I've lost count of how many people have asked Angel not to interfere with this case tonight."

Willis smirked. "Pastor, before you start claiming our dear Angel as your Eve, ask her to share the story about the last good man who lost his soul to protect her."

A swirling of spitfire rage, sorrow, and horror enveloped me. Before I could stop myself, I lunged forward. Justus grabbed me and swung me away from Willis. I wanted to claw that joker's grin off his face.

"Go home, Evangeline. Think hard about what I said, because I won't proceed if you're lurking under my shadow or trying to stab me in the back."

I waved back and watched him disappear down the path toward the entrance.

Justus placed his hands on my shoulders.

I began to cry; then I stopped myself. "What?"

"Do you want to grab some breakfast before Elvis calls?"

"I want to go home and hold my child."

"I thought you wanted to meet Elvis."

"Did you hear Roger Willis?" I asked.

"I did."

"Then understand that our play detective adventure is on a tentative hold, at least until Ava gets released or charged. I need that guy to free her."

"So you're not dropping the case?"

"Not even. Why would you think that?"

"Well, you look defeated after your match with Attorney Willis."

"That's because I'm tired. I haven't gotten any sleep in a few days. Bella was sick earlier this week, then my time at the ER, now Ava . . ." I pivoted and began walking back toward my car. "I don't want to speak to Elvis. He's not going to tell me what I need to know. Willis is right. They're probably brainwashing him right now. "

"Don't say that." He walked behind me.

I guessed my pace must have been pretty fast. He was panting a little once we reached my car.

"Give me my keys. I'll drive home." I held out my hand.

"As your sidekick, it's my duty to ignore you." He unlocked my door. "Now get in."

"Where are we going?" I asked.

"Nowhere. Well, not yet. Not until you see the light."

"And what exactly does that mean?"

"It means pull out your pen and paper, and let's mind dump everything that happened tonight so we won't forget what you need to say to Elvis once he calls."

"Mind dump?" I twirled the word in my head. I liked it. I smiled at Justus. "How do we start?"

"Over smothered and covered, diced and sliced."

14

Friday, 7:00 AM
The Waffle House

"There's something you don't know about me that may change the way you feel about me being your sidekick," Justus said.

He had hid most of his face behind the white laminated Waffle House menu, which was stuck to the table when we arrived. He should have hid his eyes. It charmed me in the way that the old Eastern Diamondback snake that lived in Aunt Doe's collards and cucumber garden did to Ava's pet rabbit Shirley the summer we were ten years old. An intoxicating danger.

I placed my menu back down flat on the counter. "You killed Devon? Case closed."

"No, guess again."

"Can you do that after I take your order?" the waitress said to both of us.

Her tone of voice rubbed me the wrong way. I checked her with my eyes until her neck stopped rolling at me. Her name tag said Cherlie ironically. She smacked her lips when she chewed her gum. I eyed her some more. She pushed the gum under her tongue or swallowed it. I don't know, but whatever she did with it made it disappear. Good. Because I wasn't in the mood to be dealing with a salty chick.

I decided to let Justus respond, since his mouth was already open from watching me and Cherlie. He gave Cherlie his eye-lock thing, ordered their bottomless cups of coffee, and then apologized for keeping her from her other nonexistent customers. She told him she would give us a few more minutes and walked off whistling. I wanted to take my shoe off and throw it at the back of her head.

I shook my head. "Please tell me you're not a woman whisperer."

He chuckled. "Not like that."

"Then tell me quick because I'm starving and I don't want Cherlie spitting in my food; then I really will be going to jail tonight."

"I'll pretend that I didn't hear that." He poured coffee into my cup.

I watched him pour. "I guess that is a sidekick job?"

"It could be or something more, but not a job, a perk for being my friend." He grinned.

I blushed and lowered my head. "It's getting a little warm in this hot box."

"Are you feeling better?" he asked.

"Do you mean if I'm still sad, confused, and defeated?"

He reached across the table and held my hands. "Yes, all of that."

"First, tell me this secret of yours before I give you an answer."

Cherlie coughed. I looked up at her. She had returned and now she had her hands on her hips. I looked around the small rectangle of a dining hall, to see if there were any witnesses just in case I dove into her chest. We were the only ones there except for two Decatur policemen sitting in the station near the door. They were busy reading an *Atlanta*

Sentinel and chopping it up with each other about its contents. I sighed. I still missed my old job.

Normally, I would have checked Cherlie's attitude despite their presence, but I didn't have the heart to do it. Instead, I ordered. As hungry as I was, I didn't have an appetite. I chose, instead, another bottomless cup of coffee, a bowl of grits, two slices of raisin bread, and a plate of bacon. Not my customary batch of hash browns or waffles on my plate. I observed Justus's plate. It was sparse. I couldn't imagine a man his size and masculine build would eat so little.

"What's wrong with you?"

"I'm good." He picked around his plate with his fork.

I sipped some coffee. "Are you going to tell me your issue, or do I have to add that to my long to-do list?"

He wiped his mouth, glanced at the sheriff, then responded, "I told the detectives how we really got inside Ava and Devon's home."

"What did you tell them?" I reached for another sip.

"I could have told them that you jammed the keypad to disarm the security gate."

I sprayed some of the coffee over my pajama top. I looked around. Cherlie giggled.

I winced at her and wiped my mouth with a napkin. "How did you know that, Justus?"

"I know a lot of things. That's what I'm trying to tell you," Justus said.

One of the policemen glanced at us, then waved for Cherlie to service them. She sucked her teeth and walked toward their station.

"Well, at least you waited until I ate to tell me." I wiped the spilled coffee off the table. "What else do you know?"

He leaned forward. "Why didn't you tell me that you were banned from the McArthur estate?"

I tensed. Willis was right. Salvador did think I had something to do with Devon's death. What if my shenanigans further add to evidence to support the DA charging Ava for Devon's murder? I felt more defeated than ever now. I pulled a napkin from the dispenser, to wipe the tears falling from me again.

"I'm sorry. I was worried about Ava. I thought her life was in jeopardy. After what you told me about Kelly and your concerns for her, I know you understand where I'm coming from. I didn't mean to hurt anyone, especially Ava."

"If that's the case, then why do you continue to lie to me?"

"Why are you doing this to me? Why confront me about this now and here? I thought we were supposed to be mind dumping or whatever that is?"

"We are. We're clearing the air and cleansing our souls with the truth." He outstretched his hand to me, but I didn't take it.

"I told you not to sneak your sermons on me."

Cherlie had returned. "Are you done with your order?"

"Very . . ." I stood up, grabbed my purse, and walked toward the door.

I needed some air. I'd catch a cab to Big Tiger's or take the bus. I had to get out of here and away from Justus.

"Angel?" Justus called after me, but I wasn't responding.

As I bounded for the door, I glanced at the *Sentinel* in the officer's hand, then stopped. The headline read: THE PASSION OF A MURDERED PASTOR. Then I fainted.

"How are you feeling?" Justus asked.

"Foggy. What happened?" I looked around. We were in the car.

"You fainted in the Waffle House. You came to before I was about to take you to Dekalb Medical," Justus said.

"Dekalb Medical?" I sat up. "There's no time for that."

"I knew you would say that, so I'm taking you home." He looked at me while he drove. "Are you sure you're okay?"

"Yeah, let's get this mind dump down before something else weird happens."

"Good." He handed me my notebook and a pen from his pocket. "Let's run down what we know so far before we get there."

I thanked him for the pen and opened my notebook.

"Why does my sister care more about her husband than her kids?"

"I don't think it's that simple."

I looked up at him. "She could have stayed at my house with me instead of going to the McMansion, and now she's playing sleepover at the Dekalb County jail. Sounds simple to me, right?"

"Wrong. Not when you're in love with someone. You'll do anything to protect them, to protect what you have together. A woman and her man have to put themselves first."

"I don't know if you know this or not, but you have a way with words."

"No, I don't know, but you can tell me about it when you call in that rain check. Now rest. It's going to be a long day."

"Okay, but I have one question."

Justus rubbed his forehead. "One."

"So you think that Ava was trying to protect the kids by bringing them to my house?"

Justus placed his arm over my headrest. "What do you think? She'd been calling you repeatedly the last couple of days. She swung by your house and scanned the place before she brought your niece and nephew. I think she was seeing if it was safe for them."

"Yeah, she was making sure that they would be okay. That makes good sense, sidekick." I nodded. "She waited until they were asleep before she brought them over. Didn't put on any travel clothes. Didn't waste any time . . ."

My heart became heavy thinking about the lengths Ava took and what was going through her mind on the drive to my house. I should have figured this out sooner.

I sat up. "Justus, she wasn't leaving Devon like Terry told Salvador. No, she was coming back. Why remove the children unless Ava knew something was going down last night."

I closed my eyes and squinted. I used to do that when I wanted to visualize a sticky situation. But even through that I still couldn't get a full view of Ava's yesterday.

"Have a clue what that was?" Justus asked.

I shook my head and opened my eyes. "No, but Terry or Elvis might."

"Don't forget, Elvis should be contacting you and you don't have Terry's contact information."

"Yes, I do." I slid my phone out of my pocket, texted him, and put the phone back.

"Should I ask how you got his number and what did you text?"

"I would, but I think now's the time for me to follow Willis's advice and not wreck anything. I want to also see what he can do for Ava first."

"You're that confident in Willis?"

"I don't like him, but I respect him. He has contacts in both high and low places, something a murder defense needs. And a church as large as Greater Atlanta can't take two huge scandals in less than five years. They'll get Ava off."

"Are you sure about that?"

"I'm too tired to think anything else."

"What does your heart tell you?" Justus asked.

That my crush on you has become more complicated.
"To sleep on it. I'm not good when I don't have four good hours."

He laughed. "Four, huh?"

"Yep, from two to six. The hours of mom power."

"You need more than that."

"Not going to get *that* today either, but thanks for showing your concern."

He smiled. "Good to see you calming down. The kids will need that today."

I nodded. "I'm curious. You're just as bright and bubbly as you were at yesterday's Communion. Aren't you the least bit exhausted?"

"Angel, I'm the pastor of a small church. I'm always exhausted."

I looked at him. I wanted to thank him, kiss him, something for going all out of his way for me and for talking a little sense into me. I missed having someone like that in my life. *Oh my.* I turned away from staring at him and focused on our mission.

"Justus, I have a friend who knows the city well, even the part we don't see. He may know if Devon was in some sort of trouble. I'll call him on the way home and ask him to do a little digging. That way you can get back to the church and I can get to the children."

"Would that friend happen to be Big Tiger?"

I looked at him. "What is it with you and Big Tiger? You haven't met him."

"Don't need to. The fact that he wasn't waiting at your bedside in the emergency room after you were almost killed to keep his money in his pocket was all I needed to know about the guy."

"You don't understand, Justus. Everything isn't as black and white as you make it out to be."

"There's no gray area for protecting the women in your life, regardless of the nature of the relationship. It's a man thing that you don't understand, Angel."

"Sounds like you're jealous to me."

"That's what's wrong with society today. Women read into things that aren't there. It is my job to protect you. It is every man's job. If they don't believe it, then they're punks."

I chuckled. "I'll add you to my prayer list before I take this nap, because you need some."

"True. After a week like this, I know I need it." Justus nodded. "That reminds me. I have to pray over the soup kitchen this morning."

I gasped. "Justus, I'm sorry for keeping you out this late."

He shrugged. "It's not your fault. Crap happens."

"Crap . . . I know a better term, but out of respect for you, I won't say it." I scoffed. "But I'll say this. Devon's death is more than crap. It's just not fair."

"Angel, you of all people know that life isn't fair."

"I do, but he didn't have to die like that. No one deserves to be treated like that."

"Think about the rest of this world and how they're treated, huh? Africa, Asia, places where children die every day because they haven't eaten anything since the moment they got here. Don't get me wrong. What has happened to your family is tragic, but we can't let it break our spirits. Your brother-in-law wouldn't want that."

I looked at him. He had some nerve. I felt more tears rising up in me. I huffed and puffed them back down. After all, he did have a point. "What do you know about anything?"

"I know that Sugar Hill is a slice of heaven compared to the last place I served."

"Where was that?"

"Darfur."

I took my eyes off the road to glare at him. "Say what? You gotta be kidding me."

"No, I'm not. Three long, soul-searching years. That's the reason why I'm in Sugar Hill right now. I thought I needed some time to restore my soul. That my sister and her family are here is a bonus. They need me, especially the twins, and honestly, those kids make me happy. Little did I know that you were here waiting to help me rub the rest of my hair out." He chuckled.

"You think my situation resembles that madness over there?"

"Of course not, Angel. But wow . . . your life is more fantastic than praying over biscuits and fried chicken on Sunday mornings."

"It's a bit rich, I guess . . ." I rolled my eyes.

We laughed until I remembered what and who was waiting for me at home: Whitney and the kids, with Mom on the way. "Maybe we can go through the Krispy Kreme drive-thru and get something for the house. That'll calm everyone down a bit." *Yeah, right,* I thought.

We stopped at the 24-hour Krispy Kreme in Lawrenceville before we reached Sugar Hill. I bought a box filled with chocolate éclairs for Big Tiger, too. I didn't feel comfortable sharing that information with Justus. He clearly didn't understand my relationship with Big Tiger, and I wasn't in the mood to be defending an old friend against a new one. I needed them both right now.

15

It was a quarter 'til nine by the time we returned to my home, which meant I had about one minute to sleep before the kids realized they needed something only I or Ava could give them, two minutes before Mom broke down my door, and no time to prepare for Big Faith's media fallout. No justice. No sleep. I smoothed my ponytail with my hand, searched for my garage door opener that I kept in my purse, and pressed it.

As we pulled into my garage, I noticed Justus's truck. It was parked in front of my yard under the brightest lit street lamp on the street. I imagine my nosy neighbors watched his truck all night and came up with some very messy conclusions about it.

I eyed him out of my periphery. He had a smirk on his face.

"Don't worry. No one noticed my truck in your yard."

"And you know this because . . . ?" I turned off the ignition.

"I haven't received one call from my meddling members." Justus slid out of the car and walked around to my side.

He opened my door for me.

I turned my head toward him, then toward the warm doughnut box resting on the backseat. The gooey sweet smell lulled me to recline on the head rest. "Can I just sleep right here?" I asked him.

He leaned down and looked at me. "No, gotta get you and these hotties inside."

"I can't go in there."

"You have to. You have family obligations and so do I. I need to check on Trish, Kelly, and the boys."

I saw Vicki Mehnert's porch light turn off through the rearview window. I know she's been watching my house all night.

"Back up." I pushed him back.

I tried to see if she was peeking out to spy on us. Vicki didn't care for me. Rumor around church was that she wasn't too hip to our new hot-chocolate preacher either. If she saw us together, he'd be pink-slipped by tomorrow.

I grabbed the doughnuts, scrambled out of the car, then crouched beside it. "You'd better leave now."

He leaned over. "What are you doing?"

I hit my garage door pad. "Keeping you out of trouble." I didn't get up until the garage doors closed us in.

He shook his head and folded his arms. "The coast is clear. Now please explain why you're acting like a sixteen-year-old skipping curfew."

I leaned on my car and whispered, "If the church knew that I got you involved with a murder investigation, almost got you arrested, mind you—and let's not talk about you rescuing me after my escapade at Night Candy, ha!—they'd push you to hell in a handbasket. I couldn't live with adding more scandal to this week. But I haven't figured out how to get you out of here without anyone knowing about it."

"Too late. My truck has been parked outside your place all night. Remember?"

"Right. All night . . ."

He nodded.

I laid my head on my hood and groaned. "Not good."

"It's fine." He grinned. "Let's go inside."

It took Whitney a millisecond to get down the stairs.

"What took y'all so long?" she asked. "I've been itching to turn on the television. What happened?" She looked from me to Justus.

"Devon's dead," Justus said softly.

Whitney gasped so loudly I was sure the neighbors heard her. She looked at me and then at Justus again. "Where's Ava?"

"Ava's been arrested and charged with Devon's murder. I wanted to call you, but—"

Whitney grabbed me. Her face began to fall apart. She laid her head in my chest and cried. I brushed her hair with my hands and mouthed to Justus, "Help me."

Clouds from the southwest rolled in for a morning shower to cool Atlanta off. Ava was still in jail, and the bad news looming over my house would not let me rest. The children would be up jumping on my bed soon, and of course, the reporters and my mom never slept. Thank God she didn't fly.

I sat on my bed without a clue of where to start. How would I tell my niece and nephew what happened to their parents? And why—for all that is holy in this world—couldn't I stop thinking about my night with Justus?

He'd stayed a few minutes after I went upstairs to get a few winks. Whitney needed some counseling from him. We all would need some.

Someone tapped on my door. I prayed it wasn't the kids. "Can I have a few more minutes, sweeties?"

"No, it's me, Whitney, but I'm still your sweetie."

"Come in." I pulled my pillow from behind me and hugged it over my chest.

Whitney slid between the door, hopped under the covers with me, and laid her head on one of my free pillows. Before Bella was born, she was my cuddle buddy, but then she grew up and couldn't stand me. Now everything had changed again.

I patted her head. "I want you to go to school and take your final exams. Devon would have insisted, and Mom will have a fit if you don't. I'll handle the kids, but you need to leave now before the vultures arrive."

She whispered, "They already came and left."

I peeled my top sheet off her face. "What do you mean 'came and left'?"

"Your old work buddies showed up at the door a few minutes ago. That's what woke me up, but don't worry." She opened one eye. "Your boyfriend/pastor took care of them."

"My boyfriend/pastor?" My chest tightened. "Justus? When? Where?"

She pointed at the floor. "He's downstairs. Ask him yourself. I'm starving."

I stood up and snatched the covers off my bed. "Get up. Go to school. Mom will be here in about an hour."

"Nope." Whitney pulled the sheets back up on the bed. "Justus is making pancakes and I'm hungry. We can't get through anything today on an empty stomach. Did you say Mom was coming here?"

"Did you say Justus was making pancakes?"

She nodded. "And they smell good, too. Better than yours."

I sniffed sweet butter and apples. "You gotta be kidding me."

"But they do. No offense," she said, as I jumped up and reached for my robe.

I couldn't stick my arm through it. I circled around myself two more times before I realized the robe was inside out.

I huffed and plopped back on the bed. "Why's he still here?"

Whitney patted my back. "I think he likes you."

I scratched my head. I think I like him, too, and that's a problem.

"Seriously . . ." I slapped her leg. "Why is Justus still here? Didn't you see him out this morning?"

"I told him to stay."

"You did?"

"You were tired after dragging me up the stairs." She mumbled underneath the covers. "You were very sad, too. We both were—are. I thought he could help us until Mom or Ava comes home. I mean, this is too much for us to handle on our own and he *is* our pastor."

Unbelievable. I sighed. Not only had I lost my focus, but my natural-born mind. Maybe it was the extra hormones I inherited from the Mother Angel after Bella was born or the fact that my twin was sitting in the pen, mourning her husband and being charged for his murder. Lord, did she kill him?

I peeled the sheet from Whitney's head again. "Our family is spinning and I might be hor-motional right now, but we're going to stay on course. We don't need a man to help us do that. So get up and go to school. I need you to be the only right thing today."

Whitney sat up. Her hair was all over her face. "That's sweet, but I don't have to go. Justus called the dean of the college this morning and told him everything. I can reschedule my exams before next semester starts. Now I can help you. Isn't that sweet?"

I slid on my slippers. My chest beat faster now. I could barely see my shoes. My eyes hadn't gotten in complete focus. "It's not sweet; it's ridiculous."

Whitney lay back down. "Tell that to your boyfriend/pastor. I'm sure he agrees with me."

"Yeah, right." I walked out of my room.

"Did you say Mom was coming?" She yelled after me.

I reached the banister and smelled apple pancakes. My stomach growled. I looked around. What happened to all those doughnuts? Then I heard Bella, Lil' D, and Taylor downstairs. Awake. My head throbbed. I sat down on the top step. I wasn't ready. My chest ached. Couldn't breathe. Something was wrong.

I heard a thud on my front door. I stood up. From my location on the stairs, I saw a few moving shadows hovering on the porch.

"Reporters." I ran down the stairs.

Before I yanked the door, Justus slid in front of me and smiled. His smile was brighter than the sun.

"Good morning." He carried a cup of coffee in his hand.

He looked phenomenal, even though his shirt was more than likely standing on its own now. Yet, I didn't feel comfortable. I was angry that he was here. I didn't want to be, but I was. I've never had a man stay in this house. I've never had a strange man around my daughter. I knew it wasn't his fault, but he's a minister. Shouldn't his super godly sense have told him that?

I looked down at the coffee mug, then looked away. "What are you still doing here?"

"You didn't ask . . ." His voice fell. "I thought you wanted me to stay."

I could smell myself making a stupid mistake. "I asked you to help me, not sleep in my house."

He placed the mug on the foyer table and took his dear time returning back to our conversation. He stood in front of me. No, he towered over me. Even though I still hadn't looked at him, his body language told me that he was looking straight through me.

"I didn't sleep. I've been watching over your house as *you* slept."

I looked up at him. The sun was gone, but his words and those bloodshot eyes almost melted me. Almost.

I looked over his shoulders toward the door. The shadows still lurked. "How many are out there?"

"I don't know." He turned toward the door. "But the kids are eating. Your breakfast is on the table. I'll remove the trespassers from the house. Call me after you wash the egg off your face."

He opened the door. The shadows had familiar faces. Justus walked out into the rain. He also left his mug.

I lifted the coffee cup and spoke to it. "I'm sorry."

"I guess this is, like, the worst first date you've ever had, huh?" Whitney asked between sausage chewing.

The kids were dancing to Hip-Hop Jack, a Saturday morning children's television show, in the family room while Whitney and I convened in the kitchen. Stress made me ravenous. I could eat everything in this house.

"No, more like a confirmation that I'm going to hell."

"Girl, you're crazy."

"No, I'm not. I've crossed the line . . . again. Now I don't know when Justus is doing his ministerial duties or trying to be my man." I threw my hands in the air. "Lord, forgive me. I'm going down a shame spiral."

"What's wrong with dating Justus? I like him and he's stupid sexy."

"I don't date the man. He's my pastor. Why are we talking about this anyway? I have tons of things to do today, and don't say sexy and pastor in the same sentence. That's a no-no."

Whitney leaned forward. "But you want a date with him, right?"

"Whitney, cut it out. So will you watch the kids while I handle things for Ava?"

"I will if you answer one question for me."

I sighed. "As long as it isn't about Justus."

She nodded. "It isn't."

"Okay, go."

"So why were you at Night Candy the night you got hurt? You know Lark works there."

Lark Samuels was her best friend, who wasn't old enough to drink, but could DJ in every bar in Buckhead. The girl knew too much.

"If nosy Lark was there, then you know why."

"Big Tiger was late."

I nodded.

"But Justus showed up on time. Right?" Whitney snickered.

I bowed my head. "Okay, I'll apologize to the man."

She hopped off her stool. "Good. Now count that as your one good thing for today." She kissed my forehead and went in after the kids. "I got the kids. You got Mom."

"Nope, Miss No Finals Today. You have her. I'm going to get dressed to meet Elvis Bloom, and hopefully pick Ava up from jail."

"Elvis who?"

"Devon's assistant." I coughed, then shivered. *Please tell me that I'm not catching a cold.*

I walked into the family room. The kids were having so much fun. Bella beamed. She hadn't spent this kind of time with her cousins in a long while. The kids, however, I could see were watching the door. They expected the people outside to be Ava and Devon. The thought angered me. *They can't be here. Those children can't hear that their father was dead.* I wanted those reporters gone now.

Bella ran up to me. "Morning, Mommy."

I knelt down and hugged her. "Morning. I love you, baby."

She looked right through me, then pursed her lips. "Why are D and Taylor here? I haven't seen them all my life."

When a child talks to your soul, you can't help but tell the truth. I shook my head. "Your aunt and uncle had plans that didn't involve them."

"Okay." She nodded, then ran back to them. I'm always baffled over the innocence of children. What happened to adults to make us so cynical?

I stood up and walked over to Whitney, then steered her toward the window. I peeled back the curtain. We both glanced outside. Five white Gwinnett County Police sedans lined the street in front of my home. Television station vans began to move away, while a black Crown Vic pulled up in the drive. A man stepped out of the caddie. He walked toward my front door and skipped up the porch steps. Salvador.

I clutched the blinds. "Not now."

If the kids saw him and his entourage, they would know something was very wrong.

I nudged Whitney. "Take the kids upstairs to get dressed. I'll take care of them."

She nodded. "Hey, kids, let's go upstairs and get dressed." The doorbell rang. I cringed, then peeked into where the kids were. They were still bopping around to Hip-Hop Jack, putting up their toys. I sighed. There must be TV in heaven. I waited until Whitney and the kids were upstairs and then answered my door.

"Good morning, Salvador."

16

"**M**orning, Angel. May I speak to you for a moment?" Salvador smiled.

Today he wore another pinstriped suit, navy with tan stripes. In the daylight, on my doorstep, in my eyes, he was Antonio Banderas. Mom would have a hot fit, if the circumstances weren't so bad and she wasn't a newlywed.

I shook my head. "Can you call your guard dogs off?"

He looked behind us and shrugged. "They aren't mine. I thought they were yours."

Justus. I cringed. He was a man of his word; I was a buffoon.

"Well, since you all are brothers in blue, can you ask them to leave? The neighborhood is going to wonder."

He smirked. "I'm sure they already know what has happened because your brother-in-law's murder is already breaking news."

He pulled a copy of the *Atlanta Sentinel* from behind him and held it up in front of me. Front and center sat a large photo of a wild-eyed Ava wearing that peach robe splattered with Devon's blood on it. Ouch. I winced.

Salvador handed the paper to me. "Have you changed your mind about that talk now?"

"I still don't have time."

I took it from his hands, folded it under my arm, and stepped outside. I was about two minutes from crying again. I gestured for him to follow me toward my rocking chairs on the front porch. I sat down and didn't say anything until he sat beside me. I wasn't going to let him tear me down in my own home.

His PDA buzzed. He didn't look at it. He looked at the yard. "When I go home after a day and night of observing scum, I garden."

I didn't say a word.

"You can find me at eleven o'clock at night in my yard tending to rose bushes." He chuckled. "I don't go to sleep until I get my hands dirty."

"Well, that explains it." I wrapped my robe tighter around my waist. "Look, Salvador. I don't have time for metaphors. I don't have time to wash my hair, so whatever it is you came by to say, you need to get on with it. Or do I need to have an attorney present?"

"No, else I would have called before I came."

"And why did you drive out of your jurisdiction to see me?"

"I need to ask you a few more questions about last night."

"And you think coming over here, where my niece and nephew are, will make me want to say anything to you?"

"I need to see your last case file."

I stopped rocking. "What are you talking about?"

"The one implicating Greater Atlanta for tax fraud."

"What would that mess possibly have to do with Devon's murder?" I asked.

Salvador shook his head. "Hopefully nothing, but in cases like this, we have to cross all our T's."

"More like, point crosshairs at my sister."

"You dug that ditch back when you wrote that story."

I cringed. He might as well have taken that deadly Wüsthof knife and stabbed me with it.

"You're asking me about something that never was. The story never inked. It's no good."

"Just because the *Sentinel* didn't run it, doesn't make it unimportant. Anyway, I live fifteen minutes from here, so it wasn't a problem to come by. Plus, I wanted to check on you and the family."

"You're the first." I tightened my robe more. Justus's disappointed face popped into view. "I meant the second who thought enough to check on us."

"No one has called from Greater Atlanta?"

I sighed. He was digging for clams right on my porch. But he didn't need to be. Ava looked more guilty than any possible suspect I had ever seen. He was searching for something else, or he knew Ava didn't kill Devon.

"What else can I do for you besides giving you my old story, Detective?"

"Come on now, Angel. Let's not do this dance. You have something I want. I can take it by force if I need to."

"The kingdom of heaven suffers violence, and the violent take it by force," I said. If Justus were here, I imagine he would chuckle.

"Now's not the time for Bible quoting."

I turned to him. "Hasn't this family suffered enough today? What you're asking could ruin Devon's legacy. Do you know that?"

"I know what your investigation alleges."

"But that's beside the point. It's apparent that the church

has taken a position to support Ava to the fullest. Willis, the lawyer. You know full well he'll make her crooked straight. Besides, you have a very strong case. Manslaughter One. You don't need that story to make that happen."

"You're so wrong." He stood up. "I need the story. Can't tell you why, but I need it, and for Ava's benefit, you need to come up with it."

My heart was doing laps at Daytona. I caught his coat sleeve. "You think it has something to do with Devon's death, don't you?"

"Don't know."

I stood up. "Then neither do I."

He shook his head. "Okay, then I'll let the assistant DA subpoena you, and let's see how far that'll help your sister."

"You don't care about my sister and that little reluctant gardener shtick of yours, you could have kept that for Oprah."

"Are you going to cooperate or what?"

"Why should I?"

"Because we're both after the same thing."

"Can't be the truth."

"Must be. That's the only thing that keeps us both up at night."

"Even if that truth means my sister is innocent?"

He nodded. "If that's what we determine."

"Let me stop you right there. She's innocent and I'll prove it. So you don't have to tell me what you already know. I'll find out on my own."

"So you already know that as we speak my partner is picking up a search warrant for your home?"

My throat singed. I wanted to kick him off my property, but I couldn't.

"If I tell you what you want to know, can you do a favor for Ava's children?"

"Out of respect for you, I want you to know that we will come search your house later today." He checked his watch. "You'll have enough time to have an attorney here with you."

"Thanks, at least you're courteous enough to give me time to get the children out of the house so they won't see."

He coughed. "I'm going to have to speak to the kids."

"What?"

"It's best if I speak to them here instead of bringing them to Decatur."

"Do you know what that means? Do you realize the kids don't know anything right now? They think Devon and Ava are on a trip. "

He rubbed his fingers. I could have sworn I saw dirty soil sift between his fingers. "It's for the best."

A huge knot lodged into my throat. "You know my sister didn't kill him. Don't you?"

His handheld went off again. He pulled it from his belt, looked at it, and grunted. "What is it going to take for you to cooperate with me?"

"Release my sister."

He chuckled. "I can't do that."

"Keep me in the loop, so I can find the real killer."

"I can't do that either."

"Well, what can you do?"

He laughed. "You haven't been married before, have you?"

"What does that have to do with the price of milk?"

"I've been married for fifteen years. Married my high school sweetheart. She's still my sweetheart. You know why?" He went on as if he hadn't heard my last question. I rocked in the chair and folded my arms. "Do you know why?"

"Clueless."

"We both learned early on to listen, something you, Ms. Crawford, should know very well, but you don't do so well right now."

I stopped rocking. He had my attention. "Can you tell me who killed Bella's father, then?"

He chuckled and stood up. "I have to go. I hope that by the time I return you will have a copy of that old case file. I'll see you later today, Ms. Crawford."

I watched him pull out the drive and then wave when he tipped his hat at me. So much for going to meet Elvis at ten. I had to uncover my own dead and find a place for my family to go while my house was trashed, but where?

I came back inside and went upstairs. The children were giggling and playing. I went into my room, shut the door, and locked it. Television shows, movies, and sometimes the Holy Bible showed people living through a romantic sort of tribulation. They do the right thing even when they don't want to. They find illumination during times of struggle. Endings are always happy. There's a light at the end of the tunnel, and sometimes Oprah invites them to her show.

But I didn't feel any of that. No. Not a bit of faith like that. We were in trouble. Big trouble. And there was no way God was placing the burden of solving Ava's issues on me.

"What makes you so special?" A voice that sounded very much like my great-grandmother spoke through the air around me.

I ignored her voice. I wasn't trying to be disrespectful, but I knew my limits. I didn't know how to make things better. I didn't want to get out of bed, and I definitely, definitely didn't want to go to the self-storage facility to retrieve that case file.

I paid good money to keep the skeletons in my closet there. My soul needed those skeletons to stay there. And so my cry came and began to crumple me down to the floor. I needed sanctuary.

But, of course, my doorbell rang. I peeked through my window and fell out of myself. Mom was here. What a mixed blessing.

Virginia Carter, our mom, had her hands on her hips looking like a Diahann Carroll knockoff with her salon-colored mahogany coif to boot. Her eyes steamed at me. She had a few more bones to pick, and by the strength in my arm when I swung my door open, I had a limb to break off myself.

"Evangeline Grace Crawford, why do you look like death warmed over when your sister is fighting for her freedom in the Dekalb Hotel?" Her nickname for the jail.

I sighed and opened the door.

She stepped into the foyer and dictated. "Tell Whitney to get my things out of the car. Move her car out of the garage, so you can park mine next to yours. And where are my grandbabies?"

"Before I even consider honoring any of your requests, I need you to do something for me."

She pursed her lips. Somehow her hips became wider, because that leg she rested on dug into my hardwood. "Let me remind you of the Fifth Commandment: Honor your mother."

"Let me remind you of the Fifth Commandment: Honor your children; Actually, honor everybody."

Mom slammed her purse on my foyer table. "I didn't come here to be disrespected."

"Mom, that's not what I meant. I need you. I'm glad to see you." I peeked over her shoulder. "Where's my new daddy?"

She exhaled and smiled wide enough to match the sun.

"He's making reservations for us to stay at the Hilton down the street. I fear if we go back to Marietta, we won't make our honeymoon after all of this is settled."

"There's room here. You don't have to stay in a hotel."

"Sounds like a full house, not a good thing for newly-weds. We're noisy at night." She walked around me, then stopped just short of me becoming dizzy. "What have you heard from the investigators?"

"Actually, not enough. That's another reason why you need to be here. The house is going to be searched in a few hours. I'm going to ask Whitney to take Bella to my church to swim and play while they're here."

"And what about Taylor and Lil' D? Why aren't they going?"

"Because the detectives want to talk to them?"

"Hell no." She reached in her purse and pulled out her cell phone.

"Mom, how can you quote a commandment and curse at the same time?" I palmed my head. "Never mind."

She closed the phone and took my hands in hers. "Let me tell you something. Those kids are going to that church and swim. I'll take care of the detectives."

"What are you going to do?"

"I'm going to introduce them to your new daddy."

"And what does he have to do with the price of eggs?"

"He's a retired police chief. I think that says enough. He can man the house while we take care of business." She kissed my cheek. "I missed you, Angel."

I kissed her back. "You know, I have to admit that I missed you, too."

"Just as long as you do, then you'll be okay." She released my hands, then walked toward her purse. "Now get upstairs, get pretty, and wash the spunk back into your soul. I heard a rumor that your pastor's a dreamboat."

"Who told you that?"

"Who else? Whitney."

"Don't you think I should get my no-name stepdaddy up to speed about what's going on first?"

"Not looking like that you won't." She scrunched her nose. "I hope you weren't dressed like that when you were out with the pretty pastor."

"On that note, I'm going to take my shower now."

17

Friday, Noon

Newsflash. My midday shower didn't wash the spunk back into my spirit like Mom said. But I knew what would. I pulled my shower blinds up and peered through the window. Sugar Hill Community Church and Justus. That's how I found Sugar Hill—looking past the Duluth skyline toward the possibility of something greater. Devon deserved a better death than what he got. Hopefully, I could give him a better homegoing, if I got Ava freed in time.

The rain disappeared soft and slippery into periwinkle-perfected sky. A brighter, crisp blue day stood behind the morning's veil. And I watched the world transform all around me. But as peaceful as it looked, I felt my own peace slipping away.

What happened to Devon? Although I had a hunch that Ava didn't do it, it was hard for me to see how Ava's not guilty. Maybe I'm out of focus.

While in the shower, I looked a mile straight down our backyard toward Sugar Hill Community Church. It stood white, compact, traditional; safe and solid; small, but a place of solace. I saw my new friend Justus standing at the top of the church steps, waving at the joggers and looking toward my house. If I looked at him any longer, I would have to take another shower—an iceberg cold one. I couldn't. I had to get the kids out the house in half an hour.

Yet to say that I had a crush on him would be an understatement. This past Sunday he proposed to the congregation that we have a fast, to put a protective covering over London, as it mourned over those lost in last week's bombing attack. We could choose anything to fast, but he preferred we fast from something that had some power over us: chocolate, soap operas, cigarettes, etc. My fast was going to be to stay as far away from him as possible.

I'd failed twice so far, and now with this Ava/sidekick thing, I might as well call this fast a bust. I needed some spiritual guidance, and with Ava's drama stretching into my home, I had no choice but to bop over to the church. At least Bella would get more "soldier-chicken-airplane" swimming lessons in the church pool.

I put the shower back on. Alaska cold this time.

Someone knocked on the door.

Mom. I could feel her spirit sliding inside the room. If I were my great-grandmother, I'd have sworn Mom had about seven other spirits tagging along with her.

"There's another bathroom in Bella's room." I spoke through my shower curtain with my back to her, the shower running, but me not under it. I wanted to look outside at Justus a little while longer.

She said something weird.

Couldn't make sense of it. I turned the shower spout off. "Huh?"

She mumbled something again.

I slid the shower curtains back and looked at her. "What did you say?"

"Do you think your sister killed my son-in-law?"

Looks like it. "No."

"Has anyone told the children?" She opened my medicine cabinet, more than likely rummaging around my cosmetics container for makeup to try.

"I don't know how to, Mom."

"Good. Avalyn can tell them herself once she's out. Meanwhile, we'll give them a parade, take them all over town. It'll keep them off thinking about their momma and daddy."

"You and Whitney will have to do that. I decided to help my stepfather prepare for Detective Tinsley's visit and I have some work to do." Wouldn't dare tell her that Ava might not get out today.

"So you're going to stick your nose in the fire again?"

I huffed. Here we go. "Mom, please . . ."

"No, thank God for you." She paused and sniffled. "You never should have stopped writing for that newspaper."

"I have my own business now."

"Girl, please. I don't know how long this little charade of yours will last. Bella needs to see you at your best, not see you laid up in some hospital after chasing thugs and the bad element. You need to be like Anderson Cooper, honey. All over the place, seeing the world for what it is."

"Mom, my work pays well and I see the world I want to see."

"I'm sure it does, but, honey, you were born nosy and with your ear to the ground. You can't sniff around on a computer all day, and hunting down men who aren't meant to be fathers is a waste of your good time. You have to be right in the middle of it." Mom sniffed one of my colognes, then turned her nose up. "So what do you think the detective wants with the kids?"

I stepped back. "They were the last ones to see Devon alive. If I were investigating—a hypothetical if—I would search my house to see if Ava left anything damaging and talk to the kids, because they have no reason to lie. The lead guy is good. His name is Salvador."

"Who cares what his name is?"

I shrugged. "I don't know."

"But what if you ask the kids before he gets here? Why don't you ask them? No." She hit the shower curtain. "I'll ask them myself, while you get dressed. But while you're at the church this afternoon, could you ask your pastor if he could come over tomorrow and make some more pancakes?"

And there went the last bit of peace I clung to. I slid the covers back, of course, not worried about standing naked before my mother. "What did Whitney tell you?"

She didn't look at me, but I knew she wore that all-knowing smirk on her lips. "Not much outside of the fact that your pastor should be my son-in-law. Mind if have this lipstick? It looks divine on me."

I shut the shower curtains; I wanted to shut her out.

Friday, 2:00 PM
Sugar Hill Community Church

"You're beautiful . . ." Justus said those words to me, sweet and perfect, like good loving on Sunday morning.

My knees shook, which wasn't good since I carried a three-pound box in my arms, my case file. I exhaled. I placed the box on the end table closest to the door, then ran my hand down my straightened hair. Mom insisted I use a blow dryer and flat iron today. In my opinion, now was not the time for hour-long beauty regimens, but as I looked at Justus beaming over me, I changed my mind.

He stood up from behind his desk and walked toward me. He stopped a pace in front of me, extending his arms, wide and inviting. I folded into him. ". . . and you're late."

Way to kill a mood.

I sighed and gave him a Sunday school hug, the kind where neither of us touched below the shoulder.

"I've been thinking about you since I left," Justus said. "I need to apologize to you. Forgive me for acting like an eight-year-old boy earlier. Guess I was tired after all."

I took his thinking-about-me line and obsessed over it until my stomach churned. "I wasn't exactly myself either. It's amazing what two hours of sleep can do."

He came closer. "No more butting heads. Deal?"

I touched the tiny knot on my forehead, nodded, and then he came closer. My breath flew out my lungs. My wobbly knees staggered forward and obliged. We hugged. This time we hugged like kindergartners. He smelled so good and his hold of me could put me to sleep right now. But I hadn't come here to relax.

"Justus, let me go," I mumbled.

He released me slow, looked down at me, and melted me some more. "My bad. I got a little carried away again. Didn't I?" He smiled.

"You do have a problem with giving off mixed signals."

"Oh, I thought I was quite obvious about my concern for you," he said.

I shook my head. What in the world was I going to do about this man?

Men and I didn't mix well when romance was involved. Men and I didn't mix at all when my investigating cap came on. Justus and I had a definite thing developing and I didn't want to slow down the buildup. More importantly, I didn't want to lose my new best friend. I needed him.

"I can't answer that question, only you can." I stepped away. "But I know you have a meeting this morning, I was just stopping by to tell you that my mom is here now and . . ."

"She finally made it." His eyes twinkled.

"Yes, she's at home waiting for me. Whitney's here with the kids. They'll be at the pool for a while. Salvador's coming."

"Coming to the church to swim?" Justus asked.

"No, to my house. He'll bring a warrant to search it for clues. He also wants to speak with my niece and nephew, but Mom's handling the latter."

He rubbed his head. "I knew I should have canceled this meeting this morning."

"No, you did the right thing. I can handle Salvador. He's a sweetheart."

"Didn't seem like that to me last night, and it definitely doesn't sound like that now."

"I didn't sense that from him."

His eyebrow lifted.

"What?" I shrugged.

"How do you know Detective Tinsley's on his way here?"

"Salvador stopped by my house and told me he would be coming."

Justus folded his arms over his chest. "When?"

"A few minutes after you left."

"What a coincidence." He chuckled and shook his head. "That man is going to charm your sister's conviction out of you so fast. You know what?" He walked back toward his desk. "I'm canceling the meeting. I'm coming with you."

"No, you aren't."

He frowned. "Are you trying to tell me what to do?"

"No, I'm not." I pointed my index finger upward. "But He'll agree with me. Handle the church business, and let me handle mine."

He pouted. "I'll be there first thing after the meeting."

I nodded. "Yes, of course, Pastor."

"I flip a few flapjacks and now we're back to you calling me pastor?"

"No, just keeping the lines drawn."

He unfolded his arms and walked back to his desk. "I take one step forward and you push me two steps back."

"I'm sorry. I know you mean well. I'm just not used to it."

"You have a lot of people depending on you right now. Why don't you allow Christ to take some of that burden from you? The church and I are here to do that. Stop making things so complicated. Get used to me looking out for you."

I should have known he wasn't flirting with me. I wanted to kick myself for once again being selfish and thinking about myself instead of what's best for the family. Why did I continue to think this man wanted me? I needed to get focused about today. The world was falling apart and my sister expected me to piece it back together for her kids.

"I'm sorry. I won't let my pride interfere again."

"No, you will." He smiled. "But I hope you hand it over every now and then, and let the experts handle Ms. Pride."

"Okay." I looked around the room. I didn't feel comfortable enough to ask for help.

"So what's today's meeting about?"

"It's about our fasting project. It seems that other churches would like to participate with us. We are meeting with the heads from those churches. Isn't God good?"

"Very."

"Now that you're comfortable talking to me, are you participating in the fast?"

No sense in lying in church. "I was fasting, but after what happened yesterday, I just can't seem to meet my goal."

"Hmmm. I didn't see your name on the fast commitment roster."

"I didn't think I needed to put my commitment on display."

He sat down. "The only person who would've seen it was me."

Exactly. "I didn't know you well enough then." My cheeks were burning now, and if I kept this up, so would my soul. I sat down in a chair in front of his desk.

He looked out his window toward the church's water park. "So how confident are you with Bella's swimming skills?"

"She's not good yet. This is her second set. Why?"

"I remember overhearing how anxious you were when she began taking swim classes and how you didn't feel that Craig Foster was old enough to train children."

"Have you been stalking me?" I asked.

"No, nothing like that. But you must admit, before the events of the past week, you were a mystery here. You sit on the last pew. You're the first to leave service. The only time we see you at length is when Bella participates in an activity or when you're at the Ladies' Communion and Brunch."

"I've caused so much drama in church in the past, I just don't want to bring down any more unnecessary attention, especially the kind that could harm Bella. I keep to myself and lay low. So far, so good."

"I hate to burst your bubble, but you must know that you command a great deal of attention around here, even though you don't try." He cleared his throat. "Any man would spot you from a mile away."

"They would? I do?"

He grinned. "You know you do."

Awkward silence from me. I lifted myself from the seat so I could peek at the kids through the window behind him.

"Whitney is at the pool with the kids. She has lifeguard training, so I feel confident."

"I didn't know that." He turned back to me, then observed the clock on the wall above my head. "So what did your mother say that brought you over here?"

I pressed my hair down again, then moved closer to his desk. *Please don't mention the pancakes,* I told myself.

His PDA buzzed. He looked down, then tugged one twist of his hair. "My meeting. Can we table this discussion for dinner?"

"Dinner?"

"Yes." He stood up again. "The church is going to provide dinner and a prayer meeting for your family tonight if that's okay with the family, unless Greater Atlanta is coming. Are they?"

I shook my head. "No, and you didn't have to do that."

"We want to. You're grieving a heavy loss, and you're family. Remember?"

"Family . . ." I nodded. "Thanks for reminding me. I need to get back to mine. Salvador's probably there."

"I'll pray for your visit with the detectives, and I'll come over soon as I can. Is there anything else I can do for you?"

"Yes. No, I'm waiting for Willis or Big Tiger to call. Ava has to come home today or I'll lose it."

"Big Tiger as in the guy who left you alone to fight that criminal Cade?"

"Justus, it's just as much my fault for not waiting and believing I could take him out alone. Besides Tiger can walk Ava out of the jail faster than anyone."

"Will he bring Ava to you?"

"If I'm bailing her out, he'd better."

His eyebrow lifted. "The church isn't paying her bail?"

"To save face, I'm sure they will." In my mind I wondered what the Board of Trustees was doing right now?

Were they preparing for a press conference? Were they pondering over an appropriate interim pastor? Were they blaming me, hiding things I needed to clear Ava's name? I sighed. "I don't know."

"What about Elvis? Have you spoken to him?" Justus's questions interrupted me.

I jumped. My head throbbed. "Not yet. I wanted to meet him today, see what he can tell me about Devon and Ava's daily routine, maybe feel him out, see what he knows, but I can't. This Salvador thing has thrown me for a loop. Now there are so many things to do, not do, and not say."

"Why don't I have Mrs. Lewis call them for you? Reschedule with Elvis for later this afternoon so I can take you."

Mrs. Lewis had been Sugar Hill's office manager for over twenty years. She could handle church folk in her sleep.

"That would be great. Oh, the reason why I came. I need some items couriered to the Dekalb County Homicide Division Office." I pointed at the box that sat on the table. "I would've done it from my home, but there are some reporters lurking around. I don't want them digging around, paying off the courier."

"Mind if I know what those items are?"

I shook my head. "I've talked about enough skeletons in my closet for one day."

"Maybe later, then?"

I shrugged. "Maybe. I won't lie in church."

He placed his hand on my right shoulder and looked deep down into me. "There is nothing in that box God or I would hate you for."

"So why do I hate myself?" My lips trembled. I didn't want his empathy. I wanted to erase what was in the box. I wanted Devon alive. "I can't fix this. It's too late."

"Don't cry." He hugged me. "I believe that God didn't

bring you this far to leave you. If this case wasn't personal, would you be able to solve it?"

"Definitely not." I wiped my eyes. "Okay. Maybe I can do this."

"Yes, you can." He smiled. "Glad I could at least help you realize that."

"No, you've done more than you think. The kids thought your pancakes were a hit." I winced. I wasn't supposed to mention those.

"Well, that's something." He chuckled. "Why don't I bring my nephews over, too, tonight? They can play with the kids."

"Sounds good. We're trying to keep them distracted, but it's hard. Kids aren't stupid. They know something's up, and if Ava isn't released today, the kids are going to lose it. They're missing their mom and dad. And I have to find Devon's killer like now. But I can't because my house is a madhouse. Not only is my mom there now, but her new husband is on his way. My suggestion, of course."

Justus scratched his head. "Sounds like we're two peas in a pod."

We both looked at each other in a way that made the hairs on the back of my head stand up.

I looked away from him. "By the way, thank your friends for clearing the press out of the yard this morning."

"Oh, no problem. They said they would patrol your block today and tonight."

"That's some good news for today." I thought about Whitney's request.

"Maybe I should cancel my meeting. You don't look so good."

"No, take care of church business. I need sleep and you do, too."

He came from behind his desk again. "Well, then I'm yours for the next forty-eight hours."

I gasped. If he only knew how those words sizzled in me.

We hugged again, and this time I didn't have any impure thoughts, more like fear. I was scared. What did my case have to do with Devon's death?

18

Before I walked back into the house, I forgot Elvis offered to bring food over tonight. I'd forgotten much since Bella was born. I wondered why pregnancy books never told you that you would lose brain juice after childbirth. Lord knows, I needed mine back in order to find Devon's killer, to keep my niece and nephew in good spirits until Ava returned, and to deal with Mom.

Having a catered dinner tonight would appease Mom for sure. I dialed Elvis's number. There was no answer. I got his voice mail. I left him a message accepting his offer to feed us.

Once inside, I found Salvador and a woman I assumed was his partner in my living room. They sat on the sofa while Mom pinched juleps into a pitcher of peachy tea in the kitchen. Had I not heard the police officers stomping around upstairs, I would have thought we were having brunch. I tiptoed through my foyer, hoping Salvador didn't see me.

"Ms. Crawford?" Salvador asked.

I waved my hand. "Hi, are y'all comfortable?"

"Yes, we are." He nodded.

The woman looked at me, but said nothing. She was a rude, little something-something.

I wanted to say something smart to her. Instead, I said, "Give me a sec and I'll be with you."

Salvador nodded; the woman stared. It took all the angels in heaven to keep my neck and eyes from rolling. I scampered toward the kitchen, peeked inside, and inhaled my once frozen key lime pie that was now sliced and set on saucers. I frowned.

"Mom, what are you doing?" I hissed.

"Being a gracious host."

"And what does that do outside of upsetting me, of course?" I took a seat on one of the island stools.

"It convinced Detectives Salvador and Dixon that the kids were too young and too asleep to know what was going in their house last night. So they don't feel the need to question them anymore."

I exhaled. "Thank goodness."

"And this nice evening tea that includes your pie also helped me stall for more time, so that you could get here and handle these people." She leaned toward me. "How are the kids?"

I bent backward to see the detectives chatting with each other. Dixon smiled, totally catching me off guard. "They're having fun, but have asked me twice about their parents."

She pursed her lips, reached for a handkerchief that she had to have taken from my curio, and wiped the corners of her eye. "Have you heard from Ava?" she asked.

"No, Ma. Have you?"

She grabbed my wrist so tightly it burned. "How could I? You turned all the ringers on the phones off in here. Why?"

"Because the phone had been ringing off the hook." I removed her hold on me. "Mom, everyone wants a story. Besides, where is your phone?"

"Including you?"

I looked at her. "I'd been waiting for when you would blame this whole thing on me."

"I wasn't, but you girls get yourselves in these situations with men that boggle my mind. This is a real doozy, baby, a real one."

"Speaking of doozies . . . Where's my new daddy?"

"He's stuck in traffic. Where's your man?"

"I don't have a man."

She lifted her left eyebrow. "Honey child, please. Do I need to go down to that little church to meet him?"

"Ma, he's just my pastor."

She looked me down and pursed her lips even tighter. "Uh-huh."

I shook my head and didn't say a word.

"Let's get back on task before our children come home." She picked up the tea tray. "I have a fresh batch of tea cakes warming in the oven. Get them out and come visit your friends."

"You've got to be kidding me," I said.

Mom had already walked away. By now, I had rolled my eyes so much that my head began to ache again. Great.

Mom continued her hostess diva routine in my living room, while I pretended to appear calm. I hadn't heard a word from Willis or Big Tiger. Something was up, but I wouldn't learn what it was until after the pinstriped detectives left my house.

Francine Dixon, Salvador's partner, wore a fierce black and lavender pinstriped skirt suit that made me envious for not taking a few laps around the pool today myself. She stuck her nose in the air when she looked at me. I scoffed.

She didn't have to bother with the theatrics. I knew she didn't like me, but why I had no clue.

"Have you found what you're looking for?" I asked Salvador.

His mouth was full of tea cakes. "We're working on it."

I sat down in the love seat across from them. "Would you mind telling me what you're looking for exactly?"

"We're not at liberty to say," Francine snapped.

She looked me up and down. Girlfriend looked like she was ready to fight. I didn't have a clue what her problem was, but I had a feeling she had a gripe about me.

"Detective Dixon, do you have a problem with me?" I asked.

Mom stood beside Francine. She held the tray over her head, but wouldn't say a word. The way she leaned into her hip in that mother defense stance told me what she was really saying was that Dixon better not have a problem or the food may fall on her head.

Francine didn't pay Mom any attention. "I don't have a problem with you. I just don't understand why my partner"—she turned to Salvador—"is giving you certain privileges."

Mom asked, "Did my daughter have to allow you inside her home?"

Salvador looked up. His eyes widened. "Ma'am?"

Mom didn't move. "You heard me. You were over here this morning. You drove off when I pulled up. You and my daughter sat right on that porch. I saw you. You could have gotten what you wanted then, but you come back with your salty friend here, who should have checked herself before she walked through the door. Privileges? Try rights."

Dixon turned to Salvador. "You were here this morning?"

Salvador coughed. Tea cake spewed all over my dirty carpet. I wanted to crawl into Francine's weave and melt.

"That was a courtesy call," Salvador said.

"And me stuffing your face with cookies I only bake for my children—one of whom is sitting in that stank tank down at the jail—doesn't seem like a courtesy. Does it to you?"

"No, ma'am." Salvador eyed me. "Detective Dixon is new to Atlanta. She isn't familiar with Ms. Crawford's past relationship with the police force."

"Well, you'd better get her up to speed." Mom pursed her lips. "But before you do, my daughter asked you a question." She referred to Francine. "Did you find what you were looking for in her house?"

My mouth dropped. I had no words.

"My apologies, Mrs . . . ?" Salvador waited for Mom to share her name. I wished he hadn't.

"Mrs. Crawford Curtis Carter, widow of Bishop B.T. Crawford of Calvary United Church of Atlanta, Georgia, widow of Reverend Dr. Augustus Curtis of Piney Grove Community Church of Lithonia, Georgia, and now wife of retired Fulton County Chief of Police, Carrolton Taylor Carter."

Francine's eyes widened and so did mine. Carrolton Taylor Carter, what kind of name was that?

"My apologies, ma'am. I came by earlier when the children were here and we—your daughter and I—agreed that the situation was inappropriate for them to see."

"It's appropriate for me, so bring me up to speed. What are you accusing my daughter Avalyn of? And what are you looking for in Evangeline's home?"

I relaxed. Maybe this new marriage had turned Mom into the woman we had needed a few years back.

"We're looking for items your daughter may have brought

with her when she came over last night. We're bagging them now as potential evidence."

"Now, that's more like it." Mom smiled and walked back toward the kitchen.

I turned to Salvador. "Thank you for relaxing on the kids."

"We're not relaxing, Ms. Crawford. We don't think we need them to prove our case," Francine said.

I wished Mom brought that tea tray back in here, so I could smack this lady one good time. Girlfriend hadn't eaten any of Mom's cookies or my pie. Her sourpuss attitude needed some sweetness. I wanted to kick her out of my house. *God, help me be better.*

I looked her in the eye and smiled at her like any Georgia Peach would. "Whatever the reason, I'm very thankful, Detective."

The police officers came down the stairs and met us in the living room. One handed Salvador two clear plastic bags labeled EVIDENCE. I rolled my eyes. The bags had the clothes the children wore yesterday. Unbelievable.

Mom stepped into the room. "What the . . . Oh, so when my grandkids come home and wonder where their clothes are, what appropriate answer should I give them?"

"Today would be a good time to take them on a Grandma shopping spree," Dixon said.

"What did you say?" Mom walked toward Detective Dixon.

I stood up and jumped in front of her. "I hate to say this, but y'all have outworn your welcome. Let me show you to the door."

My phone rang twice, which meant a text message was coming in. I peeked at it, then swallowed a squeal. Big Tiger calling.

"Mom, I need to take this call in my office," I said. "Please escort our guests to the door and be nice."

"You don't have to ask me twice. I'll show them what real nice is." Mom sashayed past me toward Salvador and Francine.

"Goodbye, Evangeline," Salvador said.

I waved one hand in the air, then closed my office door and dialed Big Tiger back.

Big Tiger grew up with Ava and me when we lived in East Lake. We lived near St. Phillip AME Church, a quieter area than his. He lived in the East Lake Meadows projects and got himself caught up in the dope game until the late, great Hosea Williams helped him find Jesus. Rumor around town was that he had found the devil, too. Now he was one of the biggest and shadiest bail bondsmen in Dekalb County, and he paid me well. I didn't trust him any farther than I could throw him. But I knew he could get Ava out. Plus, he once had a crush on me. From the giggle in his voice, he still kept that crush flaming.

"How much is the bail?"

"Don't know," he said.

"Why don't you know?"

"She didn't get into the rotation to see the judge this morning for her prelim."

I felt defeated and began to cry. "So tomorrow. She'll be ready?"

"Check with your boy, Roger Willis. I had to track that joker down. Angel Soft, I was ready to pop Avalyn out of there when he finally called me back. He didn't sound good. So I don't know about Ava getting out anytime soon."

"What? Why don't you think so?"

"You know full well why, girl. This is a capital murder case. Ava and Devon weren't just any couple. They money.

Holy money with an angel jet on top. She could fly right out of here. Heaven bound, honey. Give me one good reason why any judge would grant her bail?"

"She didn't do it."

"Did she tell you that?"

I gulped. "She didn't have to."

"After the way you two fell out, I'm surprised she left her kids with you."

"Thanks, Big Tiger. I don't know what I would do without your honesty."

"I'm just keeping it real. Your sister disowned you. And we all know Greater Atlanta Faith's got some secrets. That was a dumb move she did with you."

"Well, that is the past."

"You think, because I heard something else."

My old case. My heart raced. "Like what?"

"You know I don't talk particulars over the cell, mademoiselle, my Belle."

I huffed. Big Tiger was talking to me in one of his ridiculous codes. Didn't make sense to live on the straight and narrow when you act like you're an old gangster. I was too old and out of touch to know the latest phrases.

"My bad, Big Tiger. I forgot." I paused. "So what do I need to do to get her on the docket for tomorrow?"

"Pray."

"I'm prayed out. Can we come up with something else?"

"Like your grandma always said, where two are together." He chuckled. "We'll meet before you visit Ava."

"So I can visit her?"

"Yep, she has an orange suit now. Baby girl has a visitor's list, a cell, and a roommate now. Want 'em?"

"Gladly." My heart fell. "One more thing."

"Yep?"

"I need you to send a D-boy to my house. Tonight."

"Are you having a cash-flow problem, because I can help you out with the bail."

"No, are you crazy?" I rolled my eyes. Big Tiger was leaning too far on the other side of the fence if he thought I would ever cross that line. "I just need you to send me a normal, clean kid to pick up some files to deliver to my storage place."

"House crowded?"

"Too crowded?"

"I have a proposition for you."

I smirked. "I bet you do, but I have some more calls to make."

"Look, Angel. I need to tell you something, but don't tell Ava you heard it from me."

"And what is that?"

"I heard that Devon had a mistress."

"Yeah, and so does every male minister in the world. That rumor is as old as Christ and Mary Magdalene."

"This girl was one of Ava's armor bearers."

"Come again?" This was the second time I had heard that phrase.

"One of her assistants. I thought you did op-ed on church investigations. You know what I'm talking about."

"I just learned what an armor bearer is today. I don't remember when Daddy was alive he used the term in that way."

"True. It has been a while for you, and the church has changed. But don't worry about what an armor bearer is. You need to find out where this one went and if the rumor is true."

"Wait a minute. Why are you talking about this to me on the phone?"

He chuckled. "I wouldn't be telling you this if the police

didn't already know. Ask Detective Tinsley. He knows about it."

I took a slow breath. "You know what, Big Tiger? Scratch the duffel bag boy request. I have a better place for my things, but I will need something else from you later."

"You know I got you, Angel Soft."

"I hope that's a good thing." I shook my head. "I'm going to bed early or late, if you don't count that I hadn't slept since Tuesday."

"You do that. 'Cause tomorrow will be a long one."

"Not long enough if Ava isn't released."

19

Being a good investigator not only required analytical skill, but the ability to smell a good lie. I'm a pro at both, and Big Tiger's offer had my nose itching. I sat up in bed and thought about what he said some more.

Clearly, Ava held back something important about what happened Thursday night, even Big Tiger saw that. Had Devon's murder been a crime of passion, she would have been more than vocal about it. Her behavior made me believe that she was covering something up, but what? I decided to mind dump all the information I had so far before the frenzied world outside my bedroom made me forget. The kids would be waking soon and I hadn't figured out what to say about my absent twin.

If only Ava cooperated with me, then at least I would have a direction to take. I checked my cell on my nightstand. Perhaps I could get Roger Willis to talk to her, make her understand that unless she shared her secret with someone, she was as good as convicted. I texted him my request.

So far I'd come up with little. Someone close to Ava and Devon had to know about Big Tiger's mistress rumor or why Ava had planned to leave Devon, if that were the case. Terry, the bodyguard, said she was leaving him, but that belief was based on Devon's statement. Or was it? I needed a more solid account. Elvis. He definitely had to know about this armor bearer person, but would he admit it?

Elvis and I had chatted last night. I wanted him to bring dinner over tonight since Mom was bringing our new stepdad over, and he had agreed to help learn more about Ava's case. Elvis invited me to stop by his restaurant today after I hopefully visited Ava, to look at his menu. Before I saw them both, I reminded myself to stop by Big Tiger's. I knew if we sat kneecaps to kneecaps, he would tell me some other things that he wouldn't dare express over the phone. I just hoped they weren't too damaging. The toll of this makeshift investigation not only made me feel guilty, it made me fear to think. What if Ava did kill Devon? Could she have done it? I didn't want to be in the position to believe that could happen. I decided to see Big Tiger before Ava.

I still didn't feel completely awake, so I lay in bed a little longer with my pad and pen in hand, of course. I tried to recall the events of the last two days, then dozed off. The chirp from my cell phone woke me up. I read the caller ID. It was Willis. A surge of energy zapped me straight up.

"Did Ava add me to her visitor list?" I asked.

"Yes, your sister wants to see you."

I dropped the phone.

"Oh no!" I gasped, then reached to the floor to pick it up, then placed the phone to my ear. "Roger, are you still there?"

"Yes . . ." He cleared his throat. "I wondered if something happened to you. Everything okay over there?"

"It depends on whether Ava's wanting to see me also means that she has been charged for Devon's murder or that she's in custody with you?"

"I'm sorry, Angel. She refused to answer any questions, including mine."

I'm too late. I began to cry. I wiped my eyes with my hands.

"So how do you know she wants to see me?" I sniffled.

"Because you're the only other name she wrote down on her visitation log."

"And who was the other?"

"Your pastor boyfriend, Justus."

"He's not my boyfriend." I sighed. "I'll get down there as soon as I can," I promised, looking around the room for something clean to wear. I hadn't washed clothes in a while. Before I could sort out the day's clothes, my phone rang again. I leaned toward my nightstand and read the caller ID box. It was Justus. *God, thank you.*

"Justus Morgan calling in, reporting for duty, ma'am. What can I do for you this morning? I have the whole day free," he said.

"I had forgotten, but I'm glad you didn't. There are so many things we need to do."

"Like?"

"I know this sounds cornball, but the first thing I need is a good breakfast. I dreamt of your pancakes last night . . ."

"Mission accomplished. I was thinking the same thing," he said.

My doorbell rang.

"Don't tell me you're standing outside my door."

"Well, then, how about . . ." He paused. "I'm carrying a basket of fresh flapjacks, red-hot sausage links, and a bottle of sugar cane syrup in my arms while I stand on your porch. By the way, the cane syrup is a hometown favorite for you, right?"

My stomach applauded with a large growl. I rubbed my tummy. "I'm on my way down."

* * *

After the family, Justus, and I stuffed ourselves with more pancakes, he and I stole away to my private office. I wanted to talk with him about my upcoming visit to see Ava. I hoped he could come with me. Perhaps she would tell him why she doesn't want my help, since he was a minister.

My private office wasn't inside my home, but stood behind it. Our house came with a cute guest bungalow in the back. The previous owner's bachelor son lived in it before he inherited this home from his parents four years ago. Apparently, the bungalow was his parents' first home; then they made the home we live in shortly before their deaths when this area became a subdivision. He sold me the home after he married some burlesque dancer he met in Las Vegas with a strict stipulation that he would never share with me or anyone I knew the details of his bachelorhood in that bungalow. Yet, I was a bit curious of what foolishness happened back here.

I had the bungalow renovated with some of the money from my severance package from the *Sentinel*. It now had a secured weapons room, a sparring room, my cased antique weaponry collection in the foyer, and a property surveillance station where the dining room was, definitely not cute or open for boom-boom room performances anymore. But I did keep the stripper pole.

My best friend, Charlie, said it was great for exercise . . . which reminded me I needed to call her. She would not believe what has happened the one week of the year she was out of town. Then again, with my life, she might not be surprised at all. But Justus walking beside me in my backyard toward my inner sanctum would turn her world on its axis. No one came back here, not even her.

See, this was my spot. What I loved the most about it was that it was quiet here and not too far away from the kids. Besides, I could see everyone's room from here except Whitney's. She had more privacy than me, to some extent, but that's a perk for being single, parentless, and our little spoiled sister, I guess.

I led Justus past my garden. The office was on the other side.

He stopped short of the tomato patch and knelt down. "Is that a vegetable garden?" He touched the leaves.

I nodded. "It's my idea of sustainable living short of a chicken coop and an outhouse, but I do have a well, no prying pump, though, and no water in there either. But I've been thinking about dropping a pond back here to help with the irrigation for these tomatoes. Maybe put some bass and perch out there, so I can teach Bella how to fish."

He got on all fours, then frowned. "Are those disposable diapers in there?"

"Yes, they keep the soil moist so that I can grow bigger tomatoes."

He chuckled. "Are you serious?"

"I'm the daughter of a country preacher, Justus. I'm very serious. The price of tomatoes makes it very serious. Why?"

He squinted at me, then looked around my backyard. "Angel, you're so interesting. Every day it's something new about you that makes me wonder."

"Wonder about what?"

"Why your backyard is so much larger than mine." He stood up, brushed the dirt off his knees, and came to where I was standing. "And . . . why I haven't gotten to know you sooner." He smiled.

"Well, wait until you see what's inside my office. You might not feel the same way."

I placed my "Don't Ring Unless Your Life Depends on It" door knocker outside before I closed the door behind Justus. If his mouth dropped any lower, he would look like the film poster of *Scream 2* mounted behind my desk. The film was shot at Agnes Scott College while I was there. Covering the filming for the *Sentinel* while I interned there launched my journalism career and helped me discover that I had a fascination with the tongue-in-cheek slasher films and knives. Justus's shocked expression and heavy sighing as he studied my antique dagger collection made me wonder how he would react once he saw the pole. Did he have the mindset to be my sidekick?

It was dark, always dark in here except for the cabinet lights in the weapons display case, which I liked, but being alone with Too-Hot-to-Be-Holy Morgan, I had to find the light.

The lights came on. I turned around.

Justus stood by my lamp. "What's up with the knives?"

"I like them and they're daggers by the way." I shrugged, then walked passed him toward the blinds. "It still seems dark in here. Usually I have the blinds open, but with the media outside, I've had to keep them closed."

"Why are you changing the subject? What's wrong, Angel?" he asked.

"Because I can see your mind turning and I don't want it to get stuck on stupid . . ." I paused. "I'm just tired."

He stretched out his arms to me. "Come here."

The way he looked at me made me step back.

"What now?" he asked.

"I don't want to get used to you and me like this."

"Why not?" He came closer.

"Because of the look of despair in Ava's eyes. I know what that feels like, and I don't want to feel that again." I moved farther away from him and stood on the opposite side of the room, near my hammock. I laid in there, to strategize. "I called you in here because I need to tell you that I spoke with Roger this morning. Ava has added both our names to her visitation list. Visiting hours start soon. I'm going. Do you want to come with?"

"First, tell me about Bella's father. What happened?"

"You're not going to judge me?"

He held his hand out. "Have I said anything about the stripper poll?"

"Okay," I said. I took his hand in mine. "But let's get going to the jail first." I left out that I was dropping him off to visit with Ava while I stopped in to see Big Tiger.

20

Saturday, 9:00 AM
DeKalb County Detention Center

I dropped Justus off at the jail, then went to see Big Tiger. Avondale was a tiny Shakespearean-inspired district nestled inside the city of Decatur. The neighborhood front yards always bloomed with every flowering plant, perhaps the source of the great smell in the air. Houses with wraparound porches and sidewalks wide enough to push a double stroller through waved at you as you drove past. "Come on over and swing a while," they called out to me. I thought of home.

More historic downtowns in the Atlanta vicinity had begun to mimic what Avondale had always done. My new hometown, Sugar Hill, was one of those cities. I didn't notice the resemblance until now.

I made another left now onto Covington Walk near the Kensington MARTA train station. Ava and I once rented a townhouse over there. It was nicer then than what I saw now. Bunches of young girls wearing barely-there shorts, tank tops, and so many tatts on their bodies you couldn't decipher where one ended and another began. Some of them had small children, who clung to the arms of white tee-wearing men, whose pants hung and sagged well past their waists. They all stood there between bits of trash that sanitation services missed or refused to pick up, all gathered in clumps along the curbs. I wondered where the older people were. Had disinvestments pushed them out, or was it the sad reality of what I just witnessed that had broken their hearts, too?

I sighed. When did being poor mean not having pride?

Ava and I used to walk to this MARTA station to meet our dates. She met Devon and I met whomever he dragged along with him.

Mama had advised us the day we moved here to never let a man know where we lived. Ava followed Mama's wisdom for about three months. I lived by that with one exception, Justus. Had I not been tired, angry, stressed, and in need of much prayer—shoot—I would have let him in.

I parked in front of Big Tiger's office. It was an old brick ranch remodeled into an office that sat off Covington Drive about two minutes from the jail. I walked inside and smelled mint and bleach. Maybe the older people were over here.

"Angel Soft . . ." Big Tiger yelled out the screen door and swung it open to greet me. "How about that girl?"

He was Justus's height, dark rich skin that smelled and resembled Noble muscadines, a broad physique that could choke a rock, but dressed as if he were stuck in a time warp. He dressed like the old Dope Boys from East Lake Meadows back in the early 1990s in a crushed velvet track suit and overpriced sneakers with a sick gold chain. I noticed the wedding ring on his finger, then smiled. Now I knew what had the office smelling like Granny's idea of clean.

"Hi, Big Tiger." I hugged him and walked inside. "Where's the wife?"

"I'm looking right at her."

"No, you ain't." I patted his shoulder. "Where's Mama D?"

"She's in the kitchen eating. We're making chicken dinners for Mama's church building fund. You know how I do." He licked his lips and looked at me as if he would serve me up next.

I felt a little warm. "You've seen Ava?"

He nodded. "Girl didn't look like she'd eaten soul food in decades. Shoot. She looked like she hadn't eaten any food since high school. And I know ain't no real food out in the boondocks where you live, so you'd better get a plate."

"Thanks for the offer, but I can't."

"What's wrong with you? You've never turned down Ma's plates before. And I ain't never known you to be this quiet except when . . ." He looked me up and down, then leaned back. "What's his name?"

"His name is tell me more about this mistress rumor."

Big Tiger sucked his teeth. "To be a preacher's child, you sure is rude, Angel Soft."

Big Tiger called me Angel Soft because he thought I was softer than Ava, although everyone around me—everyone—thought I was a bad seed. He was the first to see the good in me. Don't get me wrong. He was also the first man to bring out my bad.

"I'm not trying to be, just want to get Ava home before her kids have a meltdown. Why don't you have kids by now?"

"Don't know, unless your little angel is mine."

I punched him in the gut, walked toward his front window, and peered outside. A black SUV had made a right onto Memorial Drive. That was the third one of its kind I saw on my way here.

I checked my watch, then turned back to Big Tiger. "You didn't tell anybody that Ava would be coming here, did you?"

He folded his arms over his chest and tilted his head. "I

might be black, but I ain't stupid. I slip in and out of the Dec with no pigeons chirping. I'm a shadow, baby."

Oh, brother. I rolled my eyes. Big Tiger had the most colorful language, and his words sang out of his mouth like a jazz poet's. He always stayed abreast of the hottest slang, but slid in a few of his own signature catch phrases, like the Dec. It was short for Decatur. I once could listen to him for days. Today I didn't have the time.

"Angel Soft, I didn't stutter when I asked you what's the joker's name who has you so bent out of shape? Is he the baby daddy?"

"No, joker. Ain't no dude—" I caught myself. Now I'd begun to sound like him. "Devon's dead, Big Tiger. That's messed up. My mind is all over the place trying to make sense of this. I'm just tired. Ava being home will help me rest easy, okay?"

"Nope, I'm not buying that." He shook his head. "You got me confused with them snobs up in the hills where you live. I remember when you staked out Pretty Tony's place for five days in that old Hyundai Excel you used to live in. Your eyes didn't blink until your camera stopped snapping shots of him, Kevin Dobbs, Cherry Jenkins, and them lost girls from the Avondale Children's Shelter. So sleep ain't your problem. Something else is. What is it?"

"Besides the fact that you talk too much . . . That was back then and I'm not dealing with pimps and preteens anymore." I caught myself again. The other night with Cade wasn't too far from back then. "I'm dealing with Big Faith again. You know what happened the last time I messed with them, huh? My sister disowned me."

"Yeah, but something ain't right about how that all went down either."

"Detective Salvador agrees."

"Why doesn't he ask the *Sentinel* for theirs? That's not your responsibility anymore."

"Unless he already did and he didn't find what he's looking for."

"And what do you think that is?"

"I don't know, but if I have to dig it up for him, I might as well take another look at it myself. I'll be up all night, though."

"Why don't you ask your sister first and save some time?"

"I can't ask her . . ." My eyes rolled. I stopped myself. "I promised her I wouldn't snoop around."

"So now you're keeping promises, too?" He chuckled.

"Nope." I huffed. "Motherhood makes you grow up a little."

"Good thing I'm not one." He chuckled and sat down. "What about what I told you yesterday? You think there's some truth to it?"

"You tell me."

He leaned back in his chair and looked out his window. "I heard she was a member of the church, a young girl, groomed to be an armor bearer for your sister."

"If she's no longer a member of the church, where is she? What's her name?"

He straightened up, leaned forward, all eyes and gold teeth on me. "Her name is Rachel Newton, and I don't have a clue where she is, but I know someone who does."

"Who?"

"Your girlfriend that owns the beauty salon near Stone Mountain."

"Halle?"

"Yep, I used to see Rachel all the time when Mama had me drop off a few dinners to her shop."

"When was the last time you saw her?"

"A few weeks ago. Two weeks ago, to be sure. She was in the office in tears. I remember now."

"Have any idea why she was crying?"

"What else, a man." He reached his hands to mine. "Don't let this new dude put your nose up in the air. Bella needs a daddy, and I'm willing and able."

I stood up. "I know that. Thanks for the offer, but Bella has a father, and like I said before, I don't have a man."

He raised his hand in the air. "Put your gun back in your holster, Angel Soft. I was just offering you a better alternative."

"I don't have time for propositions. I need to find this Rachel girl like yesterday."

Big Tiger folded his arms over his chest. "Well, I'll do a little chirping on my own and see which birdie is flying."

"Would you?"

"For sure, and if you need a Dumpster diver, I know a good girl who can decode a credit card number off a coffee-stained receipt while it's stuck between the napkin and the coffee cup."

He handed me a card. I slid it into my purse. "I have to see her do that myself."

"Let me know and I'll set it up."

I looked at the card. "Her name is familiar to me."

"Give yourself a little time. It'll come back to you." Big Tiger turned toward the back kitchen door. We heard voices coming. "You sure you don't want a plate?"

21

Saturday, 10:00 AM

There was a stench in Dekalb County jail's visitation hall that added aggravation to an already disturbing situation. It smelled like dirty peaches, urine, and souring trash, an odor that cataloged the pity I felt in my gut. I looked around the room and saw the smell scowling on the faces of those waiting in line with me. Then I asked myself, Why would my sister want to be here if she didn't have to?

Before I could see Ava, I had to prove I was worthy to be in this godforsaken place. It was worse than getting in the VIP lounge at Night Candy. See, just like a nightclub or a country club, in order to receive a visitor's pass to visit a jail inmate, your name had to be on a visitation list. The catch was the inmate had to add you to the list, which meant that the person had to want to see you. I'm not sure if Ava wanted to see me, although she did have me listed.

Yet by the time I had fought for a parking spot and found a locker for my purse that actually locked, I expected to be on that list. Call it rites of passage, my psyche playing tricks on me, or just plain old peer pressure, but I didn't want to be turned away at the visitation check-in station.

Besides, whether I wanted to admit it or not, there was

something evocative about being so close to danger. In my years as an investigative journalist, my best work was comprised spending much time here recruiting new informants, many of whom spent more time here than in their homes. So I wasn't surprised when a few folks standing near me waved and smiled. I had probably done a favor for them at some point in my past. I had done so many I had forgotten.

As I watched a young blonde step out of line and come toward me, I hoped she could do a favor for me.

"Paige." I remembered her name the moment she hugged me. She smelt of cheerios and milk, like she did when she was eleven years old. "What are you doing here, girl?"

She stepped back and gave me a bittersweet smile. "Jack's in trouble again."

Jack was her big brother, an old informant who helped me on an exposé about the emergence of meth labs in Gwinnett County country club communities. He was once a good boy who led the young adult ministry at a popular church. He fell in love with mixing rock salt and cold medicine. I had hoped that his last rehab stint got him back to his old self. I guessed it hadn't.

"I'm sorry. Meth is hard to beat. I'll keep praying."

She shook her head. "Naw, meth wasn't his problem this time. He killed someone." Her voice was matter-of-fact, not even surprised or fearful.

"Oh . . ." My heart ached. He would never get off those drugs in prison.

"Still going to church?" I asked.

She bobbled. "Yes, ma'am. Got Jack set up with one of them prison ministries that have a legal defense fund. He said he didn't kill the guy."

"Well, let's hope so. What prison ministry is assisting him?"

"Your brother-in-law's church. Greater Atlanta Faith."

"You're kidding me."

"Nope, that church thinks that my brother can get out. Never would have thought about them if it hadn't been for you and what you said the last time I saw you."

The last time I was a member of Big Faith, Bella was growing inside me. I cringed. It wasn't that the church was bad. The church was great, what church wouldn't be? I had to move away. Unfortunately for Jack, Ava, and a boatload of members I never spoke to again. I had forgotten them. I had forgotten Paige.

"Remind me. What did I say?"

"You said that I needed to be a kid and let God handle my brother. So I did. I'm attending college in the fall. The University of Georgia. Pre-law." She smiled as she talked.

I touched her hand. "I don't know what to say."

She took my hand and held it. "Say nothing. I came over here to thank you, Ms. Crawford. You saved my life, and if there is anything I can do for you, I will." She handed me her business card. "I'm a paralegal now. I could be of help."

"Thanks, Paige. I might have a job for you. Give me a few hours to get in touch."

The older man behind me tapped my shoulder. "They're calling you."

I took Paige's card and walked back toward the registration desk. My shoulders slumped. I was scared all over again. I presented my identification to a visitation officer. She gave me a number and made me wait in a new line with another, but smaller group of people. We waited until she called our number; then another prison officer directed us to an elevator and a booth number. To my dismay and amazement, the elevator stank, too. I had assumed the lobby smelled because of all the babies and whatever, but in the elevator toward the visitation booths . . . Should I be afraid?

I received that answer as soon as the elevators opened. The visitation room was the size of two phone booths. Inside it was a mounted table and a chair. There was a black phone mounted to a steel base on the right wall. In front of me was a huge window that at first made me think I was looking at a mirror until I saw something behind it. I looked over the table, squinted through the window's glare, and gasped. I saw Ava's temporary home, a two-story, loft-like concrete and steel compound. The bottom row was a plastic lounge, much like the waiting room. The top floor contained caged rooms the size of a clothes closet. Their doors looked like freezer drawers. My throat tightened. Below, I saw more cells, more officers, and more inmates. But where was Ava?

I checked my watch. I had only fifteen minutes with her and seven of them had already passed. I bit my lip. I was aggravated and anxious now. What in the world was she doing?

Ava stepped into the room two minutes later. She wore an orange jumpsuit that complemented her complexion. I made a mental note of the color for myself.

She sat down and reached for the phone. I wanted to berate her for showing up so late, but a rush of mercy swept over me. Her life was bad enough. I wanted to make her feel better.

I smiled at her. "You have some nerve looking like an Aruba sunset up in here."

She brushed her hair down with her hand and chuckled. "Even in here I refuse to be undone." Her voice held a sadness that touched me.

I placed my free hand on the window. "I love you." It was the first thing my heart needed to say to her.

"I love you, too." She sniffled. "How are my children?"

"They asked for you and Devon. I told them that you

were away, which is kind of true, but to a child, it's a bold-faced lie. I was hoping and praying that you were getting out yesterday, so you could tell them yourself. When do you see the judge?"

She pursed her lips. Tears fell fast down her face. She stood up. "Tell my children I love them."

"Wait!" I jumped up and patted the window. I yelled, "Where are you going?"

I forgot she couldn't hear me without the phones. I picked up my phone and motioned for her to sit back down. "Please, don't go."

She shook her head and refused to sit down.

"Where are you going? We haven't talked about your case, Devon's funeral, anything."

"Why should I talk about something that's not in my control?"

"Okay, then why don't we talk about things that are in your control, like how are you feeling?"

"I'm holding on to what I believe in. God will show his face to me, soon. I know it . . . I miss my children; I miss him so bad." Her hands trembled as she held on to the phone.

"I know." I wanted to remove the Plexiglass that separated us and hold her. "Did anyone in there tell you when will be your first appearance before the court?"

She shook her head. Her tears trickled onto the steel counter. I whimpered against my will.

"There's such a backlog here. All I've been told is that it may take a day, a week, a few weeks." She wiped her eyes. "I'll be fine."

I wiped my eyes. "We're not going to let you stay in here no longer than today. Trust me on that."

"Don't ruin yourself trying."

"Don't you want to get out?"

She looked at me. Her eyes were calmer than I'd ever seen. "I can't control those things, so I can't tell you the answer. The only thing that I can control is my mind and my children's safety. I sent them to you because that's what you do best, protect our family. All that other stuff, leave it to God, Angel . . . Leave it to God."

I leaned toward the glass. "Why are you protecting Devon?"

"He's dead. What kind of protection could I give him now?"

"Protecting his precious image from being tarnished."

"Angel, you don't know what you're talking about. I'm not going to be a party to scandalizing my husband, especially not for my sake. Isn't that my duty as his wife?"

"Your duty should be to your children. They need you now. They have no clue their father's dead. I don't know what to say to them, and neither does Mama. And if I don't bring you back today, she's going to kill me. I need you to want to get out of here. You don't have to be in jail to honor Devon. You need to be out here to help me find the real murderer. You need to be out here to save your church, because they haven't been out here to see about you. Have they? They're meeting, Ava, about you right now. They met about you last night. What do you want me to do?"

Her body trembled now. She closed her eyes. Her mouth parted. She sighed. Then she opened her eyes again. "You want to get me out of here, then listen. I cannot appear before the judge until I receive a docket number. I don't have one yet. I'm in a holding cell. It's an overcrowding thing."

I exhaled. "Not good."

"Willis has encouraged me to make a plea." Her eyes wandered off. "I think I'll do that and make all this go away. I'm sure my drama is putting a toll on the church and you."

"No, you won't!"

Ava wouldn't look at me. "I've allowed your friend Justus, to come and pray with me. I'm not ready to see my—"

"Your armor bearers?"

She turned back to me. Her eyes blazed red. "No, my children." She cleared her throat. "So you have to tell them. Tell them the truth about me and their father. The sooner the better."

"No, uh-huh . . ." I yelled. "Are you crazy? Are they giving you a sedative in here? I will never let that happen. I'm calling Willis as soon as I get out of here. You are not making any pleas."

"I requested the pills, Angel. I did it, okay. So stop searching for someone to blame. Blame it all on me. "

My heart skipped. I saw my sister, but I didn't know her. I didn't know her at all. I tried to relax my breathing, calm my nerves, something. I wanted Granny's sage voice to return, but nothing. I had nothing, no prompt to guide my next move. *God, where are you?*

"Should I blame Devon's extramarital affair on you, too, or your armor bearer?" I blurted.

"Whatever will give you peace, Angel. But I do have one point of advice for you."

I sighed. "What is it?"

"You need to go to Halle's for a new hairdo. That plain Jane look doesn't impress your minister boyfriend. Tell her I sent you. I love you and I have to rest now." She put the receiver down, blew me a kiss, and disappeared behind more glass.

I wanted to crawl under the phone booth and cry, but instead, I sat in that visitor's booth stunned. I couldn't move. I couldn't think.

See, I knew Ava, just like I knew the smell of a good lie. The booth stunk. Her trembling hands stunk. She must have forgotten that I'd known her longer than anyone on this planet. I knew what a mad, jilted, love-crazed Ava looked like. Me. Avalyn didn't have that look when we found her hovering over Devon's body two nights ago, and she didn't have it just now. But she was pissing me off by insulting my intelligence. Oh, I was going to find this Rachel chick. Oh, I was going to find out why my case file was important to Salvador. And oh, I would get her raggedy, pill-popping behind out of that stinky, stank place.

I sat there huffing and puffing and planning until the guard buzzed me to leave the floor. I knew just where to start. Elvis.

22

I stepped outside the jail, took a long, slow cleansing breath, and checked my watch. Elvis would be expecting us around 12:30. I reached for my phone to text Justus and let him know I was ready to go.

I definitely needed to get his take on Ava before I met with Elvis. Most importantly, I needed someone to speak some peace to me. I was furious. Lord knew I was capable of hurting the next person who tried to give me the runaround.

So when I looked up to see Detective Dixon chatting with Justus a few paces in front of me, I was fit to be tied. She'd better watch out. I smelled a catfight coming on.

They stood near the staff parking area. She had one hand on his elbow and the other on her chest. Her blouse was half open, exposing her inappropriately placed detective's badge that hung on a gold chain. How tacky. She had looked classier in my home. She laughed and tossed her long brown hair back. I wish I was close enough to yank a track out. A few hours inside the joint had me talking like a cast member from a television series set in a prison.

I called Justus's name when I was within earshot of them.

He squinted and then waved at me. She leaned forward until she saw me, then straightened her back and her blouse. What was she doing before I got here? Giving him a peep show?

"Angel, guess whom I ran into," Justus said to me as I approached.

"Detective Dixon, who would have thought I would find you here?" I extended my hand to hers and gave her my don't-start-with-me squint. I was still simmering from my visit with Ava. It wouldn't take much for my attitude to jump to flaming blue hot right about now.

She rubbed her hand on her skirt, then shook my hand. "I'm fine, Ms. Crawford. How's your family?"

Dixon had some nerve. I tried to squeeze her bony hand raw. "Don't ask me a question you know the answer to. What do you really want to know, as if I would tell you?"

I paused. Roger Willis had said the same thing to me the morning I met him at the jail. It didn't dawn on me until now. Why didn't us polite, southern girls ask the questions we wanted to know? Perhaps it was the same reasons Ava had yet to answer any of mine. Sometimes we don't want to hear the truth, because we wanted to confirm whatever fantasy we needed to stay sane in this broken paradise. But other times we were just shooting the bull like Dixon was trying to do with me right now, so I had to set her straight.

Justus coughed, then wrinkled his brows at me. "Did you receive my text? Are you ready to go?"

I shook my head. "In a minute." I kept my attention on Dixon.

"Did you receive the file y'all requested?" I asked her.

She grinned. "Yes, thank you."

"Did you find what you were looking for?"

"I believe so."

"Good. Is there anything else you need?"

"No." She shook her head and looked to Justus. "Besides, Pastor Morgan has given me more than I need."

"I'm sure he has," I said. "How about the location of Devon's mistress? Did he give that to you, too?"

"Out of respect for my partner's friendship with you, and not to embarrass you in front of this great man standing here, I'll pretend I didn't hear you telling me how to run our investigation." She frowned. "You're treading on dangerous ground, Ms. Crawford. If you keep this up, you'll give us another motive why your sister wanted to kill her husband."

She walked toward Justus and stopped too close to his face in my book. "If you have any more pertinent information for me, J"—she handed her business card to him, then smiled—"please, call me."

I took the card out of his hand, then handed her mine. "If you want to speak to Ava's family or him, you speak to me."

She chuckled and walked away. I knew I should have snatched a hair track.

Justus tapped my shoulder. "What was that all about?"

"Nothing." I watched Dixon until she disappeared around the corner.

"Angel, I asked you a question. What's up with you?"

"Justus, don't go there. Okay?"

"I don't know why I asked." He threw his hands up and chuckled. "So you ready for lunch?"

"Nope." My mouth was so tight I knew I had rubbed all my lip gloss off. "I'm not hungry anymore. Maybe we should take a rain check on the lunch at Elvis's?"

"You're not going to see him?"

"Yes, I am, but you're not. You have unfinished business with Detective Dixon."

"Are you jealous? Is that why don't want me to go with you?"

"Yep," I said. I didn't care. "Which is stupid because there is nothing going on between us, but the gall of that woman. I don't like her. Yeah, that's what it is. I don't like her and you know I don't like her, Yet, you make nice with her and give her that smile and now she's jocking you when she needs to be finding my brother-in-law's killer. "

"But there is something between us, Angel. Why won't you admit it?" He caught my purse with his hand and pulled me closer to him.

I clutched my purse in defense. "Because I shouldn't."

"Why would you say that?" He didn't let go of my purse until his arm was wrapped around my waist.

"Justus, every Thursday at the Ladies' Communion, you want to know what I pray about?"

He bowed. "Sure."

"I ask God to stop making me want a man's touch. I'm tired of wanting to be kissed. It's a time waster and gets me in trouble, ergo my slippery relationship with you. You're my pastor and now my friend . . . I need to stay clear about those boundaries." I wiggled out of his grasp. "I'm doing the best thing for the both of us, you know?"

He noticed the passersby staring at us. "Maybe we should talk about this in the car?"

Justus took my hand in his and ushered me out of the crowd.

"Wait. I wasn't done."

"In the car now," he said. "Don't say another word until then."

I obliged.

Once inside, Justus locked the door, then turned to me in his seat. He sat in my driver's seat again. I made a note to myself that the next time we go anywhere else together, he would drive his own car.

"Justus, now is not the time for this. Can we table this discussion for later? Let's say . . . after I find Devon's killer?"

He cupped his hands together, then placed them in his lap. "I would think that a woman prays to be kissed and more."

"Not if she doesn't trust her judgment."

"That's another issue, which has nothing to do with wanting to have an intimate relationship with a man. Now, I'm not a woman, obviously, but wasn't she created to feel kissable?"

"I don't know. Maybe . . ." I huffed. "It's all a mystery, but at times like this I wish I didn't want to be kissed."

"Why now?"

"Because I'm not married, and the prospects are pretty slim for black women, so what's the point? Why wish for something with such bad odds?"

"Marriage isn't something to gamble on," he said.

"Nor is it to wish upon a prayer about. It's not fair. It's too much pressure to be married."

"I'm not married and I don't feel any pressure."

"But you don't wish for it either. You know why?"

He shook his head. "I'm sure you'll tell me."

"Because you're a brilliant, successful, gorgeous, single, God-fearing man. . . . A catch. You can choose whomever you want. But me, I feel like the last person to be picked in middle school P.E. I don't want to feel like that all my life. I definitely don't need to feel like that about you, not right now, especially not now."

"I think I understand what you mean a little." He lowered his head; his smile had vanished. "I hope I don't sound out of line, but after all of this is over, I want to take you somewhere that will change your mind about you and me."

"Can I see an old friend about Rachel first?"

"Who?"

"Devon's alleged mistress. Her name is Rachel."

"You can't be serious." He huffed and turned to the face the steering wheel.

"I wouldn't bring it up if I wasn't."

"Before you do that, you need to talk to Elvis to confirm. This could just be one of those generic rumors about philandering pastors. It's an old trap to keep you off the right path. Don't fall for it."

"But it's a lead."

"Does that mean you have to follow every bad thing you hear?"

"If I'm worth my salt, yes, it does."

"Seems like you're losing your salt if this is your way."

"I get what you're saying, Justus, but I don't think you understand how things work here."

"Hold up. Don't treat me like that. I understand. I just don't agree with the tactics."

"So is that why you're here, to keep my crooked straight?"

"No, I want to help you find Devon's killer. That also means I want to make sure your soul isn't compromised in the process."

"That's very thoughtful, but I don't need a protector for my soul. Right now I need a clue and I have one, but I will take your counsel and talk to Elvis first. How 'bout that?"

"Good, and don't think I didn't notice that you changed the subject about us," Justus said. "This conversation isn't over."

"I'm sure you will bring it up again." I gulped.

Truthfully, I was afraid to go any further in this conversation than we already had. If we weren't racing the clock to clear Ava's name, I'd have to deal with my feelings for him. That scared me more than running out of time to find Devon's killer.

As we pulled out of the parking lot, I observed Justus. My sitting so close to him made things harder. I wanted to touch his smooth arms. His physical beauty was beyond my comprehension, and my attraction to him was almost unbearable. But his passion to find the goodness in people and his relentless quest to shepherd my soul made me dizzy. I was seated and spiraling, falling hard for the man. I couldn't concentrate on Ava like this. I couldn't focus on what mattered for wanting to make him pull over, so I could kiss him hard. Maybe I should reconsider keeping Justus on as my sidekick. I closed my eyes to keep from crying about it.

After my conversation with Elvis last night, I remembered his family's restaurant was a stone's throw away from our alma mater, Agnes Scott College. When passing by the west façade of Winship Hall, I immediately remembered some of the crazy things Ava and I got ourselves into. She met Devon there.

He attended Georgia Tech back then and came to one of our Kappa Alpha Psi Sweetheart parties in the student center. As a matter of fact, he danced the first dance with me. When I left the dance floor to add more sherbet to the punchbowl, he searched for me, but found Ava. They've been dancing together ever since. Thank God, because he couldn't dance worth a good split.

By the looks of the all the trash strung across the campus quad, I could tell that a fierce bash went on there last night. I chuckled.

I made the left onto College Avenue, and I wished I could go back fifteen years just for a minute, when life was real breezy and new and Devon wasn't dead.

The Biscuit Depot was located a few minutes from the jail and right across the railroad tracks from Agnes Scott. It was the easiest place to spot, because it was once an old Southern Railway caboose and painted granny apple green for good measure. When I was in college, it was called Eddy's Attic Tavern; then it became a few other restaurants. The restaurant look suited it well.

When we pulled into the parking lot, I had to step out and look around. Downtown Decatur had poshed up since Ava and I lived here, thanks to urban sprawl and community displacement. Most of the dilapidated buildings, dope boys, and poorer Decaturites had been run out of this section of town. Now trendy lofts, boutiques, and restaurants nestled themselves between azaleas, dogwoods, and every pretty blooming plant in Georgia. It even smelled good in the air now.

Justus stepped out the car and extended his arms to the sky with a big bowed stretch heavenward. I turned away from watching him. Again physically frustrated.

I looked around and the parking lot was empty.

"Do you have the time?" I asked Justus.

"We're not late, but it looks like the restaurant is closed," he said.

"Can't be." I walked up to the door. A pink note was attached to the restaurant: *Closed to public due to bereavement. Catered customers only.*

I threw my head back and wanted to scream, but I didn't want to bring any attention to myself. I was sure some newspaper intern was observing me from the Dairy Queen across the street.

I walked back to Justus.

"What's up?" he asked.

"They're closed due to bereavement, but open for their

catered clients. I'm going to call Elvis and let him know I'm here."

"Wow. You brother-in-law's death has impacted more than the congregation. It's impacted the town."

"I guess." I took out my phone. "But that's not my concern. I need to get Ava's case on the docket. I'm hoping Elvis can help me with that."

"It would be good for her to get out of there. I'm concerned for her."

"How was your talk with her?" I began dialing Elvis's number.

He sighed. "As you know, I have a limited history with your sister, so I knew going in our conversation was going to be introductory. But to my surprise, she opened up to me."

I stopped dialing. "She did? What did she say?"

"Don't be angry, Angel, but I can't tell you that."

"Understandable, but can you give me a clue why she doesn't want to go to trial?"

"Maybe she doesn't want a sensational court drama putting a huge cloud over Devon's legacy."

I gasped and looked at him. "Now you sound like Detective Dixon."

"Just trying to give you another perspective on things."

"Thanks, but I didn't need or want that one."

"You don't know what you need." He folded his arms over his chest.

"Well, I know I don't need weak thinking. That has never worked for anybody, and certainly not for me."

He stood up. "Are you insulting me?"

"No, I said you were thinking weak. It's a common trait with you minister types."

"I know you're anxious about your sister's problems, but there's no need to bash me or the laity."

"I'm not. I'm stating what I have witnessed and ac-counted for the past fifteen years. A mega-church's goal is to weaken individuality. Stifle a decent thought. My sister has been brainwashed into believing that her life doesn't matter. That a church, who hasn't visited her according to the jail's visitor's log—at all—which hasn't called or come by to offer condolences, but which has been on every televi-sion, radio, and podcast they could rake or scrape up in less than seventy-two hours is suspect to me. She didn't speak to me for months because I tried to show her the truth about them. But she still can't see it, and neither can you."

He sighed. "You can't judge people like that."

"Maybe, but I just think about the people Ava's trying to protect. They're not thinking about what's best for Taylor and Lil' D. They're not thinking about Ava quivering in that jail. All that they care about is that their agendas and expected fiscal growth aren't changed. I'm not okay with that. I think it's weak." I slapped my right leg. "No, I change my mind. It is weak."

"You have issues, but blaming the mega-church for them is unfair," he said and walked toward the restaurant.

"I know." I pouted. "But they're such a great punching bag. Don't you think?" I looked toward where Justus had walked off. Two redheads, one twice the age of the other, drove up around the same time in matching pink mustang convertibles. They waved at me, then unlocked the caboose.

"Two ladies just unlocked the door at the Biscuit Depot," Justus said. "Are you going in?"

"Yeah, let me call Elvis first."

The phone rang three times before Elvis's voice mail mes-sage picked up. I hung up the phone and went to grab my purse out of the car.

A blue Mini Cooper drove up a few spaces down and parked. I stopped short of my door to see if it was Elvis. A young blond man hopped out and went inside. I checked my watch, then looked down Church Street to the front façade of the restaurant. Where was he?

I huffed and redialed. He picked up on the first ring.

"Morning, Evangeline. Have you seen Lady Ava yet?"

"Yes, now I'm at your restaurant, hoping to see you."

"Then come inside. I'm here." He hung up.

I closed the phone and looked around the place. "He's here?"

Justus shrugged. "I guess so."

All this mystery and drama had me hungrier than sugar ants near a fresh-cut watermelon. Now I realized why we women crave so much chocolate, because we didn't get enough sleep. We do too much stuff. It's probably why we struggle with our weight. At least I struggled with mine. Ava never struggled with anything until now.

Justus locked the car and we went inside.

The Biscuit Depot smelled like maple sausages, fresh coffee, and steamy butter-me-not biscuits. *Have mercy.* Like the exterior, inside the place resembled a railcar. Table seating was placed in rows of three. White chrysanthemums sat in mason jars on every white linen tablecloth. The place charmed me. I smiled.

I looked toward the baker's counter where the older redhead was lathering icing on a hot batch of cinnamon rolls. One whiff of them told me that the woman stuck her foot in every dish she created.

It reminded me of the time Mom tried to teach Ava and me how to bake biscuits. We were ten and the kitchen floor was covered in flour and our tiny footprints. I covered my heart with my hands. If Elvis didn't show up soon, this cute place would make a blubbery mess of me.

"What's wrong?" Justus asked.

"I'm tired from yesterday." I was two sniffles away from

balling my eyes out, but there was no time to be weak. Actually, there had never been time for me to be weak, but whatever . . .

Justus's phone rang. He peaked at his phone. "It's Trish. Let me step outside and see what she needs."

"Sure, I can handle this on my own."

"I know, but do me a favor." He stood at the door. "While I'm outside, please don't scare or flirt with the man. You're dangerous in both ways."

I smirked. "I can't promise you anything, so you better hurry back."

He pointed at me, then stepped outside. He sat on a bench near the handicapped parking area. From the look on his face, I suspected the conversation had something to do with Kelly and her phantom boyfriend.

"May I help you, madam?" Red asked.

"Is Elvis here?"

Her eyes brightened. "Yes, wait right here."

She walked through the dining room, turned toward me, smiled, and vanished into their office, I assumed. Now the only other person in the dining room with me was the blonde.

He sat in the last table near the exit. I couldn't help but notice him. The restaurant could have been crowded and any woman with a speck of vision would have spotted him from across the room. Even from where he sat, I could tell his eyes matched the color of the smog-free day outside, a perfect baby blue.

He was far younger than me in appearance, but those eyes belonged to an old man, Cary Grant or Gregory Peck or Paul Newman. And they looked extremely wrong for me to be admiring at a time like this, especially with Justus near. More trouble. He had warned me.

If I wasn't focused before, I was on point now. Pretty

men can make a woman forget herself and her troubles. The trick was you couldn't let his troubles creep up into yours. Because I promise you, pretty men come with plenty ugly trouble.

"*Get it together.*" Granny's voice shivered through me. "*Devon and Ava need you.*"

I turned back toward the counter and reached for a menu on the service counter. I was definitely getting those cinnamon rolls.

"Evangeline Crawford?" some man asked.

For a minute I thought my desperate need for something sweet and my lack of sleep had me hallucinating, but then again . . .

I looked behind me. "Elvis Bloom?"

He stood up and wiped his eyes. It was the white man with the blue eyes. He had been crying. Those blue eyes probably resembled rain and sky now.

I grabbed one of those cinnamon rolls off the tray on the table and popped it in my mouth. I needed quick comfort.

Elvis left his table and walked toward me as I chewed and swallowed. I took note of the time. It was 1:00 PM. Not good. I needed to get ahead of Salvador's investigation. If my memory served me right, he and Detective Dixon were lunching with the coroner. I had to know what they knew.

Elvis and I hugged. He smelled like figs and something sweet. I couldn't put my name on it, but it was original, too.

"Sorry to meet you under these circumstances," I said, still chewing.

"Same here." He stepped back and looked me up and down. "I know I sound redundant, but you and Lady Ava really are twins."

"I assume you've seen my sister without her makeup."

He chuckled as he pulled out a counter stool for me to sit on. Then he sat down beside me.

"I know we don't have much time, but what happened?" he asked.

"Someone stabbed Devon. Ava called the police and was charged with his murder."

His eyes watered more. "It can't be that simple."

"Simple enough. I arrived just before the police. We all found Ava holding Devon's head in her lap." I thought about the bloodied knife lying at Ava's feet and trembled. "It was horrible."

"I cannot imagine . . ." He reached over the counter, pulled some napkins, two teacups, and saucers, then sat a pair in front of the both of us. "I need some tea to calm my nerves. What about you?"

I took some napkins to wipe my eyes. "That's not necessary, as you said, I don't have much time. Family matters. *I'm just telling you what happened from my point of view.*"

And trying to get a clue why Ava didn't add you to the visitor's list. I kept that question to myself. Mama taught me a long time ago not to disrespect the hand that fed you, else they might spit in your food.

He nodded, while pouring tea in his cup. "Do you think she killed him?"

I shook my head, but I would be lying if I didn't have my doubts. "She's not the killing kind."

He poured tea in my cup. "Then you're going to need something to drink."

"Why?"

He placed the tea kettle back in its place on the other side of the counter. "Because by the look of things, you won't be getting any sleep anytime soon."

The younger redhead came over. She placed a basket of fish and fries in front of him. Justus returned to the dining hall. He spotted us and walked toward the bar.

The woman turned to me. "Would you like some fish and chips, miss?"

"If I ate that, I would fall a sleep where I sit."

Her face wrinkled. "But you eat it all the time."

Elvis touched her hand. "She's not Lady Ava. This is her twin, Angel. Angel, this is my sister, Emma. Emma, this is Evangeline." He made my name sound like a British dream.

She wiped her hands on her apron, then held out her hand. "Nice to meet you, Angel. So sorry for the confusion."

She had a sweet, shy voice and very soft hands.

"Nice to meet you. Don't worry about it. I'm far from being an angel for sure."

She giggled. "Well, if you're anything like Lady Ava, then I beg to differ. But I should have known you weren't your sister."

"Why's that?" I asked.

"She rarely came here and never for tea."

"Sounds like you're in the wrong profession." I drank my tea after all. "You could be a detective."

"Or a reporter," Elvis said. His eyes were locked on me.

"No." I drank my entire cup quickly. "She's too decent for that."

Justus stepped into the group and introduced himself. He ordered a black cup of coffee. He didn't look at me.

Elvis whispered something in Emma's ear. She nodded and walked away. I wished Ava and I were that in sync with each other. We used to be. A shiver ran through me.

If we were close, then I could have prevented this disaster. She would have trusted me with her fears about her marriage. Maybe if she had stayed at my house instead of jetting off into the wee hours, this never would have happened. Then my heart sank into my gut. I almost dropped the tea. Had I not told her the truth about the *Sentinel* investigation, Devon would be alive today.

I shuddered.

"Are you okay?" Elvis asked.

I nodded. "Just had a tiny gut check. I'm good."

"May I ask? What is your gut telling you?

I turned to Elvis. His voice was gentle and reassuring. His head was tilted, he was no longer crying, and his body language oozed calm. I sighed and breathed him in. Those dreamy blue eyes blazed a reserved confidence. At first I thought my mind was playing tricks on me, but I could read a man better and faster than I could read my twin sister.

And it led me to wonder . . . What was a successful white restaurateur doing moonlighting as an assistant to the largest black church in the city and the state?

"My gut tells me that your role at Big Faith is more than Devon's assistant."

He grinned. "Your sister was right. You have been out of the loop for a while."

"Why do you say that?"

"Because I'm sure when you were working for the *Sentinel* you would have known all about me before we met."

"Then you can rest assured that I don't think you're a suspect."

He sat up. "For the bishop's murder?"

"No, for framing my sister."

"You don't believe she did it?"

"You know my sister. God himself would have to come down, put the knife in Ava's hands, then bless her to kill and force her hand to do it."

Elvis's eyes widened. "Blessed to kill? Wow . . ." His eyes wondered off. "So you're searching for another suspect?"

"I want to, but Ava insists that I don't."

"Why?"

"I was hoping you could tell me that, among other things."

"I don't follow."

"Ava and I haven't been close in a long time."

"Since the article you wrote about the bishop?" he asked.

My chest tightened. I turned to Justus. "Yeah, that."

Elvis patted my hand. His were warm and steady. "You were just trying to protect your sister like you're doing now. In fact, I wouldn't be working here had it not been for that investigation. Besides, from what I hear, the church grew stronger and you resigned because of it, right? Why would anyone hate you for that? I don't understand why you haven't returned to the church. From what I hear, they missed you . . . miss you."

His eyes didn't flinch. I wanted so bad to believe him, but I didn't trust Big Faith's hired men. God was still working through me on that one.

I checked my watch. "We have to go, but I'll talk to you later."

"Of course."

We stood up. Justus walked me toward the front, his hand on my back again. I welcomed it. I turned toward him and smiled. He smiled back. Our first fight was over.

Emma stood at the exit. She handed me a white box, which felt very warm in my hands.

"Emma packed you some cinnamon rolls to take to the kids," Elvis said.

"That's sweet. Thank you," I said to them both.

Emma handed me a Styrofoam cup. "And some peach tea for you."

I couldn't help but laugh. English tea was not my thing. "Thanks again. I wish I were here under better circumstances, like to eat all this good smelling food . . ."

Elvis smiled. "Once everything's settled. You are more than welcome to visit again."

"That would be nice. But before I go, can I speak with you outside for a minute?"

"No worries . . ." He opened the door.

I didn't have time to do any adequate research on Elvis Bloom, but so far I could conclude he had just charmed the stress right off me. He followed us to my car. I unlocked the door and placed the rolls in the backseat. I wished I ordered something to take on the road for myself. That cinnamon roll and tea hadn't quite hit the spot.

I turned to Elvis. His eyes were tearing again. Devon's death must have him pretty shaken up. "I need to ask you something that you won't like."

Justus cleared his throat.

Elvis blinked. "What is it?"

"Is Greater Atlanta distancing themselves from my sister?"

His cheeks reddened. "Believe me, it was not my decision."

"I don't know if I can believe you like Ava does."

His jaw clinched. Ooh, I hit a sore spot. "Are you accusing me of something?"

"I don't know you well enough to do that, Elvis, but what I do know is you're not just Devon's go-to guy. And I know you wouldn't dare share those problems with me."

"Is that all?"

"I also know you love your sisters, so I know you understand how I felt this morning when I was told that the church—the one my sister and my brother-in-law founded and devoted their lives to—would let her sit in jail another day."

He lowered her head. "I told them that was a mistake."

"You told who?"

"The trustees."

"No, you were wrong."

He looked up. "I was?"

"You go back and tell them it's a publicity nightmare."

His brows creased. "Are you going to talk to the press?"

"No, Elvis. I am the press, and this kind of story would definitely get me back on the good foot with the *Sentinel*."

Justus mumbled, "I thought you didn't want that life anymore?"

I shushed him. Justus cleared his throat and turned away from us.

Elvis tucked his hands in his front jeans pockets and sighed. "What do you want me to do?"

"Get Ava on tomorrow's docket. Apparently she still doesn't have a number. And bring some of that delicious food out to the house for the family later this week. My partner and I are going to be too busy finding the real killer to be cooking."

Justus mumbled something I couldn't understand.

"That's all?" Elvis asked.

"No, do you have contact information for Rachel Newton?"

He shook his head. His eyes didn't flinch, but his pinky finger twitched. "No, I don't."

"I don't believe that either."

He walked toward me, leaned toward me, and whispered, "I want to help you, but that information I don't have. I've never had it; only your sister and the bishop had her number."

Weird, I thought. "Do you know why I'm looking for her?"

He nodded. "I've heard the rumors."

"But you won't confirm or deny?"

He nodded. "I'm the bishop's assistant, not his confidant. That would be Lady Ava."

"Or his armor bearer?"

"One and the same." He grinned and looked back toward the restaurant. "I would like to be more of service, but I have to help my sisters complete an order. They have a wedding to service today."

"Could you do one teeny favor for me? It won't take long."

He stepped back and straightened his collar. "Of course."

"Who's this Rachel person?"

"She's just a member of Greater Atlanta. She was one of Lady Ava's armor bearers."

"Do you think I could speak to one of the armor bearers? I need to purchase some nice clothes for Ava. What she wore when the police took her into custody wasn't meant to leave the bedroom."

"And what Angel left for her to wear wasn't meant to leave her car trunk." Justus scoffed.

I glanced at him. We had gotten a bit too comfortable with one another. I nudged him.

"Will do," Elvis said.

"Thanks so much." I shook his hand. "Can you have that person call me tonight?"

He nodded. "I can do better than that. If you want, you can meet them tonight. The armor bearers usually have their weekly meeting tomorrow, but with our tragedy, the women have been wanting to pray for Lady Ava, the family, and the church. Your presence could bring joy and confidence in this time of sorrow. If you like, I could request they come to your home tonight in lieu of tomorrow evening's meeting."

Boy, he knew how to lay it on thick. He reminded me of Devon for a minute.

"I would love to, but the kids are there, and they don't know what has happened to their parents. And I don't want them to know just yet."

Justus reached into his pocket, pulled out his wallet, and

handed Elvis his card. "Have them come to our church in Sugar Hill. They can meet and pray there without the children being involved."

No, we won't. I gasped. *We can't meet there.*

Elvis turned to me. "Are you all right?"

I didn't realize he heard me or that my mouth had gaped open again.

Justus cut in. "No, obviously she's under a lot of stress today and with little sleep." His eyes were still on Elvis. "We'll see you later. Thanks for your time."

Elvis nodded and returned back inside.

After Elvis left, I turned to Justus. "We need to talk."

"Not here we don't. Let's go. We have some things to do before the ladies come to Sugar Hill tonight."

Oh, no. He didn't just shush me. I threw my hands on my hips. "We're not meeting at Sugar Hill, and I don't need an escort or someone to think for me. Did I ask you to do that?"

"You didn't have to, but let me tell you something." He came closer. His nose almost touched mine. "I'm helping you, not because I'm feelin' you, but because you need it. Lord, help me. You need my help."

"You have a crush on me?"

"Isn't it obvious?"

"I don't know. Sometimes, like now, I don't think you like me."

"I don't like your views about the church, but that's mainly because you don't know any better."

I looked at him. "Say what?"

"You don't know everything, Evangeline Crawford."

"But what if it's true? We're living in hard times right now. Gas is high, the price of eggs is high, jobs low, mortgages . . . Come on now . . . People need Jesus. So they go on a hope and a prayer that they'll find him there, and what do they get? Some power hungry nut job squeezing the last bit of faith out of them all for some pocket change to hide in an offshore account on some poor island."

"Where are you getting all this from?"

"At church. Why aren't you getting it? What's wrong with you?"

"What's wrong with me?" He lifted my chin with his hand. His eyes blazed. "Is this what you used to do? Watchdog churches? These are men of God. I'm a man of God. That's what's wrong with me. I'm offended."

"But I'm not attacking you, Justus. I'm not." I stuttered. "I've seen the bad things that good people do to ministers. I saw my father lose his life trying to clean up other minister's messes. I saw those same deep-pocketed ministers snicker at his grave. They made our daddy's life a joke. They made God a joke. You don't know . . ." I began to cry.

He pulled me closer into his arms. "I'm sorry for your father. Sounds like you and Ava are one in the same."

"How?" I said between sobs.

"She's trying to save her husband's legacy because she wants to correct what happened to your father. While you were at the *Sentinel,* it seems more apparent that you were trying to hold churches accountable for their actions to correct what happened to your father. You both need to realize that only God can do that, and He will, if you back down and let Him."

Just then my heart opened wider. It felt like an earthquake rippled through me. I trembled and held on to Justus until the pouring stopped. Granny would have said that it was the Holy Spirit moving through me. I don't know what it was, but it felt good.

"Justus . . ." I whispered.

He released me a little and looked in my eyes. "I felt it, too."

He leaned closer to my face. I relaxed in his arms before I caught myself.

"Good. At least I'm not entirely crazy." I slid out of his hold. "Just light-headed."

"So am I, but I know what's wrong with me." He blushed.

"Well, you're going to think I'm very crazy when I do this."

"Do what?"

I looked around the parking lot, caught Justus's hand, and reached up toward his ear.

"What?" He jerked away a little, then grinned.

"Stop moving." I leaned closer and whispered, "There's someone else in the Biscuit Depot watching us."

He grabbed me in another embrace that felt really yummy. "I know. I saw a shadow in the men's restroom earlier."

"Did you see who it was? Could be an employee. Right?"

His warm breaths caressed my neck. "No, It's Terry, Devon's bodyguard."

I shuddered. "Why didn't you say something?"

He held me closer. "What was I supposed to say? Potential suspect in the restaurant with another potential suspect? I was trying to keep you out of trouble."

"So you think Terry and Elvis are suspects? What motive?"

"Don't know." He released me and took my arm. "That's why we need to leave this place right now. I need to take you somewhere."

"You can't. Remember, you're hosting the armor bearers of Greater Atlanta tonight."

23

"I've been meaning to ask you," Angel began. "How well do you know Detective Dixon?"

Justus replied, "Not before you tell me what was in that box you brought to my office? I've been waiting on an answer about that since yesterday."

"I'm not going to lie to my pastor, but I'm not telling you either."

"I thought I was more than your pastor by now."

I stopped writing. "Turn the car around."

"Why?"

"Because this isn't working."

"What do you mean?"

"I can't think straight. This thing between you and me has got to stop. Do you realize I almost kissed you outside Elvis's parking lot."

He smiled. "Now you tell me."

"Well, I'm not done." I ran my hands through my hair. "You're a fine man, Justus. Whew, you're fine. But the way I feel is beginning to make me feel like some bad girl from the Bible. And I need to focus on my dead brother-in-law." I sighed. "I can't take this kind of pressure."

I threw my head in my lap. I couldn't breathe.

Justus pulled the car over, then shut off the ignition. "Sit up, Angel."

I sat up, gasping for air. "I'm losing it."

"Well, find it, catch it, grab it, because we need to clear some things up. Right now."

The power in his words made me feel like I was five years old. I folded my arms over my chest, stuck out my lower lip, and wouldn't look at him. " 'Kay."

"Look at me, Angel." He took his hands off the steering wheel and ran his hand down my arm. "I need to know you hear me when I say this."

I shook my head. He must be crazy. I wasn't looking at him.

"Evangeline?" His voice was stern, but the way he said my name made me want to melt.

"Nope, go ahead and say it. So I can wash the embarrassment off my face and we can get this show on the road. I can take it."

"Obviously you can't, since you're not giving me your undivided attention and your panting episodes are cracking me up a little. Come on. Let's be adult about this . . . Let me talk to you like a man, not your pastor, not your friend, a grown man."

I took a deep breath and looked at him. His eyes were set right on me; his gaze clutched my heart. I shivered. "I'm sorry. Please don't be mad at me."

"I don't want to hear an apology from you." He touched my cheek. "We're attracted to each other. Let's admit that and move on. Okay."

My cheek tingled at his touch. "I knew I shouldn't have worn that dress the other night."

"It wasn't that ripped-up thing you had on in the emergency room, woman." He chuckled.

I still couldn't look at him. "Then what was it?"

"The question you need to ask yourself before we go any further is, how do you feel about me?"

"Up until a few days ago I thought I was the one with the crush."

"You haven't answered my question."

"I've never liked a man so much in my life, too much to make good sense. Don't you agree this thing is a little too much, too fast?"

"It's only moving fast because you won't slow down."

"That's the thing." I lowered my head. "My life is fast. It's not the life you want."

"Don't tell me what I want. I know what I want . . ." He gripped the steering wheel. "This doesn't seem like divine intervention to you?"

"Nope, or love at first sight either. That's romance novel crap."

He turned my car on again. "You could be right. I don't read those, by the way, but what if you're wrong? What if my coming to Sugar Hill was also to find you?"

My heart raced. He was saying all the right things, but I was a coward. All I could see was Ava holding Devon's bloody body in her arms, me holding Bella's father's breathless body in my arms, and Mom dressed in widow black for the umpteenth time. Although I said before I don't believe in superstitions, I didn't want to take another chance. Not on any man, and definitely not on Justus. I needed to do a better job at pretending to be unaffected by him before I hurt him any more than I already had.

I reached for my shades in the glove compartment and put them on. "Then you would take your sidekick duties more seriously instead of having us now behind schedule."

If my car could fly, it would have. He drove so fast down 95 South back to Sugar Hill, I couldn't feel the wheels touch the highway. I knew he was upset about my reply to his love confession, so why wouldn't he just go home?

"How do you know Ava?" I asked, hoping he would slow down when he answered.

"I met her a few months after I came to Sugar Hill."

"I don't believe you. That's too much of a coincidence, if you ask me."

"I'll put my money on divine intervention." He smiled. "We met at Gospel Fest. She attended my class about race and reconciliation, and I caught the end of Devon's workshop on guilt-free leadership."

"Did she mention me at all?"

"No, but I have to admit I knew she was your sister when I saw her, so I was a little curious."

"Why didn't you ask her about me?"

He smiled. "Isn't that obvious?"

"Oh." My heart fluttered. "So what did you learn in Devon's workshop?"

"That my post here wasn't a punishment."

I gasped. "Why did you ever think that it was?"

He shook his head. "I'm not as perfect as you think."

"I never thought you were perfect, but the church has definitely grown from the inside out since you've been here. That's pretty good."

He frowned. "Don't do that."

"Do what?"

"Compliment me. When a man likes a woman who obviously doesn't share the same sentiment, compliments hurt."

"I do like—" I huffed. "Let's get back home. I'm missing my child."

24

"It's about time you got home."

Whitney sat on one of the kitchen stools nibbling on a stack of leftover cupcakes Sugar Hill's grief care team brought over for the family yesterday.

"Where are the kids?" I asked.

She shrugged. "Mama has them around here some-where. You know she took them to the Suwanee Water Park soon as you left this morning."

"She what?" I gasped, thinking about how dry Bella and Taylor's hair would be by now.

Since Mama had been sporting wigs and weaves for the past quarter century, she must have forgotten that our hair kinked and twisted like cotton caught in an April wind after a good head soak.

"Did you oil Bella and Taylor's hair?"

"Do I look like Fraulein Maria?" She smacked her lips and rolled her eyes. "No, I did not. I was hoping you were bringing Ava home with you, so you two could fix your own children's hair."

"I wish." I slapped my purse and flopped on a stool next to her. "She may come home tomorrow."

"What are we going to do if she doesn't?"

"Don't worry. Willis is going to fanagle Ava onto some judge's docket, so she'll be going to court first thing in the morning. I'm sure she'll be released."

"Good." She sighed, then turned to me. Her eyes made mine water.

"What is it?" I asked.

"Some funeral home called here, soliciting to handle Devon's funeral."

"I don't need this crap." I laid my head on the table.

"If Ava gets out tomorrow, then you won't have to." Whitney brushed my hair with her hands. "It's okay."

As she continued stroking my hair, I realized how Ava must have felt when I combed her hair with my fingertips. Thankful.

Justus said he would meet me in two and a half hours. That was thirty minutes ago, and I still hadn't changed my clothes or snuggled with Bella. I rummaged through my closet for the tenth time. There wasn't anything remotely close to an outfit Ava would wear to a prayer meeting. Now I wished I had snuck around the McMansion and yanked a few things out of there like Ava's purse—which reminded me, I needed to call Salvador. He should have combed my old case file by now. I hoped I hadn't left anything that would hurt Ava's chances.

I plopped on my bed and sighed. Would these women tell me anything relevant tonight? I looked down at my clothes. Not with me in jeans and a dirty T-shirt, they wouldn't.

I walked into my bathroom and turned on the shower. Mama had returned my cologne, but placed it on the sink. I shook my head and put it back in my medicine cabinet. She hadn't been a young mother in years, so she had forgotten the lifestyle.

Then I gasped. Mama! She had clothes befitting a Black American Queen. I headed toward her room.

I popped into Bella's bedroom, but she wasn't there. I shrugged. She and the kids could be out in the backyard playing. But I didn't have time to run outside and check. I checked my watch and sighed. I craved a pudgy kiss on my cheek. I wondered if she was missing me at all.

I reached my guest room and knocked on the door.

"Why are you knocking on your own door, Angel?" Mama shouted from the other side of the door. "Get in here. Your child needs you."

"Bella?" I opened the door.

"Hey, Mama." Bella waved.

She sat on the bed next to Mama and barely glanced at me. She didn't jump up to greet me like she usually did.

"Can I get a hug?" I asked.

She nodded, slid off the bed, then ran toward me and buried her head in my stomach. I leaned down and kissed the top of her head, but shot back up. I blinked. Her Power-puff Girl-inspired ponytail had been replaced by cornrows with gold beads dangling at the end circa 1990s tennis pro princesses, the Williams sisters. It complemented her summer bronzed skin. I didn't want to act too surprised, but I was. She looked beautiful.

I looked at Mama. "When did this happen?"

"I took the girls to the salon. They needed to look presentable." She lowered her gaze at me. I knew exactly what she meant. The girls needed to be properly coiffed for Devon's funeral.

I nodded. "What salon did y'all go to?"

"Halle's." Mama picked up some magazine she was reading. "You know she's the only one in Atlanta that I let in my hair."

I smirked. Her hair was buried under all those weave extensions.

She looked up at me. "You would look good with a fresh new look, too."

"I know, but I don't have time."

"You'd better make time," Mama said.

"Oh, I will. Halle and I have some matters to discuss anyway." I returned my attention to Bella. I stood back. "Is that a new dress?"

She nodded. "It's for tonight, Mommy."

"Tonight?" I frowned and looked back at Mama. "What's going on tonight?"

Mama touched my shoulder. "I'm taking the kids to meet their new granddaddy."

"Oh," I nodded. "Maybe I'll meet up with you guys later."

"No, you won't, Mama." Bella shrugged and walked off.

Mama watched Bella, then me. "That baby will take your bad ways, if you don't stop her."

"Long as she don't have the ones you and I share, then I'm good."

"I pray she never develops your inability to know when you need to make a hair appointment."

"You're right!" I spun around toward her. "I just forgot. I need to go to Halle's right now. Kiss the kids for me. I'm out again."

I ran out the door. I hoped I could get down there on time, find out what I needed to know, and get back before the armor bearers arrived.

Saturday, 4:30 PM
Halle-Do-Ya Spa & Salon, Stone Mountain

Halle scheduled me for an emergency wash and set. Perfect. If anyone living in Dekalb County wants to know the

latest scoop and the gospel truth of a matter, then book an
appointment at Halle-Do-Ya Spa & Salon on the corner of
Hairston and Memorial Drive. Halle's salon sat in a Kroger
Shopping Plaza sandwiched between the grocery store and
an AMC movie theater. It was a great location for her.

Seven years ago, Halle and I met while judging the Miss
Black Atlanta Pageant. She had migrated here from Louisi-
ana when her husband, Constance Capers, took on a job as
a music minister for Atlanta Faith's rival—sister church—
World Faith. Then Constance got a gig producing musical
scores for Perry David's Movie Studios. Now she styles hair
for some of the top Hollywood actresses, singers, and first
ladies in Atlanta. Because of that, the woman knew news
long before it became news. It didn't take long for her to become my informant and I her reliable Monday, 10-o'clock
wash and set, until three years ago when I didn't think I
needed her or anyone anymore. That was the worst decision I ever made.

"I thought you retired?" she asked, as she began to oil
my freshly shampooed hair with something that smelled of
peppermint and coconut. My head tingled. I liked it. Then
she massaged my head with her hands. I thought my spirit
was about to sour.

"So did I," I mumbled.

"Honey, it's a good thing, if you ask me." Her fingers
continued to work their anointing. "Maybe you'll go back
to the *Sentinel*, 'cause, child, they don't know what news is
anymore."

"Neither did I when I was there."

She reached for the wrapping lotion. It was a pink foamy
texture that smelled of strawberries. No wonder Ava's head
smelled so good.

"You know, Ava said that that place had stolen your
soul. You think she was right?"

"No, no one can steal your soul. You give it away."

"Amen, honey." She nodded. "Especially if he's fine."

The other ladies in the salon giggled. "Amen."

Halle began wrapping my hair around my head with a brush and more of that strawberry foam. Her process had me so calm I couldn't remember what I came to ask her.

"Not disrespecting the dead . . ." She leaned down and whispered, "Bishop McArthur was fine enough to lose your religion. It's a sin and a shame that man was killed like that."

The woman next to me patted my shoulder. "A man like that will drive any good woman crazy."

I shouted, "My sister did not kill Devon McArthur."

The salon shut up.

Halle said, "Oh, honey. We know that."

The salon breathed and Amen'ed some more.

"You're just saying that because I'm here."

"Honey, I don't have time to lie." Halle slapped my thigh with the hand towel that hung over her right shoulder. "Let's get you on the dryer before the wrap lotion dries up. When did you say the church folk are coming?"

"In two hours, and I need time to drive home."

I stood up and waved at the other ladies getting prepped. They waved back. As soon as I left the room, the original boom of the salon returned to its normal robust roar.

Halle walked me into another room. Both sides of the room were lined with hair dryers. She placed the towel on one of the dryer chair arms. "Sit down."

As she set the dryer to dry my hair, she said, "It's a sin and a shame what has happened. I knew Greater Atlanta was going to hang Ava out to dry the moment I saw the story about Devon's death on the news."

"Why did you think that?"

"Don't act surprised." She lowered the dryer over my head. "Ava talked about the administration's disloyalty all the time."

I lifted the dryer off my head. "She said that to you?"

"Yeah, she never told you?" She shook her head. "Of course she didn't. Ava didn't want you to know that you were right about the church."

"Right about what exactly? You know I have many gripes about the place."

"That last story you did for the *Sentinel*. You know the one about nonprofit foundation fraud, the one that made you quit. Well, Ava believed you."

My legs numbed. "What?"

She checked her watch. "You're going to have my schedule backed up with all these questions."

"And so what. You double book your clients."

"Touché. Let me get the blow dryer. It's not as good, but you don't have much time anyway. I get to try out my new porcelain dryer." She went back to her station, then returned with a big barrel silver blow dryer and a huge comb attachment.

"So why did my sister tell you all this and not me?"

"Women tell their hairstylists a lot of things. I don't know. I think it's the fact that we make you feel so comfortable, you can't help but tell the truth."

"Or could it be this place is so loud, she didn't think you heard her."

"Oh, honey, I hear everything. I even heard you are in love with your pastor."

"I didn't tell you that."

She chuckled. "We don't just listen, Angel. We see very well. So let me give you some advice."

She had my full attention. "Yes?"

"Marry him."

I laughed. "What?"

"Marry him."

By the time we were done, not only did I look fierce, but I was ready to face off with the women armor bearers of Greater Atlanta Faith. I hoped.

25

Ava's armor bearers walked inside the church at 8:00 PM
on the dot. There were three: an older woman, a young
woman who looked old enough to be barely out of school,
and a woman in her late twenties or early thirties, about my
and Ava's age. The woman closer to our age introduced herself and the group to me. Her name was Candace Johnson,
the older woman was Mrs. Loretta Stephens, and the young
one's name was April Peters. I must admit I was surprised
they weren't dressed alike or wearing the same color. In
fact, they didn't look like the modern-day Stepford Wives I
had imagined. They wore jeans and button-down blouses
just like I did. I cringed. What if they were normal decent
folk? I hoped so for Ava's sake.

To my surprise, Elvis was there. He was sweet enough to
bring over some finger food from the Biscuit Depot: peach
marmalade tea cakes, coffee, biscotti, and banana pudding,
my favorite. I hoped the pudding would take the edge off.
Justus hadn't arrived yet.

After Elvis placed all the food on the serving tables, he

walked over to me with a small plastic container in his hand. He handed me the container. "These are for you."

I popped the lid. Key lime cupcakes. I gasped. "How did you know?"

"It's a gift God blessed me with."

"What?" I giggled. "The ability to know a woman's guilty pleasure?"

"No." He touched my hand. "The ability to listen and remember. Your sister talked about your cupcake fascination often."

"She did? Talk about me, I mean?"

He nodded. "I know that you two have not been close for a long time, but I believe—I hope—that through this tragedy, God will reunite you and Lady Ava. She needs her family right now, and the children do, too."

He was so sweet. I gave him a hug. I would have given him a juicier hug if Justus and Mama hadn't walked in.

I heard Mama's voice first. "Where's Evangeline? Where's my daughter?"

"Your mother is here." Elvis released his hold. "I would love to chat with her, but I can't. I have to attend the Board of Trustees meeting tonight."

"I'm sure she will understand."

"I need to tell you two important things. One, the utensils and trays are disposable. The ladies will handle the cleaning of the catering supplies. And two . . ."

His voice quivered, I noticed. "Is something wrong?"

"I apologize, Angel, but I'm a bit concerned for you."

"For me? Why?"

Mama stopped in front of the door. "Elvis, why didn't you tell me you were in here?"

He walked toward her and gave her a hug. "Because I'm still on the clock, to my chagrin. I need to speak with your daughter for a bit longer and then I have to go."

"It's okay, sugar. We will talk soon. I just want to warn you." Mama then turned toward me and sneered. "Ava's women friends brought dishes covered in tacky plastic wrap. It takes away from the décor of the buffet table. I'm just saying."

"Okay, Mama. I'll get on it."

She nodded and walked out the door.

Elvis tilted his head as if he were looking out the door. "Mother Crawford Curtis Carter looked as if she's ready to pounce on our armor bearers."

I giggled. "She's anxious for answers. We all are, especially whether Ava makes bail tomorrow. She'll be okay."

"I pray that she will." He touched my shoulder.

I watched him. I wanted to ask him about Terry, but my gut told me to be patient and fish for something else. "You must think I'm a hypocrite."

He batted his eyes. "Excuse me?"

"I know you saw me and Pastor Morgan in your parking lot today."

"You two are a couple." His cheeks reddened. "Yes, I figured as much."

"No, actually, we're not." I looked toward the door to see if Mama was within earshot. "This isn't the right time for that sort of thing. You know?"

He nodded, but didn't say anything.

"So I'll be alone tomorrow."

"Of course." He smiled. "Nothing to worry about."

"Not even Terry? Should I worry about him?"

His eyes widened. "Terry?"

"Devon's bodyguard. I saw him today at your place. Should I worry about him when I visit tomorrow?"

"No, I'm sorry." He cleared his throat. "The church forced my hand. They sent him over because they knew you were coming."

"And how did they know that?"

"I told them." He rubbed his neck. "I didn't think it was going to be a problem. I mean, you are focused on clearing Lady Ava of the bishop's murder. What could be wrong with that?"

"So the Board of Trustees is afraid of me?"

"Not afraid, just concerned. They aren't anymore."

"What changed their minds?"

"Rachel. Your inquiry of her. The church shares similar concerns."

"What kind?"

He lowered his head. "They want to find her, too."

I stepped back and took a deeper look at Elvis. His hands trembled and his head remained lowered. He was definitely hiding something.

I touched his shoulder. "How well do you know Rachel?"

"Apparently not well enough." He looked up. His eyes had reddened. "From what I remember, she was a great girl. She did great work for the church. We got along very well. I don't have anything bad to say about her, except that she had found herself in a spot of trouble. Lady Ava wanted to help her. So did I, but unfortunately Rachel decided it was best to leave the church and resolve her issues without us."

"You worked closely with her?"

"Yes, by default, mind you." He chuckled.

"Right. Since you're Devon's first man and Rachel was Ava's assistant, you saw each other a lot."

"Exactly." He nodded. "We worked on a lot of projects together."

"Wow, you must miss her then?"

He looked up at me. "Angel, I miss them all. We were a happy family."

"I see . . ." I observed him some more. He wasn't as fidgety as he was before. "Since you and Rachel had such a close connection, did you become friends?"

"Yes, of course. She's a lovely girl."

"So you liked her?"

He grinned. "Angel . . ."

"Just asking."

"I understand, but she's not my type."

"Did she contact you after she left the church?"

"The board asked me the same question the day bishop died, but no, she hadn't contacted me. Honestly, I hoped that she bloody would have. I didn't want her to find out via cable news."

"That's very considerate," I said. "But I'm confused about why the board wanted to find her after Devon's death. Do they suspect she's involved?"

"Of course not." He sighed. "That's absurd."

"Then give me a better explanation."

"It's quite simple, honestly. Finding Rachel is a crisis management issue. The last thing the church needs right now is for the DeKalb County Homicide Unit or the Atlanta press to find Lady Ava's personal assistant."

"Former personal assistant."

He squinted. "Excuse me?"

"Rachel is no longer Ava's personal assistant. She could possibly be a material witness, but she wouldn't be helpful or hurtful to Ava at this point unless there's more. Is there more about Rachel that you're not telling me, Elvis?"

"This discussion makes me uncomfortable, especially when the conversation is with a bloody reporter."

"I'm not talking to you as a reporter; I'm talking to you as one sister desperate to free her sister from jail."

He huffed. "It's hard to believe with all your questions."

"Questions?" I scoffed. "The police don't have a reason to search for any other suspects, because my sister won't

say anything. But if Ava's silence has to do with Rachel . . ."
I touched his shoulder. "Please, Elvis. I'm begging here. Tell
me. Why is Rachel important to the church?"

Elvis folded his arms over his chest. "Rachel had problems. I can't talk about them here, for the sake of time, but
finding her is very important to Greater Atlanta, and, of
course, to Lady Ava. We don't want her problems adding
more scandal to an already scandalous situation. Do you
understand?"

"Very. When can you tell me about her problems?"

He rubbed his jaw. "Not now. I have to go to my meeting."

"So I assume you've already asked the armor bearers
about her?"

He looked at them and leaned toward me. "Since
bishop's death and Lady Ava's arrest, they barely talk to
me. I don't know why."

"Is it because you're white? No offense, but you do
stand out at Greater Atlanta. It's got to be the elephant in
the room over there."

"Actually, my father is Nigerian." He smirked and shook
his head. "Bishop McArthur was working toward changing
the dynamics in the church to something far beyond race,
more like structure and traditions."

"Would that include the need for armor bearers?"

He shrugged. "Some traditions Devon didn't think were
necessary. I don't know if the armor bearer division was a
part of that plan. All I know is that he wanted to streamline
Greater Atlanta. Take the church toward a new and better
vision, a new denomination."

"A new denomination? Really?" I made a mental note.
"So what do you want me to do?"

"I want you to find her. Maybe the ladies will talk to
you. One of them must know where she is. If not"—he

pulled an envelope out of his hand—"I hope this is enough to retain you. I know you have other ways to find someone who doesn't want to be found. It's pretty clear Rachel doesn't want to be found."

"Seems like that to me, too." I peeled the envelope open and peeked inside. My mouth dropped. There was a cashier's check for $50,000 inside.

26

When I looked up, Justus was standing behind Elvis, his eyes on me. I placed the envelope in my back pocket. He didn't need to see this. I'd give it back to Elvis as soon as I could anyway.

"Elvis, you'll be late for your meeting if you don't leave now. We'll discuss this later tonight."

He nodded and then turned to Justus. "You have a lovely church, sir."

"Thank you." Justus smiled. "And thank you again for bringing food tonight for the family."

"One of our drivers will drop off some breakfast tomorrow morning as well." Elvis walked toward the door, stopped, turned around, and looked at us. "Have a good night."

"You too," I said to him as he walked away.

He spoke to the armor bearers, then exited as quietly as he came.

"Angel, I need to talk to you," Justus said.

I exhaled. I decided that I would not lie to him anymore. Something inside me wanted to come clean. "I need to talk to you, too."

I took his hand and pulled him into an empty study room so no one could see or hear us.

Before I could tell him about the money and Big Faith's request, he said, "I can't be here tonight. I have a problem of my own."

"A problem?" I gulped. "What kind?"

"It's Kelly. Nothing to trouble yourself with. I'll be back before the ladies leave, but I wanted you to know before I left why I had to go. I retrieved your mother so she could be here with you for moral support. You'll be okay."

"My mom for moral support?" I chuckled. "Well, it was good while it lasted."

"I'm sorry, but I have to go." He kissed my cheek and then left.

"Justus?" I turned around and gasped.

Everyone stood in the doorway watching me. Mama shook her head.

I blushed. "Let's get back to the conference room, ladies."

Everyone settled inside. Justus stayed around a few minutes longer to greet everyone. I was sure he would give me the 411 about his niece's situation later. I wished I had found time to do a small search on Kelly's boyfriend, because I didn't want Justus to leave. After this meeting, I would call Paige to see if I could contract her to check up on that guy. It's the least I could do for the help I've received.

Sugar Hill Community Church may not have been as large as Greater Atlanta, but we had our own small luxuries. The room was large. The mahogany chairs were wide, comfy, and new. The round mahogany conference table glistened and glowed, and the room smelled lemony fresh. A huge bowl of lemons and limes sat in the middle of the table. Mrs. Lewis had outdone herself.

I smiled and winked at Justus before he left, then remembered I wasn't supposed to be doing that anymore. His eyes widened and he smiled back. I lowered my head and located a seat on the other side of the table. I placed my note pad down, then gathered a few snacks from the buffet table and sat down.

Mama plopped down next to me with an empty plate. She watched the armor bearers nibble their food and sip their drinks with her arms folded. I nudged her to try to get her to stop. Tonight was not the time or place to be combative. We needed answers, alliances, and bail money. I eyeballed Mama to get her attention. She looked at me, rolled her eyes, and then returned to mean-mugging the ladies. She was not listening to me. *I'm in big trouble.*

About two minutes into our reception, Mama asked, "Have any of you ladies been to visit my baby in jail?"

I stood corrected. We were in hot water.

April, the youngest of them, coughed. Candace sat in the middle. I didn't notice how large her eyes were until Mama's question. I thought they would pop out of their sockets. I took note of that for some weird reason.

But the older one, the one who sat down first, Mrs. Loretta, she didn't seem surprised at all by Mama's question. She cleaned her mouth with a napkin slowly, lowered the napkin in her lap slowly, and then looked up at us and grinned.

"Your daughter hasn't included us on her visitor's list. We hoped that you would implore her to do so. We want to be of service and support to her wherever she is."

"Mmhmm. I bet you do." Mama leaned back in her chair, then mumbled another profanity.

I cringed.

"You don't have to bet in God's house, Mrs. Crawford. God has it all in control," Mrs. Loretta added.

"No, get it right. I'm Mrs. Crawford Curtis Carter."

Mrs. Loretta smirked.

I felt nauseated. I didn't think this meeting was getting anywhere.

"Is something funny?" Mama asked.

My neck felt uncomfortably hot. "No, Mama. Please."

"No, darling. I'm stating our case. We are here because we wanted to pray with you and dine with you. We want to be of service and to help in anyway we know how. But your tone, which I understand is more fear and bereavement than anything else, is putting you in a place where God can't do His majestic work. I know you don't want that. I understand your concerns." She glanced at the other armor bearers. "All of us do, sweetheart." Mrs. Loretta possessed an old sultry southern voice that reminded me of Lena Horne. Come to think of it, she favored the legendary singer and actress, too.

"Thank you for understanding our challenge. But I have to ask—" I cleared my throat and patted Mama's hand. "Why do you think Ava didn't put you ladies on her visitor's list?"

Mama sneered. "Probably because they wouldn't answer her call when she contacted them from the stank tank at the jailhouse."

"I beg pardon, ma'am." Mrs. Loretta raised her voice. "I am called to service the First Lady. If she needed me, if she called me, I would have been there. I have committed myself to your daughter for my entire life, and that has not changed. I do not understand why you are being harsh to me. I have always been there for Lady Ava."

"Then where were you the night she apparently needed someone to watch her kids, when she felt compelled to leave her home in the middle of the night? Where have you been all this time before this ridiculous mess? Had you not seen their trouble? Had you not seen this coming? What are you people good for? Aren't you supposed to protect my daughter? Oh!" Mama screamed, trembled, and then sobbed. "My baby. My baby. Oh God, take care of my baby. Please, Lord. Please heal my soul." She turned to me and lowered her head on my chest.

The ladies gasped and jumped up to gather around us.

I held on to Mama and whispered, "Mama, calm down. She's coming home soon. I promise."

I looked at April. She was crying, too.

I returned to Mama's attention. "Remember, Mama. They're here to help us. These women are going to help us set Ava free."

"Help? They're a day late and a dollar short, if you ask me." She cursed again.

I rubbed her shoulder. "Mama, could you please stop cursing? Your blood pressure," I whispered. "First impressions and the cursing don't mix well."

"You're right. Lord, forgive me. I sound like a slap fool up in here." Mama lowered her head and shook her head. "Ladies, please forgive me. I've never cursed a day in my life."

"Now you don't have to lie to the nice people," I whispered.

She picked her head up. "I only curse when I'm scared. Okay? Is that better?"

"Sure, Mama." I kissed her head.

Mrs. Loretta touched my shoulder. "Fear makes us do crazy things, sister."

"Especially when a dead man is involved," I said.

The other ladies Amen'ed in unison.

Candace said, "But Mother Crawford, you do have a

point. We have failed your daughter." Mrs. Loretta and April rolled their necks in her direction. She continued, "And I apologize for all of us."

The others looked down, then nodded. Mama sat up.

"Candace, what do you mean when you say you didn't do your job?" I asked.

"Your sister entrusted us with protecting her. We knew she was in danger, spiritually speaking. We had no clue it was a real, physical one. But we knew that she was afraid of something."

"Did she say she was afraid?"

"Her prayers said it all." Candace looked at Mama, then at me. "They had changed from, you know, her normal requests—the kids, church business—to something more secret. I think the marriage was in trouble."

"Candy!" Mrs. Loretta huffed. "We don't gossip. It's not our place to know everything that plagues First Lady Ava, and definitely not to assume anything about the marriage between her and the bishop. We pray. We assist. We're silent."

"And your silence has murdered a good man." Mama slid in that stinging remark.

Mrs. Loretta's mouth flew open. I think I stopped breathing. She just wouldn't stop. I didn't know why Justus brought her and then I remembered he based his assumptions about my mother on first appearances. He didn't know.

"Evangeline . . ." Mama stood and looked down at me.

I couldn't read her mind, but her calling me by my full first name told me that she was just as spiritually exhausted as I was over this mess. I watched her and wanted so badly to make things better, but I couldn't. I couldn't move. I couldn't speak.

She threw up her hands. "I apologize, baby. I'm a bit too

sully tonight. I think I need to leave and let you all meet. I don't mean to offend you fine ladies. I'm just tired. I'm supposed to be on my honeymoon, you know." She walked out.

I could hear her sobbing down the hall. I wanted to follow and comfort her.

Candace touched my hand. "We're sorry if we sound insensitive. We know you all are under great stress."

I nodded. "Our mom isn't generally like this. She's usually nice to other people. It's her kids who experience her wrath. She's been holding all her frustration in. I suspect because she wants to appear in control in front of the children."

April smiled. "We know. She's been to the church before. We know that her outburst was out of character. How are the kids?"

"They don't know about their mother or father."

"Now that's very wise." Mrs. Loretta held her folded arms across her chest tighter than the lids on Granny's old apple jelly mason jars. Her lips were pursed even tighter. I rolled my eyes at her, although I knew I shouldn't have.

"Before Pastor Morgan returns, could you tell me if, outside of prayer, you saw any evidence that Devon and Ava's marriage was odd?"

"Odd like how?"

"Abusive, adulterous . . ."

"No, ma'am. He wasn't either," Candace said. "He was very sweet to her."

April raised her hand. "A little too sweet if you ask me."

Mrs. Loretta snapped, "Child, you have not had the privilege of being loved by a good man, so please keep your insecurities to yourself. Thank you."

She rolled her eyes. "Don't call me that. I'm not a child, and I have a good man in my life."

Mrs. Loretta scoffed. "I'm praying for the day your version of good changes."

"I think we're getting off the subject," I interjected. "What do you armor bearers do that helps Ava?" I asked. The last thing I needed was to be accused of inciting a cat fight in the church.

"We mainly pray with her and for her and anticipate her needs." Candace walked toward the refreshment table and added more dumplings to her plate. "But like I said—in my spirit—I felt I should have done more."

"How? And what qualifies you to do what you do anyway?" I asked.

Candace looked at the other women, then back at me. "You of all people should know that."

"What do you mean?"

She blushed. "I'm sorry. I didn't mean to sound disrespectful. What I meant was that you and Angel are twins. You almost share the same spirit, so I assumed you would know what it's like to be in sync with someone."

I stopped her. "No, we weren't in sync. Ava's her own person, and so am I. I've lived with her longer than anyone in this world and I couldn't read her thoughts. And she definitely couldn't read mine." I refused to share twin-intuition with them. That was not the same.

Something in my gut checked me. I looked up. "Let me rephrase that. When you're a twin like Ava and me, the last thing you want to be is a clone of the other. So you carve out your own identity. You share what you want to share. And you keep what you want to keep. From what ya'll just told me, Ava wasn't sharing her soul with you. She was telling you one thing and something else to you, April, and something else to Mrs. Loretta."

April shrugged. "I was too new for her to share anything

with me, but there was the woman I replaced. They were pretty close."

"No, April!" Candace shouted. She bumped against the table by accident and dropped her plate. It crashed in bits around her feet. "Oh no."

"Don't move," Mama shouted. She had returned. My heart skipped. What would she do now? "I'll get it up."

I smiled in relief. Mama couldn't stand a stain on floors. Good thing she didn't see Ava's house the night Devon died.

I returned to April. "Was that woman you replaced named Rachel?"

April nodded; the other women crossed their legs.

Mrs. Loretta asked, "How did you know about her?"

"I'm a reporter. It's my job to know things."

"Used to be," Justus interjected as he returned to the meeting. "False alarm. I'll be here after all. He cleared his throat and smiled. I tried hard not to smile back at him, but couldn't help myself. I was glad he was back.

"But what do you know about her?" Candace asked.

I sat back. "I was praying that you would tell me. Who is she and why isn't she with the church anymore?"

"Before we get to that, I think we need to pray, because some of us in this room are prone to gossip," Mrs. Loretta eyeballed April.

Candace interrupted, "Not this time, Mrs. Loretta. What's said here, stays here. Right, Angel?" She looked at me.

I gulped. Were they kidding me? I'm a former reporter. That was why I didn't like talking to people in churches. They put the hand of God over the conversation and then I couldn't do what I wanted to do with the information I received. I couldn't share it.

"Not if it will help get my daughter's charges dropped. No way am I keeping anything a secret," Mama said.

I patted Mama's back and whispered to her, "Thank you." I thanked God for an out clause on that one. Mama said exactly what needed to be said.

"I agree that this is the perfect time for prayer," Justus said.

"Amen, Reverend." Mrs. Loretta waved her hand in the air.

He looked at me. "Can we do this together?"

We both blushed at each other. If God would let me remain friends with this man, then I would learn to be satisfied. I nodded. "Let's pray."

27

After the prayer, Justus and Mama went into his office to talk about cursing in church and enjoy some chocolate while I talked to the armor bearers some more. I pulled out my pen and pad, then asked the questions I had been wanting to ask all night.

Who is Rachel?

Candace: Her name is Rachel Newton. She's twenty-six, single, been a member of Greater Atlanta since 2000. Was once the church receptionist. Devon appointed her as an armor bearer in 2005.

What was Rachel's role?

Loretta: Lady Ava had decided to facilitate leadership retreats for women alongside Devon's pastors conferences and needed a prayer cell to support her ministry and to travel with her. Rachel was hired as the media contact and events scheduler. She kept up with Ava's calendar.

Like a publicist?

No, First Lady Ava wrote her own media material. She just needed someone to get them out to her media outlets on time.

When did Rachel leave Greater Atlanta?

April: Six months ago.

Why?

Candace: She said that she had a personal obligation to meet.

April frowned. "She told me that God had called her to another service."

"Tttt . . ." Mrs. Loretta shook her head. "It didn't matter what she said. We all knew she was pregnant."

"Pregnant?" Mama yelled from the other room.

"So it wasn't a rumor?" I asked.

Candace sat down. "I had hoped it was."

"Why did you not want Rachel to be pregnant?" I asked.

"Rachel was devoted to her faith. She wanted to be married before she had children. If she were pregnant . . ." Candace lowered her head. "She would be very ashamed of herself."

"As she should be." Mrs. Loretta snarled. "Before I was a retired, old woman, I was a midwife. Did it for twenty years. I got so good I could spot a pregnant woman before those pregnancy tests could. Shoot. Come to think of it, I can, and I would tell those young girls to hold fast and wait for marriage."

I turned to Mrs. Loretta. "How did Rachel know that you knew about her pregnancy?"

Mrs. Loretta grinned. "I'm the one that brought it to her attention."

"Oh." I sat back. "Mrs. Loretta, you ever thought about becoming a private investigator?"

She chuckled and shook her head. "No."

Justus escorted Mama back to her chair. He sat down beside me.

"Now that you've relaxed, Loretta, may I ask you if you know who's Rachel's baby daddy?" Mama asked.

We all turned to Justus.

He threw his hands up. "It's not me. I promise."

"We know that." I turned back to the ladies. "Could it be Devon's?"

"No!" the ladies shouted.

"Why couldn't it be Devon's?" I asked.

"Because he's a man of God." Candace threw her right hand over her chest. She whispered, "And your brother-in-law. Do you have any loyalty?"

"I'm loyal to my sister. I've never led you to believe otherwise."

"You have a funny way of showing it," Mrs. Loretta said.

I saw Justus looking at me. He wasn't smiling or beaming at me, neither was Mama. I lowered my head.

"It's no surprise to you guys that Devon and I didn't get along, but my feelings for him have nothing to do with this question. It's important. I don't want to damage Devon's name. I don't want my sister, my niece, or my nephew to hate me, but I want to find the real killer. If there's a possibility that Devon could be the father or in all certainty, based on your statements, Devon knew who the father is, we have to know."

No one in the room seemed fully convinced.

"Well, let me give you another scenario . . ." I stood up. "Newspapers are hurting right now because of the economy. If they get a whiff of what I uncovered—very easily, I might add—then imagine what that will look like for Greater Atlanta. Would you rather that I found out and fixed things before my old buddies at the *Atlanta Sentinel* do?"

"We're not having anyone debase the bishop's good name and character." Mrs. Loretta placed her arms around me. "I'll help you. We all will. April, set out my banana pudding. This might be a long night."

Justus patted my shoulders. "Finally, you're letting someone in."

Mama whispered, "I told you that you needed Jesus."

I frowned at her, then giggled. "Mama, you're something else."

Candace placed her bowl down. "I'm not trying to sound selfish. But I don't believe our pastor fathered Rachel's baby. He wouldn't do a thing like that. He wouldn't do that to First Lady Ava. I know that in my gut."

The other ladies said "Amen" in agreement.

Mrs. Loretta added, "Angel, based on your questions, I can tell you haven't spent much time around First Lady or the bishop."

"He wouldn't allow me to," I said.

Mama poked Justus in his ribs with her elbow. "He wouldn't."

"Justus, let me get your two cents. Is that some kind of new pastor's law? Keep the women from their family?"

All the women looked at Justus. He looked at me, then folded his arms. "Pastors don't live by any marriage code different than a normal wedded couple."

"That's true," Mama said. "My first husband, the girls' father—God rest his soul—did his best to make our lives normal, but how can you be normal when everyone expects you to live like angels? I never had any real relationships until after he passed. And I don't think my children did either. Thank God they had each other . . ." She looked down at me and smiled. "Sort of."

I loved her.

"Now, my second husband. He was a pastor, too. Honey, that was a nightmare and the church had nothing to do with that. Isn't that right, baby?" She looked at me.

"I won't touch that tonight, Mama."

I turned my attention to the ladies again. "Then where's

Rachel? Why has she disappeared and given you all different reasons as to why she left? She sounds a little suspect to me."

To tell the truth, I still wasn't buying Devon's holy pants spiel. He very well could be the father of Rachel's unborn baby. It would definitely explain why Ava wanted to keep everything on the hush. She was protecting Devon's legacy with Greater Atlanta, while Rachel was hiding her pregnancy to protect what or whom? Maybe Devon wasn't the father. Pastors took concubines like David took Bathsheba, and scandal like this would definitely rock Big Faith's arc. But I'd take the high road. I'd give Devon the benefit of the doubt for now, because to tell the truth, all I had was more gossip and a missing mom-to-be. I needed some facts. I needed to find Rachel.

"But if that's the case, then none of you ladies would object to helping me find Rachel?"

Mrs. Loretta stood up. "I don't have a problem with it. I would like to know how she's doing. That baby should be due any day now."

"Have any of you visited her lately?"

They all shook their heads.

"She moved from where she once lived," Candace said. "So I haven't seen her."

April raised her hand. "I saw her last week. We both were at the McArthur mansion. I had to run an errand for Lady Ava. She was there meeting the bishop. She said she would be returning to our group after her life settled down."

"Did she say when she would return, like what month?"

"No, like I said, I didn't know her very well. It was more like small talk, I thought."

I turned to Candace and Mrs. Loretta. "Has my sister said anything to you about Rachel's return?"

They looked at each other, then at me. "No."

I didn't want to suspect that these two were not being truthful, but their responses only generated more questions for me.

"Do either of you know where she moved?"

They shrugged.

"Have you called her at all since she left Greater Atlanta?"

"Her cell phone was disconnected," Candace said. "I don't feel comfortable talking about someone when they aren't present to defend themselves, but she left the church so abruptly. I thought she had done something wrong. I admit that."

"More wrong than being pregnant out of wedlock?" Mrs. Loretta asked.

Candace rolled her eyes. "I believe Mary was pregnant before Joseph married her, so what? See. This is why we're losing members. We're too judgmental."

"Beware of the judgment is all I will say to that." Mrs. Loretta shook her head and sipped some iced tea from her glass.

"Candace, if you're such an advocate for unwed mothers, I'm surprised that Rachel didn't come to you."

"So am I." Candace looked at everyone in the room except me. "She knew that she was welcome in my house, but she chose to walk away from us all. I don't understand that. Do you?"

"No, I don't."

Justus cleared his throat. I looked up. He nodded at me to follow him outside the room. I excused myself from the ladies and followed him.

He turned around. "I know what you're thinking."

I pulled the envelope from my back pocket and handed it to him. "No, you don't."

He held the envelope in his hand and looked at me. "What's this?"

"Before Elvis left, he gave me this envelope. He told me that the Board of Trustees and Greater Atlanta want to hire me to find Rachel."

"You're joking."

"Take a look inside the envelope. There's a check for 50 G's in there. Does that look like a joke to you?"

"This doesn't make sense." He peered inside and wrinkled his nose. "Why didn't they take their reservations to Detective Salvador instead of you? Why didn't they ask Terry to find her instead of you?"

"I don't know. But the question you should be asking yourself is . . ."

He frowned. "What? What's the question?"

I looked away.

Over the years, I had received anonymous story germs— little notes, tips, snippets, and rumor bites that could, under the right conditions, turn into a full story. Most of these germs came from "my shadow people." Many of them were disgruntled throwaways who didn't want any attention, but wanted to settle scores with the people who had hurt them by disclosing their secret sins. Their stories would range from sexual indiscretion, domestic violence, money laundering to things I shuddered to mention and definitely cringed to write about. I was many things, but I didn't have the stomach to tear someone down for the sake of vendetta journalism, so I rarely used them. But I never forgot them either. As I stood in front of Justus thinking about the possibility that Rachel was removed from the church because of her unplanned pregnancy, I thought of what Justus would think of me if I contacted any of them, to know what they knew.

I liked Justus. I respected him, but if I told him my

thoughts, he wouldn't like me anymore. He wouldn't respect me. I didn't want to lose that. I missed what it felt like to have a good man respect me. To me, it was far more important than spilling the contents of my warped brain to him.

I forced a grin. "Why is finding Rachel worth fifty thousand dollars to Greater Atlanta?"

"That's a good question?" Justus rubbed his head. "I think we need to take this info to Salvador. It would help Ava's case."

"Or it could hurt."

"Why would it hurt her?" Justus asked.

"If Rachel was a part of some torrid love triangle between Devon and my sister . . ." I thought out my next words before I said them. "That kind of news would not be good for Ava."

Justus put his arms around me. "I don't believe that at all. Not the bishop."

I looked up at him. "Fifty thousand dollars, Justus. It makes sense to me."

He pulled back and frowned. "What if she's in trouble? What if she's a witness?"

"A witness? To what?" I scoffed. "I wish."

"That's a possibility."

"No, it isn't. Think about it, Justus." I came closer to him. "Ava won't talk. She demanded I not snoop around. And out of thin air, this Rachel person's name pops up a day before the church asks me to find her."

"You're losing me." He rubbed his head. "Slow down and clarify."

I pulled out my notebook and ran my fingers down my throat. "I don't know myself. I'm just talking this out to process it all. Tossing some brainstorms out to see what sticks."

He nodded. "Okay, so what's sticking? What looks like it makes sense?"

"The only thing that makes sense to me is . . ." I gulped. I didn't want to tell him, but I couldn't. I felt like I would be lying to God if I didn't. Yet, I didn't want to hear what was about to come out of my mouth. It was a stupid, stupid thought, I chided myself, but it was the only thing that made sense at this point. "I think that my sister might be the killer, after all, and Greater Atlanta wants to clean up the mess before Devon's indiscretion with Rachel becomes public record."

"You can't believe that."

"I don't want to believe it, but if Ava weren't my sister—objectively speaking . . ." I shook my head. "It's just like Salvador said. The more I snoop, the more I'm going to hurt Ava. He meant I would uncover more evidence to bury her with."

"I think you're tired."

"No, just listen. Let's take tonight's meeting with the armor bearers, for example. All we did was uncover more dirt. Rachel's resignation from the armor bearer's group was suspect. It's hard for me to believe that those nosy women in there didn't know who Rachel was seeing. They had hoped they'd removed Rachel before Ava found out, but they were too late. They're covering up for my sister."

"We don't know that."

"We don't know that they're not." I threw up my hands. "Don't you see that?"

"I don't. In fact, if—and I mean a very little if—this mystery baby is Devon's, wouldn't Rachel become a suspect?"

I shook my head. "She has no motive."

"She's in love with Devon."

"No proof. Unmarried women have children all the time and don't love the baby's father."

He frowned. "Perhaps Rachel assumed that since she was carrying his child, she assumed he would leave Ava for her, but he didn't, despite his moral responsibility."

"You're thinking like a man, Justus. I'm thinking like my sister. She loved Devon. She would have lost her mind if that man betrayed her. My sister is crazy when you betray her. I know that firsthand."

"That doesn't sound like she would kill Rachel."

"No, she wouldn't come after her at all, but Devon. . . . It makes perfect sense now."

Justus harrumphed and slumped against the wall. "You've tired me out, so just tell me what you're thinking."

"I'm thinking the person the dagger was meant for wasn't Devon. It was Rachel. What if—" I grabbed Justus's hand. "What if her life's in danger now and this money in your hand is her death sentence?"

"You can't think Greater Atlanta is behind this? That's crazy talk?"

"No, I don't think they're behind it. They want to stop it." I moved around and paced the floor. "I think there's a hit out on her."

Justus rubbed his head. "Please stop. Don't say another word."

"You don't know what depths a mother will take to protect her family."

"That's not God, and you know it."

"I never said it was, but was it Ava? That's what we have to find out."

"I'm not going to preach to you or give you some sermon. You've made it clear on more than one occasion that a sermon would automatically make you see how wrong you are about making such prejudiced generalizations against your sister. I'm not going to do that."

His jaw was clinched. He stared at me with seriousness and concern and with his free hand, he took my hand. "But I'll ask you to believe me. Do you trust me?"

"I do, but—"

"No buts. If you trust me, then call Salvador and give him this money."

"Oh-noooo." I shook my head. "I'm keeping this money."

"Why?"

"Because I need it and I'm out of time."

"You don't need it, Angel."

"Yes, I do." I squeezed his hand. "If Big Faith is looking for Rachel, then she knows they're looking for her. Believe me. If she's pregnant and has any common sense, she is long gone by now. The only way I can find her at this point is to hire someone. Meanwhile, I have to take care of the house, the kids, funeral arrangements, and picking up Ava from jail, hopefully tomorrow. This money could help me do that. I have no more time. What choice do I have?"

"Forget choice; choose faith." He raised his other hand, which contained the money Elvis had given me. "Not this. Give me until tomorrow morning to come up with a better plan for you, for Ava, and for us."

"For us?"

He took my hand in his. "Yes, the sooner Devon's murder is solved and Ava's charges are dropped, the sooner you and I can move forward *together* under normal circumstances."

"Normal?" I chuckled. "What about Trish and the kids? What about the church? You're just as overextended as I am."

"Stop searching for excuses not to surrender to the way you feel about me, woman."

"I don't know if I even know what that means."

"Give me a chance, Angel," he pleaded. "You're not supposed to carry these burdens. That's why you can't think straight right now. Don't give up."

He gave me that look that I loved and hated.

I lowered my head on his chest. "You're right. I'll return the money."

He wrapped his arms around me. "Why don't I return it for you, so you can concentrate on preparing for Ava's homecoming? She might need your help with Devon's funeral arrangements. She's going to be a bag of nerves with a trial looming over her head as well."

"That sounds great, but I'm sure her armor bearers would take care of that, and besides, Tiger will be escorting Ava from the jail for me."

"Tiger." He lowered his arms. "Your boss who put you in danger last week? That guy?"

"Yes, that guy. He's good people most of the time." I stepped back. "You know what. It's probably best that I take Elvis his money back, since I have to go to Tiger's to retrieve Ava anyway. I'll do it before I pick her up. That way she will be none the wiser."

His brilliant smile lit the room around us again. "Now, that's good news. Tomorrow will be a better day, I promise. Get rest. I will drive your mom back to your home for you."

He hugged me again. I held him tight but felt myself falling away from him. I wasn't returning that money, not until I got more answers, and definitely not until I got to the bottom of Miss Rachel. I held him longer, because I knew after tonight, he wouldn't want to touch me again.

28

A late-night fog fluffed over Decatur and my windshield. The only thing I saw was Big Tiger's Trusted Bail Bonds' chalk-white office gleaming through the muck. I wished I could turn around and have Justus ride along, but not tonight, not anymore. I sighed. This was not the time to fall in love with a good man.

"It's about time you came to your senses and called me, girl," Big Tiger said when he opened the door to greet me. "What took you so long?"

I walked inside and threw my purse on his desk. "I didn't think I would have to resort to this to help Ava."

I plopped down on the sofa. No one was here but us. I glanced around the office.

"Resort to what? Finding a killer?" he asked. "Girl, have the suburbs made you soft? Killers don't knock on your door and invite themselves over for lemonade and chocolate-chip cookies. You have to hunt them down."

"I know, but my pastor—my friend—he thinks that God doesn't need me to lower myself to solve Devon's murder."

Big Tiger sat down beside me and placed his arm over

my shoulder. His cologne smelled okay, but not as yummy and calming as Justus's. "He's right."

I turned to him. "Justus is right?"

"For sure." He nodded. "You don't have to be here, Angel."

"But just a minute ago, you said that I had come to my senses by coming here."

"True." He nodded faster.

"I'm confused."

"There's no need. It's real simple, baby girl." He removed his arm from around me and turned his body toward me. "Your man is right. Eventually, the truth about what happened to Devon will come out. It could be next week. It could be thirty years. God does what He do." He rubbed his hands together. "But you don't care about that. That's not what you want tonight. You want to find this girl Rachel. You need to know Ava is innocent, and you don't know how long God will take to answer. So it's your choice. Plain and simple."

I scoffed. "You make it sound like I don't believe in God."

"I didn't say that, Angel. You know I know you. We both come up in the church together. We both know God is real. But that don't stop us from being spoiled rotten. Some fool killed your brother-in-law and is trying to frame our girl for his murder. Whoever it is has done a good job, because they've got you spooked. God ain't got nothin' to do with that, so you gotta choose. What's best for you right now, baby girl?"

I listened to Big Tiger like he was a ghetto Billy Graham, drinking in his words like red Kool-Aid on a steamy August dog day.

"Big Tiger, get my stuff out of my car."

Big Tiger hoisted my case files out my car trunk, brought them into his office, then slammed them on this desk.

"Angel Soft, what do you think you'll find in there?"

"Salvador wanted to see my old case files, remember? So I'm thinking about Gabe's intent. There may be some clue in there about what went down."

"But that won't help us find Rachel."

"She was Ava's armor bearer at the time of that investigation. Gabe may have had some information on her that we can use to locate her." I paused. I hadn't said Bella's father's name so much in a long while.

"You never found out who killed him either. Did you?"

"Nope." I shook my head. "I'm not ready to open that case."

"For you and your man's sake, you can't keep it cold forever."

"I think we're too late for that."

"What? You broke up already?"

"We're not together. He just doesn't know that I'm here, and I want to keep it that way."

I pulled out my manila notebook that housed all the leads I had so far, my calendar notebook, and the envelope with the check Elvis gave me.

I handed Big Tiger my notebook. "I need a Dumpster diver like now."

A Dumpster diver was someone who sifted through other people's trash to find things of value: bank receipts, credit card bills, hotel keys, shredded papers, pregnancy tests, and anything that could buttress a case. Not only did the press Dumpster dive, but corporate spies and lobbyists did as well. If it weren't for Dumpster diving, the BALCO steroid scandal might not have seen the light of day. When I worked at the *Sentinel,* I ordered garbage pulls all the time. It didn't require a warrant and it never failed.

"We need to pull Ava's trash, and the trash of all the armor bearers and Elvis Bloom."

Big Tiger combed through my notebook and jotted down some notes. "Got anyone in mind?"

I nodded and checked my wallet for Paige's number. I pulled the card out and handed it to Big Tiger. "I think we have one, and she's old family."

Big Tiger grinned. "Good, then she won't need to be schooled."

I found Big Tiger's speaker phone and dialed Paige's number.

She picked up. "Hi, Angel. What do you need?"

I sighed with relief. It was refreshing to deal with people who didn't waste time and knew how to get things done without all the condemnation.

"Paige, I need you to do a garbage pull. Get letters, prescriptions, bills, receipts—snot rags, anything out of a few trash cans ASAP."

"Do you need me to locate their trash removal services, too?"

I blinked. "Why?"

"Maybe they haven't burned it, composted it, or shipped it off to the landfills yet. And you know at a landfill, things can sit for years in the same shape they were buried."

"Honey, I can't pay you enough to have a landfill excavated. Just check the trash and the recycle bins and bring them to Big Tiger's."

"Ok, give me the addresses and depending upon how far I need to travel, a few hours for each pull," Paige said.

"Cool, Big Tiger and I should be back by then, so call me on the cell when you're done and we'll meet you here."

"Where will you be? Maybe I can meet you there?"

I cradled the phone and turned to Big Tiger. He shook his head. "No."

"No, meet us here." I gave her the pulls and Big Tiger's address and ended the conversation.

Tiger chuckled. "Angel Soft, do you think you have the heart for what we're about to do?"

I rolled my eyes. "Yes, I'm ready. Why?"

"It's been a long time. You're not the same girl you used to be."

"Why do you say that?"

"Because you wouldn't have needed me."

"I'm not soft." I looked at him. "You think I've become soft?"

"It's okay if you are. You're a mother now, you know?"

"I don't need to be soft tonight. I need to get this thing done."

My cell phone rang. I looked at it. "It's Paige. Something must be wrong."

I answered. "What's up, girl?"

"I know we just got off the phone, but when you gave me the names of the people you want me to trash check, one of those names was familiar."

"Which name?"

"Rachel Newton. I've heard her name before and you wouldn't believe from whom."

I motioned for Tiger to get me a pen and pad. He slid me a yellow pad and a pencil.

"Okay. I'm ready. How do you know Rachel?"

"Charlotte," she said. "Charlotte Lewis."

I ended my call and plopped down. "Things just got real interesting."

Saturday, 10:45 PM
Canoe Restaurant, Vinings, GA

Charlotte Lewis kept a discreet escort service in Sandy Springs until 2004, a year before the city incorporated. As a favor to her for being such a great source, I warned her about an impending investigation that might involve her. Her most loyal client and boyfriend, former Georgia State Senator and the Honorable Judge Telly Milner of Sandy Springs, found her a quiet office in Vinings, ten minutes from Canoe Restaurant, where we were meeting for a late dessert. The restaurant was closing in fifteen minutes, but they obliged me as a small courtesy to Charlotte. I found her in the River Room, sipping Dom Pérignon and watching the Chattahoochee River rolling just outside the window. Her legs were crossed, but her free foot shook.

I sat my phone down on the glass table in front of us and placed my purse over the empty back of the chair across from her. Charlotte didn't move, except for that foot.

I walked toward the windows and looked outside to get a better view of the river and what had Charlotte so intrigued.

I glanced at her. She was just as perfect as the last time we met. She wore a cream linen pantsuit with matching halter top and gold bangles that showed off her authentic Bermuda tan and the fact that yoga kept women past forty forever young. I also noticed that a dried tear had ruined her makeup on her cheek.

She turned toward me and smiled. "So we're back where we left off, hmmm?"

"And some . . ." I touched her shoulder. "Charlotte, is this a good time?"

"Any time is a good time when you're here. Want a drink?" She waved for the waitress to come to the table.

I sat down. "Sure, if you're treating."

"I never treat, but Big Daddy always does."

Didn't take a wild guess to know who Big Daddy was.

I ordered what Charlotte was drinking and Whiskied Chattahoochee Mud to eat. Bounty hunters and single mothers rarely get called to Canoe's unless work was involved. So I was going to enjoy myself and indulge in some dark chocolate and Irish crème.

"My condolences to your sister and her kids." Charlotte's North Carolinian drawl dripped with sweetness and sadness as she talked. I often wondered why a woman so cultured resorted to her line of work.

I reached for her hands across the table and squeezed them tight. "Thank you."

I held on to her hand until she looked me in my eyes. "Charlotte, who's hurting you, and does it have anything to do with my sister?"

She slipped her hands from my grasp and then reached for her napkin on her lap.

"No, why would you ask me that?" She patted the corners of her eyes.

"Because I've found out some things that don't make sense, that somehow lead me to you."

"Are you . . ." She lowered her arms, cleared her throat, and straightened her back. "Are you suggesting that I've something to do with your brother-in-law's murder, Evangeline?"

"Of course not. You know me better than that." I picked up my phone, opened a recorded video, and slid it to her. "There's a girl, a missing pregnant girl, who looks very much like someone I saw before in your old place. Remember?"

Charlotte picked up my phone and reviewed it. She gasped, then nodded. "Rachel, yes, but she's not one of my girls. She's literally a good girl, a very good girl."

"Then who is she?"

Charlotte leaned forward; I leaned even closer.

"My daughter . . ." She looked around. "And Big Daddy's, too," she whispered.

I gasped and threw my hands again over my mouth. "Charlotte!"

She sat back. "Angel, bring my daughter and my grandchild back to me. Money is no object. You understand me?"

I nodded. "I need to ask you a few questions in order for me to do that."

She nodded and dabbed her eyes with her napkin again. "I'll tell you what you need to know."

Sunday, Midnight

And boy did she. Charlotte shared a secret she had been holding close to her heart for twenty-five years. She had a daughter, Rachel Dawn Newton. Newton was Charlotte's maiden name, and Rachel grew up with Charlotte's mother and father in Madison, Georgia, until Rachel moved to Atlanta a few years ago. Judge Milner knew about his daughter and helped to support her. Rachel, however, shunned them both once she realized the relationship between Charlotte and Judge Milner. She moved out of Charlotte's house two years ago, to live with some girlfriends she met at church, and Charlotte hadn't heard from her since until she called her a few months ago to tell her she was pregnant.

"Did she mention who the father was?" Tiger asked. He lay on his couch and snuggled up to one of his throw pillows.

"No, she didn't have a clue. Charlotte didn't know Rachel had a boyfriend." I rubbed the back of my neck and noted the time. "Meeting Charlotte wasn't a total waste of time. That mud dessert was really good."

"Don't be like that, Angel Soft. We're closer to the truth than we were before."

My phone rang. I pulled it from my jeans pant pocket and placed it on my ear. "Hello?"

"Evangeline Crawford, I believe you've been looking for me."

"Who's this?"

"Rachel Newton, and I've been told you want to see me."

My heart raced. Again, I was at a crossroads. I could cancel Paige's order and tell Big Tiger I changed my mind. I could call Justus and tell him that he was right about God's timing and ask him to tag along. Or I could handle this thing right now and not involve anyone else.

I closed my eyes and cradled the phone to my ear. "Tell me where."

Sunday, Too sleepy to know when . . .
Avondale Estates, GA

The lights were off at the Rogers Mill House when Big Tiger and I arrived. We cancelled Paige's Dumpster diving order for the armor bearers and Elvis, paid her for her service, and headed out to Avondale Estates. My sixth sense warned me not to come.

If Rachel and I hadn't just spoken to each other, I would have thought the place was vacant. No porch light on. No carport lights on. No car in the drive, nothing but a dark house on a barely lit, secluded street on the edge of Avondale Estates and Clarkston. This smelled like a setup to me.

It began to rain, pour, actually. Good thing I wore a tracksuit with a hood, but my cute Halle-Do would be done the moment I stepped out of the car. I didn't want to get out, and by the looks of Big Tiger, he did not either.

"Are you sure this is the place?" he asked.

I nodded. "Just as sure as I have ten fingers."

"And why are you so sure?"

I put my hood over my head and opened the door. "Cause I once lived here."

We ran up the stairs as fast we could. I huffed when we reached the lawn. I wasn't totally drenched, but Big Tiger was. It took him a little longer to get here. I told him one day all that smoking would catch up to him. I rang the doorbell.

No one answered. I leaned toward the door to hear any movement. Nothing. That bothered me.

I turned to Big Tiger. "Don't count yourself out just yet. You might have to pop this door."

I turned the knob. The door opened. It creaked when we opened it. We both stepped back. Big Tiger pushed behind me.

"What?" I whispered to him. "Don't start being protective of me now."

He put his finger over his mouth and waved his hand under his neck to tell me that for our safety, we needed to be quiet. I nodded and shut up. We didn't open the door any farther.

My heart raced. What in the world had I gotten myself into now?

I peeked inside and touched the threshold floor panel with my hand. It was soaked. Inside, the house was pitch black and creepy silent except for the creaking door. I felt like a high-school cheerleader walking into a horror flick. I stepped back again and bumped into Big Tiger.

I jumped, he caught me. "Angel, stop."

I caught my breath and then whispered, "Why don't you go in first?"

He snickered. "Oh, now you want me to lead? Your timing, Angel Soft . . ."

I rolled my eyes. "Yes, I want you as the man to lead, please."

"It's about time." He moved in front of me. "Stay back here where you belong."

I nudged him on his right side. "Watch it."

Big Tiger peeked through the door like I had just done and walked in. I stood outside holding on to the brick wall as if I could climb it if I needed to. My heart beat so fast, I thought I would choke on it.

A few seconds later, the lights came on.

I sighed. "Big Tiger, is that you?"

Nothing. He didn't respond, but a thunderous boom from inside vibrated the porch floorboards at the same time a huge lightning bolt rippled through the sky ten counts away from the house. My hands trembled, so I had to kneel down and hold them.

"Big Tiger?" I whispered.

My phone buzzed against my thigh. Before Big Tiger and I arrived, I had put my phone on vibrate mode. The way it felt against my skin made me want to jump out of my skin.

BAM!

An even louder noise, accompanied by shattered glass, pelted the porch like hail. The noise rang through my ear. I dropped my entire body to the floor and threw my hands over my head. I couldn't hear or see. I reached for my phone. My fingers trembled so bad that when I pulled it out, my hands slipped. The phone fell to the floor and flew across the porch. I reached for it.

BAM!

I scrambled back under the window and did not move. That sound wasn't thunder. It was the sound of a double-barrel shotgun, a bounty hunter's nightmare. Was Big Tiger okay? I was too scared to find out.

I heard the phone buzz again. I cringed. *Please, don't let the gunman hear that.* I prayed until my nerves calmed down.

I observed the distance from the front porch to Big Tiger's car. If I ran fast and low, I could get to it. But I couldn't drive away because I had no keys and I wouldn't leave Big Tiger. My heart sank. Maybe I could put the car in neutral and coast out the drive. A satellite police station was less than a block away. I hoped they'd heard the shots. But then I remembered Big Tiger had a few rifles in his trunk. My Glock was in my purse. I had to get to them.

The front door swung open. I cowered, then tried to be still as a statue, but my stomach wouldn't keep quiet.

Then someone grabbed my shoulders. My heart sat in my throat. I couldn't scream, but I kicked and flared my legs and arms like a wild woman.

"It's me," a familiar voice said. "Salvador."

I stopped fighting and opened my eyes until they focused on his lollipop head.

"Thank goodness you're here. My friend—" I pointed toward the front door, then tried to scramble off the floor. "He's inside. Someone inside shot at us. Big Tiger . . ." I panted. "I'm going inside."

"No, you don't." Salvador helped me up. "You don't need to come inside."

"Yes, I do. My boss, Mr. Jones, is inside."

"No, he isn't." He looked over my shoulders and tilted his head. "Mr. Jones is behind you."

I looked. Big Tiger stood behind us. There was a huge gash on his forehead and standing next to him was Ava. She wore that jacked up chiffon dress I wore to Night Candy last week.

"How?" I blinked and stumbled forward. "What are you doing here and when were you released?"

Salvador turned back to me. "Your pastor boyfriend didn't tell you? Apparently he has higher connections than you."

I smiled and thought of Justus. He told me to trust him.

"Well, your sister had been in processing all evening, but now she's going back to the correction center for good."

"What?" My head began to throb. I was confused. I caught his arm. "Why?"

"For double murder. Wachoothink?"

"What?" I looked around us. Squad cars and ambulances began to line the street. A twinge of déjà vu hit me. I turned back to Salvador. "Who's dead now?"

"Rachel Newton and her baby are dead."

I moved past him and looked inside the house. Rachel's body lay on the floor near the front door along with the handkerchief I gave Ava the night she left the kids with me.

I looked at my sister with so much disappointment and pain. I cried. She just stood there as a uniform handcuffed her. She appeared as stonefaced as she once did when Mama caught her red-handed in Granny's cookie jar. I wanted to slap her.

Instead, I shook my head and sat on the porch.

"Are you okay, Angel?" Salvador asked.

"No, man." I sighed. "How did y'all get here so soon?"

"Your pastor, he told me you would be here."

"What?" I stood up. "How did he know?"

My phone still buzzed on the porch.

Salvador glanced at it. "I think that's him. He can tell you himself."

"No, I don't want to know right now. Can I see my sister before she is processed?" I asked.

Salvador nodded. "Yeah, obviously you two will have a lot to discuss again, but keep it shorter than the last time. You can follow us to the jail again, too, unless you don't think you're good enough to drive."

"And what about Mr. Jones?" I referred to Big Tiger. "What will happen to him?"

"The EMT will transport him to Dekalb Medical for a little stitch work to his face and then he's free to go."

"Maybe I should follow him and meet you at the jail later. I'm confused."

Salvador touched my shoulder. He looked at me, then reached in his coat jacket and pulled out a silk handkerchief. He handed it to me. "It's over, Angel. I hope you see that now."

My eyes were so filled with tears I couldn't see anything. My mind was so flooded with sorrow I couldn't process a decent thought.

29

Sunday, 2:30 AM
Rachel's residence, Avondale Estates, GA.

They walked Ava toward yet another police sedan, and I sat back on the steps and dropped my head in my lap. The phone buzzed again. I looked at it, but I didn't pick it up. The only person I wanted to talk to at that moment was Ava.

I stood up and walked down the steps toward her. She stood near the squad car with her hands folded across her chest. They had taken her cuffs off. We all knew she didn't plan to run.

Salvador turned toward me. "Two minutes, then you'll have to read her statement just like everyone else."

I nodded and waited for him to walk away. I stood in front of her. She didn't look at me.

I hissed. "Why did you lie to me?"

Ava set her gaze on a button on my shirt or a necklace. Her behavior angered me so bad I wanted to ring her neck.

"Ava, look at me," I demanded. "Why didn't you tell me about Rachel?"

She looked up at me. Her eyes seemed older than Mama's somehow. "How could I?"

"How could you not? Because who's going to help you now?"

"God will help me, Angel. He's the only one who can, not me, not you."

"So why didn't you ask God to help you kill Devon instead of you doing it yourself?"

Ava sniffled. My heart began to break again at the sound of her crying. Her desperation was too new for me.

"I didn't kill Devon." She touched my hand. Her fingers were so soft and trembling. My pulse carried her fear into my heart. "I didn't kill him or Rachel."

"It doesn't matter if the only person who knows that is you." I turned away from her. "Are you ready to tell me what happened the night Devon died?"

She lowered her head and bowed. "I made a vow to my husband. Telling you would break it."

I peeled her hand off mine. "Then you deserve what you get."

Her lip quivered. "Do you really believe that?"

I looked back at her. Her stone exterior had softened considerably now. She quaked as she cried.

"Ava, I don't know what to believe. I don't even know who you are."

"You do. You know you do." She sobbed.

"I wanted to believe you didn't do it."

"I didn't," she screamed.

"Why didn't you go to my house when you were released, then? What were you doing in our old house instead?"

"I don't know." It was hard to make out her words now. "I needed to see her."

"I'm sorry, ladies." The police officer standing beside us interrupted, then looked at Ava.

She looked at me and followed the officer's request. Tears streamed down both our faces. "Believe me. I didn't kill Devon or Rachel," she said.

"Then answer my question. How did you get here?"

She sniffled. "Mrs. Loretta brought me to Rachel's."

I nodded. "So she did know where Rachel lived."

Ava nodded. She stopped crying, but the sniffling continued. "She helped me place her here."

"She what? Where is she?"

"No!" she screamed. "Mrs. Loretta had nothing to do with this. She was gone long before you two got here."

"I don't believe you."

"You don't have to, but I will tell you the truth anyway." Ava sighed. "I had been helping Rachel through her pregnancy. I had hoped . . . I didn't want her out in public in her state."

"What state? Carrying Devon's baby?"

She shook her head. "No."

"Then why take care of her?"

"Because she was my armor bearer and her predicament was partly my fault."

"Who's the father of the baby?"

She lowered her head. "I can't tell you."

"Are you protecting him, too? Come on!" I shouted. "What about your children? Why aren't you protecting them?"

"I brought them to you and Whitney for protection."

"So you knew something bad was going down the night you came over?"

She nodded. "I knew that Devon was in trouble, but he wouldn't come to me about it. I begged him to leave all this trouble behind and choose us over the church for once."

"Wow." I hadn't heard her sound like her old self in a really long time. "So why did you go back?"

"Because he's my husband. I didn't expect all this to happen, Angel." She looked around. She began to cry again. "I didn't expect to lose my husband." She whimpered. "And I didn't get to say good-bye to him."

"But if you told me or Salvador any of this—"

"I couldn't. Besides, it wouldn't have mattered. I didn't think this would happen. Rachel's death. I thought the real killer would repent and confess. I prayed and believed it. I still do."

"Did Rachel kill Devon?"

She shook her head. "I don't think so. I don't know."

"Again, is the baby Devon's?"

"I don't know." She sobbed. "I'm afraid to know."

"Ava . . ." I paused. I didn't know what to say. "I have to find the truth now, even what you're too afraid to know about."

"No!" she screamed. She looked at me and dropped her head.

I could tell she was exhausted.

"Yes . . ." she whispered. "Do whatever you have to do. Get me back to my children, Angel."

"Everything will be fine. I'll come to see about you after I make sure Big Tiger is okay. "

"Please, don't leave me, Angel," Ava cried.

I saw Salvador coming toward me. I knew it was against procedure, but if this was our last time alone together, I thought I would give it a shot. "Can I come along this time?"

Salvador nodded. "Of course. I just got off the phone with the DA's office. And according to her, you're the best witness I got. I need you to answer a few questions. Francine will talk to Mr. Jones at the emergency room. I'll have one of the guys park Mr. Jones's car in the detention center parking lot, as a courtesy to you. "

He looked at Ava. "Mrs. McArthur, unfortunately you are being charged with . . ."

Salvador read Ava her Miranda Rights again, while another officer escorted me to Salvador's car. I watched Ava roll away again, but I wasn't sure if I would see her again this time.

After Ava was booked and back in lockup, I told Salvador my account of what happened tonight, which wasn't much. I walked out of the jail with no clue where to go, what to do, or how to get it done. Big Tiger was still at Dekalb Medical having that bump on his head nursed, and Justus was waiting for me on the other side of those squad cars.

He stood in front of the revolving exit doors, leaving me no choice but to speak to him.

I didn't want to. I wanted to tell him off.

He walked toward me. My chest and lips tightened. I couldn't move. For the second time tonight, my body and my mind weren't aligned.

"I'm so sorry, Angel," he said. "I had no clue Ava would be there."

"So you wanted me to get arrested, then, or worse, killed?"

"I wanted you home in bed, taking care of your child like you promised."

"My sister is facing double murder, triple murder charges maybe. She'll die in prison, and you knew where Rachel was all that time. How could you?" I shouted.

"I didn't know this would happen. I was trying to protect you."

"How did you know where Rachel was?"

"I called Francine and gave her Rachel's name. I thought

she could find her faster than us, and I thought that this Rachel person could be the suspect we needed to help Ava's case, just like you thought."

"Francine? Detective Dixon? You told her? I should have known." I shook my head and began to walk away.

He caught my hand. "You have no need to be jealous of her."

"Jealous?" I scoffed. "You need to get over yourself. The last thing that I need in my life right now is to be caught up in a love triangle between a dumb detective and the sanctified superhero. I'm not jealous. I'm pissed off."

His eyes widened. He frowned. "Insulting me won't make things better."

"I disagree. I feel pretty good. Now let me go."

"Are you going home?"

"No, I'm not."

"Angel . . ."

"Angel, what?"

"Tell me you're going home."

"I'm sorry, Pastor, but I have to help my sister."

"Forget about your sister for a minute and think about someone else. Rachel is dead. Her baby is dead. You could have been dead. Had I not told the detectives about this, you would have been dead, too."

Whap! I slapped him. "This is your fault."

He stumbled back. "Go ahead and blame me if that makes you feel better, but I protected you tonight."

"You ruined me tonight." I was glad it was raining, because I didn't want Justus to see my tears. I turned and ran into the storm.

Have you ever found illumination sitting on the back pew? Sure, you can slip out of service if you think the sermon is full of crap. Or ogle that fine usher standing beside your pew holding the church program, but you can't get your soul fed back there or any food, for that matter.

By the time you reach the Communion table, only a drop of grape juice and a few crumbs of pita bread remain for you to swallow. It's almost embarrassing to bend your head back and take of the Body when the body was now crumbs. The only good scraps you're sure to ingest sitting on the back pew are all the rotten business going down within fifteen miles of your church. Whispers, scandals, smells—every peccadillo—float to that back pew. Believe me. I've digested them all. It's what I do, and something told me I wasn't the only one who did that, too.

Big Tiger was too weak to drive home, so I dropped him back to his house, stitches and all, and hopped in my car. Justus had called me more times than I cared to count. I didn't want to see him or hear anything else he had to say. However, I needed to see Elvis.

I knew Elvis had heard the news about Ava by now. I needed to beg him to protect Ava and Devon's kids. For the first time in a long time, I needed Greater Atlanta Faith Church.

Elvis lived in a late Victorian bungalow off Candler Drive in historic Winnona Park district. It was a beautiful place: cute little houses with bright red doors, azaleas, and dogwoods dancing on the lawns and people who looked you in the eye with smiles as bright as the sun. When I went to college, I would pass through this district and dream. I prayed that God would give me a decent job and a sweet man so that I could live in Winnona Park. It was the closest thing to heaven to me back then.

As I pulled into Elvis's driveway, I thought I saw Justus and Bella bouncing down the steps coming toward me. I blinked. They disappeared. Suddenly, I felt overwhelmed.

What was happening to me? Guilt, or worse, dread? Should I apologize to Justus again?

Elvis stood outside waiting for me. The storm had cleared and the world around me felt strangely calm. He came to my car door and opened it. He took my hand and helped me out of the car. I was so tired, and he felt so strong and steady. I let him hold me outside in the only other version of Eden I knew.

"I don't know what I'm going to do," I told him.

"Come inside. I'll make you some breakfast. We'll figure it out."

Elvis's home was immaculate. He had bookcases everywhere, modern furniture, very Ikea. There were pictures of his family, his sisters, and his parents. His father wore a priest's collar. I wondered if he were Anglican or Orthodox Christian, although neither answer would explain why Elvis worshipped at a nondenominational church.

I sat back and picked up a magazine on his coffee table. I opened the magazine and noticed something on the floor by the sofa. It was a handkerchief. I picked it up, then dropped it again. It was my handkerchief. The last time I'd seen it was at the crime scene, Rachel's crime scene. Oh no, he couldn't be. I scooped up the hankie, put it in my back jeans pocket, and hopped up.

"Elvis?" I scurried to the door.

By the time I reached the door, he was already out of the kitchen. "Yes? Where are you going?"

"I have to go. My family is calling and wondering where I am. I'm thinking they heard the bad news."

He had a look of concern on his face. I couldn't tell whether he knew I now suspected him of killing Devon and framing my sister or what.

"Is there anything I can do?" he asked.

I was so scared. I didn't want to give myself away, but I

needed to get out of there. "No, well, I don't know. This is all too much for me right now."

He nodded. "You do look very out of sorts. Maybe I should take you home."

"I can manage." I reached for my purse and keys.

"No." He snatched the hankie out of my pocket. "I don't think you're well enough to drive at all."

30

Agood woman can't be both an investigative journalist and a mother without failing the other. Both took enormous amounts of time, energy, and patience. And both—whether we wanted to admit it or not—provided a private, immeasurable satisfaction that made the long hours, incessant prying, and obsessive need to know everything pleasurable enough to do it again, if the opportunity presented itself. However, being carried down a dark hallway was not one of those satisfying moments.

I could say that I knew Devon's killer days ago, but I didn't. I couldn't. There were so many variables and twists. I didn't see this coming. But now I saw things clearly, even in the dark. Actually, I saw things clearer, because Elvis was carrying me to my death.

We reached some cold room somewhere I assumed was the Biscuit Depot. I had no clue how he knocked me out or how I'd gotten here. I did know that I shouldn't have pushed Justus away. I regretted never kissing that man.

Elvis laid me on a table, checked my pulse, and walked away. I listened to his footsteps; then the door opened and closed. I couldn't quite understand why I wasn't dead yet, but I thought that maybe I had a chance to live for another day. I slivered off the table. It was too dark to figure out where I was, but I knew I shouldn't be here, and I began to suspect that we were not at the Biscuit Depot either. The kitchen was too big.

My head throbbed. I touched my forehead. It felt swollen. That fool must have hit me on the head. Since I still had that slight concussion, it wouldn't take much to knock me out.

I staggered toward the doorway. Girlfriend had no clue how to open a locked door. I scrambled and scrambled until my mind told me to just touch the knob like Justus did the night we found Devon and Ava. I did and the door opened.

I dropped to my knees and crawled toward darkness. My weak knees had me sliding around on the ground. When I finally made a decent move, I found another opening. I pulled myself up, opened the door, and slid through it before I heard Elvis's voice.

"Where are you going, Evangeline?"

I scrambled off the ground and took off. I had no clue whether I was running away from or running toward him.

I had always wanted to live in Mama's shoes, until right now. Her Prada slingbacks caught no traction on the slick carpet. I knew I shouldn't have taken them out of her luggage. They clickety-clacked and made too much noise for someone running from a hellraiser. I was running stupid, scatterbrained, and without direction. I couldn't find the exit doors to save my life, literally. I wanted to turn around to see where Elvis was, but I was too scared.

I heard footsteps. The dude was gaining on me. I huffed and tried to pick up speed. Mom was going to kill me if I didn't make it out of here alive.

Thank God for the moonlight. I saw another sliver of a doorknob to my right, caught it, slid inside, and exhaled.

Oh my gosh! I looked around. I was in Devon's office. I was in Greater Atlanta. *Are you kidding me?*

I heard someone coming. I hid in Devon's coat closet and held my breath.

Deep inside, behind coats, boxes, and the night's darkness, I held my breath, but I couldn't stop breathing. Someone behind the door wanted me dead. I needed to stop breathing in order to save myself. How ironic.

While waiting and praying for a miracle, I thought about my relationship with Ava. Why did I work so hard to not be like her? For obvious reasons, I wouldn't wear her clothes. I had a problem with being in the limelight as she had done most of Devon's ministry. And I feared the possibility of falling in love again. I didn't want to admit that, but if I was on my last leg, I might as well be truthful with myself.

Justus was a great guy that my low self-esteem and lack of faith in myself had pushed away. And now I was in some obscure closet in Devon's former office. I was alone and probably going to die. I wished I could have told Justus the truth, that I cared for him, too.

If Ava were me, she would have told him that she loved him as soon as he called her into his office and asked her for a favor.

Then I heard another noise.

I would've fainted if I knew that it wouldn't get me killed. So I held my breath again, but I couldn't stop breathing—again, to save my life.

I sobbed without sniffling. There was mucus all in my nose and I thought I would drown. I wanted to wipe my nose with my sleeve, but Elvis would hear me if I did that.

The floor creaked closer to where I hid. My heart attempted to jump out of my chest.

Granny's voice spoke to me, *"Girl, get your gun."*

I have a gun? Oh yeah. I remembered.

After I took Tiger home, I took my gun out of my purse and hid it in my waistband. I didn't want to be caught off guard again. It was the wisest decision I made tonight. I could feel her, but I couldn't find her. Where was it?

The creaking turned into footsteps. My heart bounced up my throat now. I fumbled all around my waist. Where was that little gun?

Thud. I found it. It hit the floor just as the moon somehow found me, too.

The door opened and the moon placed his spotlight right on my head. I cursed.

"Angel, the pain in my side," Elvis said. "You shouldn't have come in here."

My whole body shook. There was no place to hide. I felt the floor for my gun.

The lights came on and Elvis stood in the entrance of the closet. It was a good thing this closet was a packed-to-the-gills walk-in closet. I heard him moving Devon's junk, searching for me. "We're not playing hide and seek, are we?"

Then I saw his eyes. I gasped.

He laughed. "You can't hide from me."

When he grabbed my hand, I sucker punched him in the nose. "I wasn't hiding."

He stumbled back. He paused, smoothed his tie over his chest, then smiled. I didn't want to think Elvis was a tad touched, but he had that crazy look in his eyes.

"Come out of this closet please. We need to talk," he said.

"No." I stepped farther back in the closet. "I want to stay in here."

He stepped forward. "We always want what we can't have. Isn't that true, Angel?"

"It depends. What do you want that you can't have?"

"I want you to not be here."

I couldn't show fear. I had to look him in the eye and ask, despite the fact that I wouldn't be able to see what he was doing with his hands. "You brought me here. Why?"

"Cut the crap, Angel. Shall we? Let's not reenact a bad episode of *Miss Marple*."

"Who?"

"It's a British television show."

I shook my head. "What?"

"BBC? Oh, you wouldn't understand." He sighed. "Let's not reenact a bad episode of *Law & Order*. Reality is much darker. Is that a better metaphor for you?"

"Yes." My legs weakened. "But I don't watch those shows, Elvis. I watch *New Detectives,* the *First 48,* and repeats of *The Closer*."

"That's not the blooming point. You know bloody well why you're here."

"Because you killed my brother-in-law and Rachel."

"What can I say?" He snickered and scratched his head. "I'm a fool in love, but you wouldn't know what that's like, now would you, especially since your non-boyfriend/pastor dimed you out?"

"If you killed Rachel, I assume you're not in love with her, which means that you're not her baby's father . . . Are you the father?"

He shook his head.

"Then who else could it be?" My mind raced. "Terry?"

"Bingo," he sang.

"But you're in love with someone. I can tell."

He smiled again.

I caught my breath. "You're in love with my sister."

His clapped his hands and grinned. "Now you're on to something. I thought you would have figured it out sooner."

"I didn't see that one coming at all. Why?"

"You should understand, since you have experience falling for someone you can't have. As I recall, the bishop was your man first."

I shook my head. "No, he was always hers. Still is."

"The bishop is dead now."

"Yes, and you killed him." Mama's spitfire surged through me now.

Elvis's face darkened, reddened, changed to something uglier than I could have ever imagined. "It was my duty to kill him, and if I recall, you've wanted him dead for a while. Is that why you came to my house, to thank me?"

His steady voice and stare scared me. I had hoped that Devon's murder was a crime of passion, but not this. Elvis had problems. I didn't think I could talk him down. My teeth chattered so hard, I bit the inside of my jaw. I winced from the pain, blinked, and the tears fell fast, which kind of relieved me. If I was going to die, I didn't want to see it coming.

His head cocked to the left. "Can you answer me? You always have a very colorful retort. Where's your smart mouth now?"

I wanted to say something smart back, but nothing made sense, except the repeating prayer to Jesus looping in my brain.

"Let me help you." He grabbed my head and began to drag me out of the closet.

Ouch. This was the second time I had been dragged by my head in one week. Something had to give.

"What was your reason for killing Rachel?" I grunted.

He stopped and turned me over. Elvis's eyes turned colder than this room.

"What do you know, madam? You're a washed-up reporter, a sham."

"You were siphoning funds from the Greater Atlanta Foundation, and Rachel found out about it during your fling together. How does that sound for washed-up reporting?"

"Shut up." His voice thundered through the room. My stomach shook. I felt the gun under my thigh.

"Devon found out about what you did from Rachel. Didn't he?"

"She ratted me out, just like Justus did you."

"So the fifty thousand was yours?"

He nodded. I looked down at his hands. They trembled.

I looked back at him. "You don't want to kill me. You didn't want to kill the others. Did you?"

"I had no choice, you see."

"Why did you need all that money?"

"For my family. My dad was very sick. But he's fit as a fiddle now."

Crazy. "You don't have to do this, Elvis."

He laughed. "I do, but don't worry. This way your sister will be free like you wanted."

"Excuse me?"

"I'm going to kill you, then blame the whole lot on you, Angel. Ava will be released and she will be with me, as she should be."

"Oh, you must've fallen and bumped your head if you think I will let that happen. Besides, Ava would never marry you. Are you crazy?"

"Watch your step, madam!"

"Get a life, Elvis." I slid my gun out and pulled the trigger.

My ears popped.

My heart stopped for a second.

I stepped back, but I never took my eyes off Elvis. He fell back, clutched his shirt, and dropped to the ground. As he squirmed over the floor, gasping for air, I felt empathy for his pain. I knelt beside him and took his hand in mine.

He squeezed my hand and winced as he began coughing and wheezing. "Why are you doing this?"

"Because I didn't for the man I once loved."

"Pray for me," he said.

I prayed and held his hand until he left.

Sunday, 6:00 AM
Greater Atlanta Church, Atlanta, GA

Justus held me in his arms when Salvador's team wheeled Elvis out of the church in a body bag. I shook and my teeth chattered. I was afraid I would be carted off to jail, too. I was too broken up to be questioned, but I wasn't too broken up to apologize to Justus.

"I never killed anyone before," I said to Justus over and over again.

"I know. I wish I'd been here to prevent it."

"I'm sorry you weren't here."

He kissed my forehead. "Don't be."

"But I am and I think you should stay away from me."

"If you had gotten sleep like you should have, you wouldn't sound so crazy." He chuckled. "Woman, I'm not leaving you."

"You will in about two days after all this craziness is over. It's called adrenaline romance. It's perfectly normal for you to feel this way."

He shook his head. "You make falling in love sound like a virus."

"You're in love with me now? When did this happen?"

"It happened the moment I saw you in that tattered cocktail dress. You looked like a broken-down Cinderella."

"I ain't no princess, Justus. I'm definitely not a pastor's girlfriend."

"And why not?" he asked.

"Because I've seen more evil than any good woman should have. I'll shame your pulpit."

"So what are you saying?"

"I'm saying if you want to be an effective pastor, stay away from me."

I stood up. He grabbed me. He leaned toward my face.

"Kissing me will not change my mind." I knew full well that it would.

Justus lowered his face toward my ear and whispered, "Only love will do that." He pulled back and watched me. I swooned a bit.

"I'm looking at you, and it's hard to tell the difference between you and your sister."

I sighed. "Yeah, she's the beautiful, spirited one. You know she's single now."

"So are you, but that's beside the point."

"Here you go with your points." I rolled my eyes. "Your point is?" My heart cartwheeled over the fact that he said he was in love with me.

He paused and trapped my eyes with his. "Love is unconditional, but it requires sacrifice and action. A man knows, understands, and will prepare for the sacrifice. It's his job. Your job is to surrender to it."

If he weren't holding me up, I would have fainted.

"All right . . ." I exhaled instead. "Go ahead and kiss me now."

"Nope." He shook his head and grinned. "You will not have your way with me, woman, not until you apologize."

I nodded. "I suspected as much."

31

Friday, one week after Devon's death, twilight
East View Cemetery, Atlanta.

Storms—the really bad ones—rolled over Atlanta like bandits, fast and furious. The clouds above my head crawled around the air in grays, silvers, zebra, and then black within seconds. Rain tickled, tucked, and tumbled over Devon's homegoing service. It poured so hard that the Kelly & Leach Funeral Home tent fell twice, and the white rose floral coffin spray had to be covered in plastic before it was laid over Devon's casket.

In African American folklore, bad storms meant a great, holy person was living in glory and the rain was tears of joy from the angels. To say good-bye to a great soul was a bittersweet moment. For me, losing Devon was worse than the taste of unsweetened dark chocolate.

See, I thought I knew him. I thought he was like the ministers I once investigated, the opportunists donning crosses in exchange for celebrity and untaxed charity, with a sloppy paper trail longer than Devon's homegoing parade. I was a fool. He was the best man I'd ever refused to know. I had so much to learn.

Friday night
The McMansion Ballroom, Lithonia, GA

As I like to say, I would've sold my soul a long time ago for a handsome man who made me feel pretty or who could at least treat me to a millionaire's martini. Instead, I lingered over a sparkling white grape juice cocktail and made goo-goo eyes at my brown-eyed Bella dancing in front of me. After all, I'm her mother. It's my job to cherish her, no matter the cost. Yet, I was wondering. Why was she dancing with my sidekick?

In lieu of the customary repast—overindulging in rich foods and desserts with the family—Ava decided to throw a dance in Devon's honor. I managed to sweet talk Big Tiger into spinning some music on his turntables.

Justus's niece and nephews were here as well. The twins were comforting Taylor and Lil D on the dance floor, while Whitney chopped it up with Kelly. Trish catered. I hoped she schooled her daughter on making better decisions with teenaged boys. Mama and our new daddy two-stepped to every dance.

"This is a lovely reception, Ava." I touched my sister's hand. "I'm sure Devon is doing his weak two-step in heaven with us."

She chuckled and wiped a tear from her cheek. "You know that man couldn't dance worth a hot cup of chocolate, but I wouldn't dare tell him."

"Well, honey, you just did." I patted her back.

She laughed. "Yes, I did."

Whitney slid over to us and threw her arms around us both. "Why y'all looking like old lushes at the bar? Y'all better get your groove on."

"I can't because my daughter is dancing with Justus."

"I can't either," Ava said. "I don't want to embarrass Angel in front of her new man."

"Oh no, you didn't! And he's not my man."

"Oh yes, I did and, yes, he is. Will you just admit it?"

I watched Justus with Bella and smiled. "Not gonna happen."

"Whatever . . ." Ava jumped up. "Tonight's my beloved Devon's night, and I think we should end it like we began. I stole him from you on the dance floor because you didn't know how to use your hips properly."

"Oooh." Whitney clapped. "Sound like a dance-off."

"If Ava had been keeping in touch with us as she should have been, then she would know that her twin has gotten some pep in her step." I stood up. "Let's do this thing, girl."

We sashayed to the dance floor just as Big Tiger put on my new favorite jam.

Justus caught my hand. "May I have this dance, young lady?"

"Yes, sir. I hope you can keep up."

"Well, let me give you something to slow you down." He leaned toward me and kissed me.

It was the sweetest, purest, downright grown womanish feeling I'd ever felt.

"It's about time." I punched his shoulder.

"I just wanted to let you know what you're missing, so you can stop fighting this."

"I'm not fighting. I just know it won't work."

"Why do you keep saying that?" He groaned.

"Because when sidekicks hook up with the lead, the series ends."

He chuckled. "You're incorrigible."

"Or maybe it's a good excuse to keep you on your toes."

He swirled me around and we danced the night away.

Epilogue

Early Saturday morning
Sugar Hill, Georgia.

I dreamt of Justus and wasn't ashamed. We were booked up in one of those VIP cabanas in Night Candy. He wore a periwinkle button down shirt that made his honey colored skin glow, even in the darkness of the club. He smelled like butterscotch and something manly.

Justus pulled me toward his lips when he said, "Knock, knock, knock."

What he said confused me. It didn't fit the moment at all.

"What?" My nose wrinkled. "Are we playing a knock-knock joke now?"

He shook his head, while caressing my cheek. "Knock. Knock. Knock."

I moved back. "What the . . . ?"

I awoke and sat up. I looked around the bedroom until I got my focus.

Crap! I sighed. Someone was knocking on my front door.

"Well, at least they had the good sense not to ring my doorbell," I grumbled. Whitney and Bella were still asleep and they needed to stay that way. I had every intention to pick up where my dream date with Justus left off, as soon as I got rid of my door knocker.

Downstairs at the front door, I looked through the peep hole. It was a florist delivery man. My heart fluttered. Flowers! I did a happy dance in my foyer. Justus was thinking of me, too.

"Hold on for a second," I said to the delivery guy, while I disalarmed the door.

Perhaps it was time I called in that rain check date with him. It was time to take a risk.

I unlocked the door, opened it, and smiled.

"Ms. Evangeline Crawford?" The delivery man asked. He held a large golden box with a red ribbon.

"Yes, I'm Evangeline." I clapped. I was feeling teenaged giddy again. I missed this feeling.

I signed his clipboard before he handed me the box.

"Have a good day, ma'am" Then pivoted back toward his van and began walking away.

I didn't see his face, because his navy baseball cap sat well below his brim. I only saw his chiseled jaw and a mole above the top right corner of his mouth. Based on that little information I could tell he was handsome. Good thing Whitney wasn't awake. She would have embarrassed herself, trying to get his attention.

While he walked down my drive, I pulled out the card stuck on the box. It was a picture of me holding Bella at the funeral. A bolt of adrenaline rushed through my body. My heart raced again. I dropped the box, gasped, and looked up. The delivery man was rounding the corner of my street.

"Wait!" I jumped off the steps and raced after him until I gave up the chase at the stop sign.

I ran back to the house, stood over the box, and panted. Fear began bubbling around me, as I observed it. I didn't know if I should open it or throw it in the trash. Obviously it wasn't a bomb or it would have gone off when I dropped it. But it had something to do with Bella. I didn't know what to do about that.

My heart beat so fast I had to sit down on the porch steps and catch my breath. I thought about waking Whitney, but I was too afraid to leave the porch. I scanned the street, while I calmed my breathing down, so I wouldn't hyperventilate.

And then I saw it. The note card. It had fallen near the porch step where I sat. I still hadn't completely caught my breath, but I was curious by default. I had to know what this all meant. My hand trembled when I turned the card over. It read:

Do you still love me?

Gabe?! I wheezed and clutched my chest. He couldn't be alive. I watched him die. I held him when he died.

"Who did this?" I tried to stand up, but couldn't. "Who sent this?!"

I looked around me again. I think I saw a neighbor walking a dog, but everything had become a blur. My head swam so fast. There were too many emotions. I passed out on the step. No dreaming, just gone.

Did Angel actually witness Gabe die?

Want to find out what happened to put Angel on bad terms with Ava and Devon?

Then join Angel on her next manhunt in Someone Bad and Something Blue, *coming in July 2012 from Dafina Books.*

DISCUSSION QUESTIONS

1. Why didn't Angel wait for Big Tiger before she left Night Candy with Cade?

2. Does Angel appear to start her own trouble? Why is that?

3. Why do you think Justus is attracted to Angel?

4. Have you ever crushed on someone who would be taboo to admit (pastor, doctor, etc.)?

5. Did you agree with Ava's reason for not telling Angel the truth?

6. Would you take the fall for someone else?

7. Does Angel's mom show favoritism with Ava?

8. Angel isn't afraid of dangerous bank robbers or a good fight, but when it comes to her family, she's a pushover. Why? Can you empathize with that?

9. Why do you think Angel chose being a bounty hunter instead of something more reputable?

10. Is it wrong for Justus to express his feelings to Angel?

11. If this were a movie, who could play Justus? Angel? Ava? Salvador? Whitney? Virginia?

12. What do you like about Justus?

13. Do you think Angel and Justus belong together?

14. Is Ava a good parent? What can she do to improve?

15. How do feel about Whitney? Is she the typical meddling little sister?

16. Why doesn't Ava want Angel to help her?

17. Do you think Devon's death would have been prevented had Ava contacted Angel sooner?

18. When did you learn who the real murderer was? What tipped you off?

19. What do you think about Big Tiger's advice to Angel about Justus and her investigation?

20. If you had a good excuse to be bad, what would it be?

Stay tuned for a helping of Lutishia Lovely's new series, which follows the hot tempers and tantalizing temptations of a family whose restaurant is *the* place for a tasty meal. . . .

Mind Your Own Business

Coming in September 2011 from Dafina Books

Here's an excerpt from *Mind Your Own Business*. . . .

"Why can't a woman be on top?" Bianca Livingston demanded, tossing shoulder-length, naturally curly hair over her shoulder. She stood over her brother as if ready to strike, looking totally capable of kicking butts and taking names. Her quick smile, short stature, and girly frame had caused many men to underestimate her—to their peril. But anyone seeing her now—shoulders back, hands on hips, and perfectly tailored black suit and four-inch heels—would believe her capable of running almost anything. "I'm as qualified to run the West Coast locations as you are, even more so, matter of fact."

"You're qualified to run the kitchen, *maybe,*" her older brother retorted. Jefferson suppressed a smile. He'd taunted Bianca from birth, and did so now. Her fiery personality was the perfect foil for his laid-back teasing. But even with his ongoing provocations, this time Jefferson's antics masked the seriousness of his quest. He had every intention of being the Livingston who moved to LA to establish the Taste of Soul restaurants both there and in Nevada. He just didn't like confrontation, or competition. He'd quietly made his bid to run the West Coast locations the same way he cooked his ribs—low and slow. "Isn't that why you spent the last nine months in Paris?" he queried to underscore his point. "Learning the fine art of cooking so that you could give our soul food some class?"

Actually, Bianca had fled to Paris to get away from the chain around her neck otherwise known as Cooper Riley, Jr., her fiancé. But only one other person knew this truth. Initially, forestalling the marriage everyone else believed was a fait accompli was also why she'd expressed interest in running the West Coast locations. But now, after months of talking with her cousin Toussaint, her confidant and the brainchild behind their company expanding out west, Bianca wanted to relocate to continue spreading her independent wings, expand the Livingston dynasty, and make the brand shine under her direct supervision.

"Need I remind you that I have not only a culinary certificate from Le Cordon Bleu, but I also have an undergrad and a graduate degree in business administration?"

"No, little sis, you don't need to remind me." Jefferson's smirk highlighted the dimple on his casually handsome face, his tan skin further darkened by the August sun. His brown eyes twinkled with merriment. "But do I have to remind you that I have a double master's in business administration and finance?" After receiving an MBA at Morehouse, Jefferson had garnered a second one from the Wharton School of the University of Pennsylvania.

Bianca, knowing that she couldn't go toe-to-toe when it came to her brother's education, tried a different route. She walked away from Jefferson and sat in one of the beige leather chairs in the artistically appointed office. Reaching for a ballpoint pen that lay on his large and messy mahogany desk, she adopted a calmer tone, yet couldn't totally drop the petulance in her voice.

"Jefferson, the only reason Dad is promoting the idea of your heading up the location is because you're the oldest."

"And the son—don't forget that. You know Dad doesn't want to see his baby girl fly too far from the nest."

"Okay, probably that too," Bianca conceded. It was no secret that when it came to her father, Abram "Ace" Livingston, she was the apple of his all-seeing eye.

"Besides, how are you even considering relocation when you've got a fiancé chomping at the bit to get married? Cooper has been more than patient with you, Bianca. Not many men would let the woman they love move to the other side of the world, even if—as you successfully argued—it was for the union's greater good. What did you call it? Increasing your company value and the marriage's bottom line? As if being a Livingston isn't value enough? No, Bianca, Cooper allowed the wedding to be pushed back once already. He's not going to delay it a second time, and you know he isn't moving to LA."

Bianca abruptly rose from the chair where she'd been sitting and walked to the window. "You're probably right," she said, quickly wiping the tears that had leaped into her eyes. "If everyone has their way, I'll be married in six months with a baby on the way in nine." *But how can I marry Cooper after what happened in Paris?*

"Hey, sister, are you all right?"

Bianca jumped. She hadn't heard Jefferson rise, hadn't been aware that he'd walked from his desk and joined her at the window.

"Actually, no, if you want to know the truth. Jeff, I—"

"Hey, man . . . Oh, Bianca, I'm glad you're both here." Toussaint Livingston burst into Jefferson's office and rushed toward his cousins on the other side of the room. "We need to roll to your parents' house right now. Emergency family meeting."

Their conversation forgotten, both Jefferson and Bianca turned and talked at once.

"What's the matter?"

"What's going on?"

Bianca's heart raced with concern. "Why are we meeting at Mom and Dad's house, Toussaint, and not in the conference room?"

Toussaint turned and headed for the door. "That's what we're about to find out. I'll meet y'all there."

Fifteen minutes later, Toussaint, Jefferson, and Bianca joined their family members in the living room of Ace and Diane's sprawling Cascade residence. Toussaint's parents, Adam and Candace, and his brother, Malcolm, were already there.

Toussaint and his cousins were the last to arrive, and as soon as they sat down, Ace cleared his throat and stood. "We've got a situation," he began without preamble. A pregnant pause and then, "Somebody's stealing company funds."

Reactions were mixed, with bewilderment and anger vying for top billing.

"Who is it?" Bianca angrily asked, ready for battle though the culprit remained unnamed.

"We don't know," Ace replied. "But it's definitely an inside job."

The family members looked at one another, a myriad of thoughts in each of their minds. *Who could it be? How did this happen? Is the guilty party somehow connected to someone in the room?* One family member even pondered the unthinkable: *Is the thief one of us?*

"What kind of money are we talking about?" Toussaint asked. "Hundreds, thousands . . . more?"

"*Several* hundred thousand," Ace replied, his tone somber and curt.

Again, responses were symphonic.

"What the hell?"

"Who could do such a thing?"

"Oh, hell to the no. We're not going to take this lying down."

"You're absolutely right, baby girl," Ace said to Bianca. "We're not going to stand for this at all. Nobody steals from our company, takes from our family, without feeling the wrath of a Livingston payback."